GOTHAM

DAWN OF DARKNESS

GOTHAM
DAWN OF DARKNESS

JASON STARR

TITAN BOOKS

GOTHAM: DAWN OF DARKNESS
Print edition ISBN: 9781785651458
E-book edition ISBN: 9781785651465

Published by Titan Books
A division of Titan Publishing Group Ltd
144 Southwark Street, London SE1 0UP

First edition: January 2017
10 9 8 7 6 5 4 3 2 1

This is a work of fiction. Names, characters, places, and incidents either are the product of the author's imagination or are used fictitiously, and any resemblance to actual persons, living or dead, business establishments, events, or locales is entirely coincidental. The publisher does not have any control over and does not assume any responsibility for author or third-party websites or their content.

A CIP catalogue record for this title is available from the British Library.
Printed and bound in the United States.

FOR CHYNNA

O N E

At a little past two a.m., Thomas Wayne was still at work on the computer in his office—the ultimate man cave—when he thought he heard a creaking sound. It seemed to come from above, or maybe behind him.

Thomas listened intently for a moment, then shrugged—maybe another bat had gotten in—and he returned to work.

This part of the house wasn't airtight, but its walls were thick, and little sound ever made it downstairs. In fact, what with its raw stone and concrete, exposed pipes, and the accompanying mustiness, it really *did* feel more like a cave than a basement. There were a lot of nooks and crannies where light never reached, and he'd seen bats down here before—sometimes hanging upside down, dormant, or flying around at night. He'd considered exterminating, but the bats didn't bother him, and they couldn't get upstairs into the main part of Wayne Manor, so he didn't see the point.

Besides, he sort of liked the company. Aside from

him, the bats were the only ones who knew about this place's existence—situated as it was directly below his first-floor study. Even Thomas's wife Martha and his teenage son Bruce didn't know about it.

A minute or so later, he heard more noise. This definitely came from above him, and it didn't sound like a bat—it sounded like a bang, as if something had dropped on the floor upstairs.

That's odd…

He wasn't home alone. It could be Bruce, Martha, or their butler, Alfred Pennyworth. But it would be highly unusual for any of them to be up and about at this time of night, and even more unusual for one of them to go into Thomas's workspace. Martha always respected his privacy and while Bruce—like any fourteen year old—got curious from time to time, Thomas had made it clear to him that his office was off-limits, and the boy usually complied. This left Alfred, his devoted employee for many years, who was the least likely to enter alone and uninvited.

Especially in the middle of the night.

Figuring he ought to check it out, Thomas left the office, closing the steel, high-tech security door he'd had installed. He kept a lot of valuable secrets here, including ones regarding his company, Wayne Enterprises, and these days, with crime rampant in Gotham, there could never be too much caution.

Creeping up the steep staircase which led to the secret entrance, he listened for any more sounds. Nothing. At the top landing he waited about a minute, but still didn't hear anything. Perhaps something had fallen on its own—that happened from time to time. Maybe a book had been precariously placed on his desk, and had somehow fallen off. Or maybe a window or a door had been slammed shut by a breeze.

Had he left a window open? The night was chilly…

After several more moments of absolute silence, he was ready to accept that it had been an anomaly and was about to return downstairs to finish up his work, when he heard voices—men's voices—coming from inside his study.

Thomas couldn't make out what the men were saying, nor could he tell how many men there were. Then he heard more movement—maybe furniture shifting. Thomas's pulse quickened. People were upstairs. They had made it past the security system, and entered his home. Bruce, Martha, even Alfred, could be in danger.

Then there was a banging, as if someone was pounding on something, and the sound of more objects hitting the floor.

He rushed back down the stairs, going as quickly as he could without falling. Into the keypad, he typed in the password—B-R-U-C-E—and the basement door swung open. He went right to the landline and tapped in three digits.

"Nine-one-one, what's your emergency?" the female operator asked.

"This is Thomas Wayne," he said, keeping his voice low. "There appears to be a break-in at Wayne Manor."

"Sorry, what's your name?"

"Wayne. Thomas Wayne."

A pause, then the operator said, "Wait, Thomas Wayne. *The* Thomas Wayne? The billionaire? The richest man in Gotham?"

I don't have time for this. Impatient, Thomas said, "What's your name, please?"

"Jessica."

"Jessica what?"

A pause, then, "Meyers."

"Send the police here immediately, Ms. Meyers," Thomas said, "or you'll never work in Gotham again." Without waiting for a response, he hung up on her. In general, he hated threatening people, but sometimes it seemed the only way to get anything done.

Thomas kept a loaded handgun in his office, just for emergencies—and this qualified as an emergency. He retrieved the Walther semi-automatic from the back of one of his filing cabinets, and then moved again for the door.

Staying in the basement, waiting for the GCPD to show up, simply wasn't an option. He figured it could take ten minutes or longer for the police to get here at this time of night. He thought about Bruce and Martha, hopefully still asleep in bed, but he had to do whatever he could to protect them. Besides, someone had broken into his property, invaded his space. *His home.* This was a violation—felt like it on a gut level. It reminded him of the way he'd been feeling at work lately—vulnerable, disrespected, irrelevant, cast aside.

He hated playing the part of the victim, and remaining passive wasn't in his nature. For centuries, the Waynes had been fighters.

Again locking the office, he headed back up the stairs, padding quietly. The door at the top led to a secret entrance behind the fireplace in his office. There was no subtle, quiet way to enter the study—once he pressed the button the shelves would part, and if there were in fact an intruder or intruders in the room, Thomas wouldn't exactly be taking them by surprise.

He listened carefully at first—didn't hear anything.

To hell with it. He pressed the entry button.

The two halves of the door parted, and he saw that the study had been ransacked. Heavy, leather-covered furniture had been overturned, drawers pulled out of the desk and dumped. Classic, valuable books, papers, antique statuettes, all had been thrown about, some shattered, and office supplies were strewn all over the floor. A massive grandfather clock lay on its side, the glass broken out. That must have been what he had heard from the office below.

What the hell? There were large gashes in the walls, and the plasterboard had been pulled away in several places, revealing insulation and exposed electrical wiring. Here and there he saw gaping black holes in the wooden slats that lay underneath.

Aiming the gun ahead of him, Thomas crept into the room. Thoughts swirling, he made his way through the study, avoiding the stuff on the floor.

Who did this? he asked himself, over and over.

Random thieves? Professional criminals? Then he noticed the empty space on the wall opposite the windows. One of his most valuable paintings—Picasso's *Le Picador*—had been taken, frame and all.

Thomas was gutted. Not over the money. True, the painting was worth tens of millions of dollars, but even if it were gone for good it wouldn't make a dent, or even a smudge, in Thomas's private fortune. It was the painting's sentimental value that couldn't be replaced. Thomas's great grandfather had bought it from the young, struggling artist himself on a street corner in Seville. Or at least that was how the family story went.

He paused a moment, and frowned. Was that what the break-in was all about? A painting? If professional art thieves had come here to steal a painting, then why ransack the study?

Unless they were looking for something else. Maybe still looking for it.

The thieves could still be in the house, even upstairs.

Intent upon making sure his family was safe, Thomas left the study. If he saw an intruder he planned to shoot first, and to hell with asking questions later—he wouldn't ask questions at all. All he needed was a good look, and he'd get his man. Cool under pressure, he was a good shot. He had never served in the army, but his grandfather used to take him hunting and skeet shooting, and he practiced at a private shooting range north of Gotham. Alfred had helped him with that, pressing his training until he was satisfied with the results.

He continued into the foyer. The only light came

from several night-lights, and he had to squint to see at all, especially as he approached the main hallway where it was even darker. Then he detected movement to his right. He shifted, and was about to fire his weapon, when he realized he was looking at the mirror, at his own dim reflection.

Feeling ridiculous, he stayed put, catching his breath. The house was almost silent—the only sound Thomas heard was his own breathing. He passed through the dining room, then the drawing room, noting that all the windows were secure and there was no sign of a break-in.

Then he saw them.

Three men coming toward him, from the direction of the kitchen—or the servants' staircase. They were all in black, wearing Halloween-style masks. There was a werewolf, a zombie, and a gorilla. The gorilla was holding the Picasso, while the zombie had something in his right hand. A knife? No, it was wider than a knife. It looked more like a meat cleaver.

When the men saw Thomas they stopped, as if surprised. They stood about ten yards away, and it was an awkward standoff—like deer in headlights, staring at one another. It seemed to go on forever, but it was no more than five seconds. Then motion. The werewolf guy took out a gun, and it glinted in the dim light.

Thomas raised his weapon, aimed it as best he could, and fired, hitting him in the chest. The intruder grunted in agony and fell back, keeping his feet.

"Come on," the zombie said, "let's get outta here.

Thomas didn't recognize the voice, muffled as it was, but the accent was pure, working class Gotham.

The zombie and gorilla took off toward the front door, but the werewolf remained and aimed his gun at Thomas's face. Thomas leapt to his right, ducking behind the grand piano. A bullet hit the piano, and another whizzed by overhead.

Leaning to his left, Thomas saw a sliver of the man, visible between the legs of the piano, and he fired the Walther, hitting the intruder again. He groaned and stumbled backward, toppling over a club chair.

Leaping to his feet, Thomas rushed past the body and went outside. Dull orangeish light coming from old-style lampposts illuminated the long driveway. The other two intruders were getting into a car, slamming the doors and revving the engine. The car sped away along the driveway toward the front gates. The night guard, Nigel, was supposed to be on duty, but the gate was wide open. Where the hell was he?

Dropping his gun hand to his side, Thomas went back into Wayne Manor and turned on the lights. He was heading toward the main stairway, to go up and check on his family, when he heard a muffled voice.

"Hey, rich guy. Where you goin'?"

Thomas stopped and turned back. The werewolf guy stood in the doorway to the drawing room. With a bleeding gash in his leg, he was aiming his gun. Thomas still had his own weapon by his side.

"You got what you wanted," Thomas said. "Why don't you just leave?"

"You wanted me to leave, you should'a thought about that before you shot me."

The werewolf guy's finger moved against the trigger.

Thomas flinched as a shot rang out.

A bullet ripped into the side of the guy's neck—knocking him off of his feet. The gun fell to the floor, along with his dead body.

Then Thomas saw Alfred on the mid-landing of the stairwell, holding his Browning 9mm sidearm, crouched a full twenty feet from his target. In his sixties, Pennyworth was still as fit as a man half his age, and possessed a lethal set of skills honed in the British Royal Marines. That was why Thomas had hired him. A butler who could make tea was easy to find. A butler who could save lives? Not so easy.

"Nice going," Thomas said, "but I had the situation under control."

In the distance, sirens blared.

"Of course you did, sir," Alfred said. "I don't doubt that for a moment."

T W O

Before sunrise, GCPD Detectives Harvey Bullock and Amanda Wong arrived at Wayne Manor.

"I should be in bed right now," Harvey said, "getting all rested up for tomorrow morning's hangover."

Harvey and Amanda had been partners for about a week now, ever since Harvey's last partner got killed in a shootout during a drug store robbery. He'd liked his last partner. Marv was a good guy, but what could you do? It seemed like Harvey went through partners faster than rock bands went through drummers.

So enter Amanda, stage left. Ideal partner?

Not quite. First problem—their personalities. Harvey was a husky, rugged Irish-American with a scraggly beard. He liked to wear old suit jackets and fedoras, and didn't give a damn if his clothes were in style now, or if they'd *ever* been in style. He lived by the adage, *"It's not how you look, it's how you feel,"* and he always felt like the coolest dude in the room. If he hadn't become a cop, he would've been a sailor, or a dockworker, or maybe a lumberjack if he lived in the woods and knew how to swing an axe.

Amanda, meanwhile, had Asian features, wore her hair in a tight bun, and her clothes were neatly pressed. If she was attractive, Harvey hadn't looked long enough to notice. She was in shape, but thin—way too thin, as far as Harvey was concerned. He liked women with meat on their bones and if they had a temper, liked to slap him around a little, so much the better. Amanda couldn't win a fight with a punching bag.

Worse, she was a snob. For example, when she was off duty, she liked to go to wine bars and to the theater and freakin' museums. What was up with that? For Harvey, it was bars—real bars, ones that sold beer and whiskey—and maybe an occasional trip to a pool hall or the racetrack.

They got out of the car and headed along the graveled driveway. Beat cops and medical personnel were working the scene, and there were black-and-whites, emergency medical services ambulances, and a Gotham TV news truck. Lacey White, the young, curvy brunette reporter was chatting with a cameraman, prepping to report from the scene.

"Never too early to break a hot news story, huh Lace?" Harvey called out.

When she spotted Harvey, her expression brightened.

"Harvey!"

She handed the cameraman the mike, then rushed

over. He met her halfway and she gave him a big,
tight hug. Damn, she felt good. Smelled good, too—a
combination of lady soap, whatever perfume she had
on, and her own natural scent. It gave him flashbacks
to the nights they'd spent together, how she'd tossed
him around like a giant beanbag and had her way with
him—just the way Harvey liked it.

He whispered into her ear. "I miss you, sweetheart."

She whispered back, "Me, too. What's wrong, Harv?
Lose my number?"

They'd gone out a few times a couple of years
back, always had a great time—hell, if they hadn't,
he would've forgotten about her by now. If he was a
relationship kind of guy, which he definitely wasn't,
she might've been the one for him. She was definitely
his type—fun, sexy, no attitude.

"Maybe I did," he said, "but I promise I'll find it
soon, sweetheart."

She nodded, and he smiled, feeling good about
himself. Not all guys could make that work—blow off
a woman, and then call her "sweetheart." Not without
seeming like a total sleaze ball. Harvey could work the
magic.

"I'd really like that," she said.

Her soft, raspy tone reminded him of the time she'd
whispered in his ear after she'd beaten the crap out of
him. *"Lacey's in charge,"* she'd said, *"and don't you ever
forget it."*

"I'll be in touch."

"I bet you say that to all the girls," she replied.

"Yeah, actually I do," he said, smiling. "Thing is, in your case, I mean it."

She laughed, enjoying the banter, as she headed back toward the cameraman. Harvey got along well with all of his old flames. As he often told people, *"Don't judge a man by his friends, judge him by his exes."* Every guy got along with his friends, but if he got along with his exes—well, that told you something about the man's character.

As he resumed walking with Amanda toward the entrance, she tossed him a harsh, judgmental look. Already he was beginning to find it familiar.

"What?" Harvey asked.

"Flirting at a crime scene?" she said. "Seriously?"

"We're not at a crime scene yet," Harvey protested. "We're *outside* a crime scene. Big difference. Huge, actually."

Amanda remained stone-faced. "When we get in there, I'll take the lead," she said. "You just hang back."

Harvey did a double take, partly because he was at least half-drunk and partly because he was thinking, *is she serious?* Amanda had been getting more and more controlling. What was up with that? She'd only been his partner for a week, and she kept insisting on doing a lot of the driving, picking the music they listened to in the car, and editing his arrest reports before he handed them in. But telling him how to handle an investigation? Was she serious?

He had twenty years in the Department, nine as a detective, and she had what, five and less than a month? Besides, she was a woman. He didn't have anything against women—like, *obviously*. He loved women, and women loved him—it was a mutual respect sorta thing, and he had a lot of, well, notches on his belt to prove it. But he didn't think women should be cops was all. There was plenty of other work they could have, so why cops? For example, was he trying out to be a cheerleader? No, he was not.

The other day he'd voiced his opinion to Amanda, and she'd called him a sexist.

Harvey had fired back, "I'm no sexist. I'm the *opposite* of a sexist. If I was sexist, I wouldn't like women as much as I do, and if I didn't like women, I'd *want* them to be cops, so they could get hurt or killed. But I don't want them to be cops, because I love women and want them to be safe."

She hadn't bought it, but it had shut her up.

Now he said, "Sorry, I had a cold last week and maybe my ears are still a little clogged. I thought I just heard you telling me how to do my job."

"First off, you're piss drunk," Amanda said.

"Whoa, I'm not at all drunk," Harvey said. "A little buzzed, yeah, okay, but not drunk. Want me to walk a straight line for ya?" Harvey managed a couple of steps, as if he were walking along a tightrope, and lost his balance. Then he said, "Or, better yet, wanna give me a breathalyzer?"

"Why do I need a breathalyzer?" Amanda asked. "I can *smell* it from here."

Attitude, Harvey thought. See? You didn't get crap

like that from a man. *A man'll stab you in the back, but he won't needle you to death.*

"Second, I'm better at a crime scene than you are," Amanda said.

"What?" Harvey couldn't believe this. "Who says?"

"It's a fact," she said. "I just am. You get too worked up, you don't ask the right questions, and this is all exacerbated when you've been drinking."

"Oooh, big word," Harvey said. "I'm impressed. When did you memorize that one?" As they headed up the several stairs, leading to the entrance, Amanda was muttering to herself. Harvey, dizzy, had to hold the railing.

Yeah, okay, he was a little buzzed. So what?

Amanda noticed he was wobbling and smirked. She rang the doorbell.

"Okay, I need to hear this," Harvey said. "So how are you better than me?"

"It's called having people skills," she said. "I have them, you don't. Honestly, your attitude embarrasses me sometimes. We're in a partnership, so it reflects on both of us."

Harvey laughed—for effect. He didn't think any of this was funny.

"I embarrass you, huh?" Then he was full-blown serious—even angry. "Look, you're lucky I'm even working with you, okay, sweetheart?"

"Sweetheart?" Amanda said. "Seriously? Who do you think I am, your news reporter ho?"

"Whoa, easy, Lacey's a classy lady," Harvey said.

"And what's wrong with 'sweetheart'? Why's that a bad thing to say these days? It's a term of freakin' endearment."

Amanda rolled her eyes. "You wouldn't work with me if you had a choice," she said, ringing the bell again.

"What do you mean?" Harvey asked. "I mean about not having a choice."

"Captain Essen told you if you didn't, you were going on desk duty."

This was true, but Harvey hadn't known it was public knowledge.

"Where did you hear this?" he demanded.

"Gimme a break," Amanda said. "Everybody in the department knows about your misogynistic tendencies."

"Wait," Harvey said, "they said I gave a massage to *who*?"

"How much exactly did you drink tonight?" Amanda asked.

"It's last night, now," Harvey said. "And not much. Not as much as usual anyway."

"If you're inebriated you shouldn't be here," Amanda said.

"No, *you* shouldn't be here," Harvey said. "You and your fancy words. *Inebriated*." He laughed. "What's wrong, people can't say 'drunk' anymore? That's too low class?" He belched then continued, "Wanna know the truth? Okay, yeah you're right. I didn't wanna work with you, and I still don't wanna work with you—but as long as we're together, I'm in charge, I call the shots. *Comprende mundo?*"

"*Comprende mundo?*" She wrinkled her face as if she smelled something foul. "That doesn't even mean anything."

Harvey glared at her, and didn't notice that Martha Wayne had answered the door. When he did notice her, he let out a soft whistle.

Talk about pretty—yowza. If you looked up "Harvey's type" in the Encyclopedia Britannica, you'd see a big picture of this lady. He'd seen her around a lot over the years, talked to her a few times at charity balls, GCPD functions, and whatnot. She was blonde, classy, okay a little on the thin side, but somehow with Martha Wayne the whole package worked. The thing Harvey liked most about her, though, was her confidence. In a weird way she reminded him of Fish Mooney.

Yeah, Fish and Martha came from totally different walks of life—it probably wasn't possible to get *more* different—but there was something similar about them, too. Fish always made herself the center of attention. Same with Martha Wayne—when you were in the same room with her, you noticed her. It was hard to look away, and she didn't just have attitude. She had the looks to back it up.

Even now, in the middle of the night, after there'd been a murder at Wayne Manor, the lady of the house looked stunning. How about that as a litmus test for beauty? Of course Martha Wayne was married, and Harvey wasn't the type of guy who would ever make a pass at another man's wife, but looking? Looking never hurt nobody.

Snapping out of it, he realized Amanda was already asking questions.

"Were you here when the shooting happened?" she asked Martha.

Had Harvey's gaze drifted down to her chest?

Yep, yep it had. Hey, he was only human.

"No, I was asleep," Martha said. "We were in Switzerland for a week, and just arrived back this afternoon, so I was pretty tired. Actually, it was the gunshot—I mean *shots*, that woke me up."

Harvey caught a glimpse of Amanda, sneering at him as if saying, *Seriously?* They stepped through the doorway and started down the hall. He shook his head a little and spoke up.

"Um, how many shots were there?" he asked. It didn't really matter; he just wanted to say something.

"Several, I believe," Martha said. "I'm not sure. When I heard them, I went and woke up Alfred, our butler." Harvey and Amanda followed her along the wide, brightly lit hallway, past all the fancy antique furniture, toward the crime scene further back in the house. He couldn't help noticing Martha's swinging hips. Even in yoga pants, or whatever she had on, her body looked in perfect proportions. Harvey didn't know how to draw, but even if he had, if he was the best damn artist in the world, he wouldn't have been able to draw a body like that.

"You're so classy," Amanda whispered into his ear. Harvey began to smile, then realized she hadn't meant it as a compliment.

As they approached a door that probably led into the drawing room, there was a kid waiting for them. Martha approached her son Bruce, who was standing there in pajama bottoms and T-shirt. Harvey had met the kid a bunch of times. Good, polite rich type. Smart too.

"Bruce, why don't you go upstairs and get some rest?" Martha said. "You've had a long day, and you're probably still jetlagged."

"I'm not tired, Mom." He glanced at Harvey and Amanda, his eyes wide, and said, "Are you the detectives who'll be in charge of this case?"

"Yep, we are," Harvey answered.

Bruce eyed him carefully, but didn't say anything more. Could the kid tell he'd been drinking? Eh, highly, *highly* unlikely. Nobody could hide his drunk better than Harvey Bullock.

"Who do you think is responsible?" Bruce asked.

"We don't know yet," Amanda said. "We just got here."

"But you must have some idea," he insisted. "I've heard that police always know who the criminals are." Something in his voice indicated that he didn't believe it, though.

"Cynicism," Harvey said. "I like that, kid." Harvey belched, re-tasting that last shot of Jameson he'd downed. And, damn, it still tasted good.

Outside Thomas Wayne's study the body remained splayed. Several uniformed cops were in the room—a couple of them talking to Thomas Wayne and Alfred Pennyworth, his butler, near the entrance to Wayne's study. Pennyworth may have looked like an uppity butler, but he had a tough-ass past—you could see it just by the way he stood, and by looking in the guy's eyes.

The medical examiner was photographing the dead guy, who was in a hooded sweatshirt and was wearing a werewolf mask.

"Who is he?" Harvey asked.

"Looks like a werewolf to me," one of the cops said. He was a fresh-faced blond guy, probably right out of the academy.

Smartass. The kid must've caught his expression.

"He has no ID on him," the cop said, "and obviously we didn't want to pull off the mask. I mean, not till the ME and you guys got here."

"This the only vic?" Harvey asked.

"Yeah, there were two other intruders, but they escaped."

"The security's tight here. How'd they get in?"

"The security system was disabled and the guard at the gate, guy named Nigel Hayward, got ambushed. When we got here he was tied up and gagged. Beaten up pretty bad, too—his face looked like hamburger meat. He's in Gotham General now. He'll live, but he's gonna take a lot of scars with him."

"We'll have to talk to Nigel," Amanda said.

"Good idea," Harvey said, the sarcasm so dry it almost sounded sincere. He got a pair of latex gloves from one of the EMS workers and squatted near the body, careful not to get any blood on his favorite chinos. Reaching out, he gripped the edge of the mask, avoiding the wound on the dead man's neck. "Time for the big reveal," he said. "Let's see who we've got under here."

The dead guy was a pudgy-faced, red-haired guy with a thick scar on his forehead.

"Never seen him before in my life," Harvey said.

"Neither have I."

Who the hell said that? Harvey looked back over his shoulder and saw that Thomas Wayne had come up behind him.

"Hey, Mr. Wayne." The detective stood up, lurching a little. "I'd shake your hand, but…"

"Do you want to tell us what happened here?" Amanda asked.

"Yes, but it's late obviously," Wayne said, "and I've already explained it all to the officers. Can't they fill you in?"

"Better if we get it from the horse's mouth," Harvey said. "No offense."

"None taken," Wayne said.

"And we'll need to speak to Mr. Pennyworth as well," Amanda said.

"Of course," Wayne said. "If you'll give me a moment…" Harvey nodded, then watched Thomas go over and whisper something to Bruce, who was still standing with Martha. A moment later both mother and son headed away, probably to get back to bed. Before Bruce exited, however, he looked back at Harvey, as if to say, *Find out who did this*.

Harvey smiled, and gave the kid the thumbs up.

A short time later, Harvey and Amanda were seated across from Thomas Wayne and Alfred Pennyworth at the dining room table. Wayne leaned his elbows on the polished wood surface, while Pennyworth sat stiffly.

"We'll make this quick," Harvey said. "There's been a bunch of other art robberies in Gotham over the past couple months, so there's a chance the same crew is behind this one. So you say there were three intruders in the house, right?" The uniformed cops had filled him in, but he wanted to hear it for himself. Besides, it made him sound official.

"That's right," Wayne said. "All in Halloween masks. A zombie, a werewolf, and a gorilla. The gorilla was holding the Picasso, the zombie had what looked like a meat cleaver."

"That explains how your wall got chopped up," Harvey said. "Do you have any idea why they did that?"

"No," Wayne said, and he shook his head. "None."

Questioning witnesses was Harvey's forte, and even when he was two sheets to the Jameson wind—as his relatives in Ireland liked to say—he could tell when somebody was holding back. He had that feeling about Thomas Wayne.

"Come on, you must have *some* ideas," Amanda

insisted. Harvey glared at her, annoyed. Hadn't he made it clear that *he'd* ask the questions?

Wayne remained silent for another few seconds.

"Well, since they're art thieves, it might be that they were looking for some sort of electrical alarm system," he suggested. "Maybe they thought the painting was wired for protection?"

No, he's reaching, Harvey thought. *But for what?*

"Do you have separate alarms like that for your paintings?" Amanda asked.

"No," Wayne said. "I thought my main system would suffice." With a smile he added, "Obviously I thought wrong."

"How do you think they disabled the main system?" Harvey asked.

"That I have no clue about," Thomas said. "Nobody knows those codes except my wife and Alfred... well, and Wayne Security, the company we employ."

"Well, they figured out the code somehow," Harvey said. "So somebody must've squealed."

He looked at Alfred.

"I beg your pardon," the butler said, and it came out more of a growl. "Are you implying that I might have any involvement in this?" Pennyworth had a British accent. It wasn't a fancy Brit accent, though. It was the kind of accent that tough guys had in crime movies.

"I like to shoot from the hip," Harvey said.

"Bloody idiot," Pennyworth said. He looked like he was ready to jump over the table. Harvey kept a hand on his piece—just in case.

"It's okay," Amanda said. "Let's just calm down."

"I'm calm," Harvey said. "It's this guy who looks like he's about to blow a gasket." Then he said to Pennyworth, "Down, boy."

The butler's face went red and Harvey saw veins in his forehead. So the detective turned back to the master of the house.

"Is it possible somebody at Wayne Security is involved in this?" he asked.

"Anything's possible," Wayne said. "I'll certainly conduct an internal investigation."

"Yeah, I think that's a good idea," Harvey said.

Pennyworth was still sneering.

"So where were you when you heard the intruders?" Amanda asked Wayne. "In your bedroom?"

Wayne hesitated, then said, "No, I was in the kitchen."

Again Harvey's gut told him something was off about the man's answer. "Didn't they have to pass by the kitchen to get to your study?" he asked.

"I suppose they were already in the house when I went down to the kitchen to get a drink," Wayne said.

He was smooth—Harvey had to admit it.

"Okay," Harvey said, "so you heard them, and then what happened?"

"I came out here, and one of the intruders—the one with the werewolf mask, shot me, so I shot him. He didn't die though—Alfred shot him from the stairwell."

"One shot from the stairwell, huh?" Harvey was

impressed. "That's some good aim ya got there. What're you, some kind of sniper?"

"Actually, I did toy with it in the military," Pennyworth said.

"A butler who knows how to kill," Harvey said. "I guess that can come in handy."

"It did tonight," Wayne said.

"Back to the walls," Harvey said. "Sorry, but I ain't buying the security system theory. These art thieves are pros—they can tell if a painting's wired or not. Without doing enough damage to raise the dead."

"Okay, so perhaps they thought I had something hidden in the walls," Wayne said. "Jewels, or money, or some sort of valuables."

"Do ya?" Harvey asked.

"Do I what?" Thomas asked.

"Hide valuables in your walls."

"No," Wayne said. "It was just another theory. I have no idea why they chopped up the walls, Detective. Maybe they're just crazy. There are a lot of crazy people in Gotham these days—just look how Arkham's overflowing. There's a mental health crisis in this town, which is why Wayne Enterprises has been such a huge advocate for mental health reform in Goth—" He cut himself off, rubbed his forehead with one hand, then continued. "Look, it's late and I'm exhausted, so can we call it a night? I'd be happy to answer any more questions you have, just as I'd love to get my painting back, but it's very late and it's been quite an eventful evening. If you'd like to come by again tomorrow and—"

"Just one more thing," Harvey said. "You said nothing else is missing, but can you think of anything else these guys might've wanted? Besides the family jewels?"

"What do you mean?" Wayne asked.

"Something else valuable," Harvey said. "Some other piece of art maybe? Something they were *really* after."

"Do you have any idea how much *Le Picador* is worth?" Wayne said.

"Let's just say I'm confident it's out of my price range," Harvey said.

"It's worth tens of millions of dollars, or more," Wayne said. "I think it's more than a big enough score for art thieves, don't you?"

"Touché," Harvey said. "But tying up the guy at the gate? Taking apart your office? These don't exactly look like the moves of professional art gangs. Too much fuss, especially when their target was hanging in plain sight."

"Can I ask you a question now?" Wayne asked.

"Shoot," Harvey said. Then he pointed to Alfred, "I mean him, not you, Sniper."

"Have you been drinking tonight?" Wayne asked Harvey.

"'Scuse me?" Harvey asked, pulling back as if offended.

"Because I think Captain Essen might want to know that one of her detectives showed up here after a night out on the town, tossing around wild, bizarre theories when he should've been trying to find my stolen property."

"What makes you think I'm drunk?" Harvey asked.

"I can smell the alcohol from across the table," Wayne said.

Harvey glared. "How do you know it's not my mouthwash?"

Amanda stood up. "Thank you for your time, Mr. Wayne, Mr. Pennyworth," she said. "We'll keep you updated on the progress of the investigation." At that she spun and marched out of the room ahead of Harvey, moving at a clip.

Leaving Wayne Manor, she was looking straight ahead, in a rush to get to the car. The sky was starting to lighten to the east, but it was still pretty much dark.

Harvey had the car keys out.

"I'm driving," she announced, and snatched it away. A headache was starting to make itself known, and Harvey didn't protest.

"Well, that went pretty well, huh?" he said as they drove along the driveway, the headlights illuminating the open gate ahead. Amanda, at the wheel, still wouldn't look in his direction. Harvey didn't get what was wrong with her, why she always had to be so freakin' moody.

"Women," he muttered.

THREE

It wasn't noon yet, but Alfred had already arranged for a crew of repairmen to fix the walls in Thomas's study. Most of the other repair work had already been done, and all the blood on the floor had been cleaned up. There was practically no evidence that there had been a shootout in the house, and a man had been killed less than twelve hours ago.

"Looking good," Thomas said to Alfred.

"The walls should be repaired by the end of the day," he replied. "I'm sorry this happened, sir."

"Sorry?" Thomas sounded confused. "It's not your fault. Like Detective Bullock said—you're a hero."

"Not quite," Alfred protested. "I'm afraid a hero would've made it downstairs much earlier. Lucky is what I was, but I assure you, I won't let it happen again."

"It was the middle of the night, and you had just taken a transcontinental flight. If I wasn't working such crazy hours, I wouldn't have heard them either."

Alfred took a few moments to absorb this.

Thomas Wayne didn't talk much about his work, and Alfred was always careful not to overstep his boundaries, but he was sharp—especially when it came to security. He knew Thomas had been having issues with work, and he could tell the incident bothered his employer more than he was revealing. The robbery very well might have been a cover, and there may have been another reason behind the break-in.

What that reason could be, however, Alfred could not fathom—and that didn't sit well with him.

"Well, let's hope the police get the painting back soon," he said.

"I'm not keeping my hopes up," Thomas confessed. "The police are overloaded these days, given the turf war between Don Maroni and Don Falcone's crews. The body count is high, and increasing by the day. How hard do you think they'll look for a missing painting? They'll take a half-hearted look around Gotham, question the usual suspects, but if the trail isn't obvious, it'll turn into a cold case by this time tomorrow."

"I can take a gander around town, if you like," Alfred said. "I do have a bit of Scotland Yard detective work on my resume, after all."

"I appreciate that," Thomas said, "but you have your own responsibilities here, managing the household, seeing to our schedules and, as last night exemplified—protecting us. But I'll need your help in finding out how the security system was compromised last night, and what exactly happened at the gate with Nigel. I know you and he are good friends. How's he doing?"

"In quite bad shape, I'm afraid," Alfred said. "His face may require reconstructive surgery, and one of his knees was shattered, perhaps irreparably. I'm going to pop over and visit him later on."

"Perhaps you can put together a care package from all of us," Thomas said.

"That's quite nice of you, sir."

"I know the police will talk to him, but perhaps when you visit him you can find out if he knew any of the intruders, or saw anything of importance."

"I will as soon as he's up to it," Alfred said, "though I assume they were wearing the same masks they were wearing last night. Do you mean if he recognized their voices?"

"Or if he actually knew them," Thomas said.

Alfred frowned. "You're not implying that you think he's lying about what happened, are you?"

"I'm saying we have to look into everything," Thomas said, not backing down.

"So first that detective, Bullock, implied that I might have leaked the alarm codes to the intruders," Alfred said flatly, "and now you're accusing my best mate of letting them on to the grounds." He gave his employer an expressionless stare.

"I'm not accusing anyone of anything," Thomas said, though his voice wasn't conciliatory. "The fact remains, however, that three dangerous men—criminals and killers—pretty much waltzed in here last night, and that can't happen again."

"I've known Nigel for thirty-five years," Alfred

said. "He'd never betray you. Besides, his face looked like beef tartar when they took him away."

"Some people will do anything for money," Thomas said.

"Nigel isn't 'some people,'" Alfred said.

"Security breaches can't happen at Wayne Manor," Thomas said, his voice rising. "Not ever again, and that's final."

The workers looked over. Wayne glared at them until they resumed working.

"Of course, sir," Alfred said. "I understand the situation entirely."

"Thank you," Thomas responded, and he walked away.

Thomas regretted losing control, and taking his frustrations out on Alfred, but he was under so much stress lately he had to give himself a pass. Besides, he and Alfred were old friends, so they were allowed to vent once in a while. In fact, their ability to get angry at each other without any lasting fallout was what made their friendship stronger.

He went to the kitchen to get a bite to eat. He hadn't slept much—an hour at most—and upon awakening he'd forgotten to eat. He felt light-headed, which probably contributed to his edginess. A roast-beef-on-rye sandwich with mustard would hit the spot, so he fixed himself one.

Unlike other billionaires Thomas knew, who lived

with a full staff—cooks, maids, drivers, and people to provide practically every other service imaginable— Thomas and Martha had chosen a different lifestyle for their son, Bruce. Aside from Alfred, the Waynes only had a few full-time employees who were involved in their daily, personal lives. A maid came several days a week, a landscaper and his staff came to work on Wayne Manor's lavish gardens, and Alfred did most of the cooking.

They didn't go overboard on buying Bruce things either. He had a modest allowance, and aside from living in Wayne Manor, spending vacations at the Wayne's family chalet in Switzerland, and visiting other exotic locales around the globe, Bruce had experienced a fairly normal, low-key upbringing.

As he ate, something still gnawed at Thomas— fueling his anxiety. It had to do with the walls in his study. The idea that the thieves had been searching for a security system seemed farfetched, indeed, but the thieves certainly seemed to have been searching for something else. Unless their goal was a hidden cache of wealth, the most obvious alternative also was the most disturbing.

Could they have been searching for Thomas's hidden office? Yet how could they even know of its existence?

If that was true, the violation of his home struck deeper than he could have imagined. Barring further information, however, it was a waste of his time trying to figure it out. He could come up with endless theories, but it was up to the GCPD to solve the mystery, not him.

Meanwhile, the sandwich had rejuvenated him. After he loaded the dishwasher, he looked out through the kitchen window to the garden, and saw Bruce out there on the veranda, writing in a notebook. Bruce didn't have many friends from school, and spent much of his time with adults... or alone. Thomas and Martha had hoped that when Bruce started at Anders Preparatory Academy he would begin to socialize more, but so far that hadn't happened.

In fact, he seemed to spend even more time alone— mainly reading, studying, playing video games, and watching movies. His best friend was probably Alfred, whom Thomas had hired when Bruce was quite young. The boy had always liked Alfred, and Thomas couldn't think of a more positive role model for his son.

Nevertheless, while Alfred took Bruce to the movies and other events, Bruce still shied away from children in his own peer group. He never seemed upset or depressed, though. He was different from other kids— but in a good way. He didn't need attention from others in order to be happy, and he didn't desire material things. He was smart, curious, determined, and had an inner confidence that was astounding for a boy his age.

Thomas went out to the garden and approached his son. It was a sunny but cold fall day. Leaves were whipping up, but Bruce was seated on the veranda overlooking the garden, immersed in his reading.

"Gripping stuff, huh?"

Bruce hadn't heard his father approaching, but

didn't seem startled as he glanced up from the classically bound hardback.

"Yes, *Beowulf*," he said.

"Ah, one of my all-time-favorites," Thomas said, "but I haven't read *Beowulf* since college. Are you enjoying it?"

"Quite a bit," Bruce said. "Particularly I'm enjoying reading about Grendel. Monsters fascinate me."

"Really?" Thomas smiled, always impressed by Bruce's precociousness, and his way with words. "Why do you think that is?"

"Maybe because it's so foreign from my own experience," Bruce said. "Sane people are easy to understand, but monsters are a true mystery. You can think you know a monster, but there's always a part of the monster that's elusive, that you'll never know or fully understand."

"Well, speaking of monsters," Thomas said, "how are you after the invasion by the werewolf, zombie, and gorilla last night?"

"I'm okay." Bruce was confused. "Why wouldn't I be?"

"Well, there was a shooting in the house last night," Thomas said. "I'm sure it was traumatic for your mother, and I just want to make sure you're not having a hard time with it, as well."

"Oh, I understand now," Bruce said. "You're worried about my psychological state." He smiled. "I'm fine, but I appreciate your concern, Dad. Thank you for asking."

Thomas didn't want to let it go. "What about when you heard the gunshots, or saw the dead body?" he pressed. "Are you sure you weren't at all frightened?"

"Nothing like that frightens me," Bruce said in a youthful, matter-of-fact voice. To all appearances he was sincere, but…

"Now I *know* that's not true," Thomas said. "You have a strong constitution, but you're not made of armor. You used to be afraid of the dark when you were younger, and you've had plenty of nightmares over the years. I remember we were at the Prado in Madrid, and there was a Rembrandt self-portrait that for some reason terrified you. You had a visceral reaction, and started crying. After that, you couldn't even look at a poster or photograph of the painting, without getting upset."

"The painting must have reminded me of something," Bruce said. "A suppressed trauma perhaps, but that was the past. I think I was just five or six. I'm older now—nothing frightens me anymore. But things do make me angry."

"Really?" Thomas was intrigued. "What sort of things?"

"When people get away with things—you could call it injustice, I suppose," Bruce said. "It angers me that people can get away with crimes, like beating poor Nigel, without being punished. My humanities teacher told our class that seventy percent of all crimes go unpunished nowadays, and the number may be higher, since many crimes go unreported. In Gotham those numbers are probably even worse. I don't think this is fair at all." He paused, then added, "Criminals deserve to be punished."

"Well, many good people in Gotham, including myself, agree with you," Thomas said. "The trouble is that there are a lot of bad people in the world, too, and the police sometimes get overwhelmed. They can't investigate cases as thoroughly as they'd like to. So don't get your hopes up too much with our break-in.

"What makes the situation more complicated is a lot of crime isn't on the surface," he added. "It's not just shootings and stolen paintings. It's what's going on under the surface that's the real problem—the deep-seated corruption on every level that pervades our society."

"Corruption?" Bruce's interest had been piqued. "What sort of corruption?"

"Well, like—" Thomas cut himself off, realizing he was talking too much about subjects he didn't want to discuss with his son. He never involved Bruce—or even Martha—in the details of Wayne Enterprises and his other business ventures, and the baggage that came with them. There were things he and his company had done, things that continued to this day, that made him ashamed, and could put his family in danger.

In many ways, Thomas retained some of his father's old world values, and believed in keeping business and family separate.

"Actually that's a conversation for another day," Thomas said. "But for now it's important that you focus on other things—like *Beowulf*. Do you have a test coming up?"

"No, I have to write a paper," Bruce said. "It's due Monday, but I don't know what to write about."

Pleased that his distraction strategy had worked, Thomas said, "It seems like you have a lot to say about monsters. All you have to do is put it into words."

"I suppose so," Bruce said. "I don't know. I like reading literature for personal enjoyment, but I don't like having to explain how I feel about books. I prefer science and mathematics. Literature's all based on opinion. Any two people can read the same book and have vastly different views of it. But science and math are precise—there's only one answer, and if you search hard enough, you can always find it."

Thomas smiled, once again impressed by his son's beyond-his-years wisdom. Then he saw Martha approaching from the house. She was wearing a red elegant dress, heels, and her dirty blond hair was pinned back. He knew why she had gotten dressed up—she was hosting a luncheon today downtown, to help raise money for the GMHCC—the Gotham Mental Health Crisis Center—a group that had received many generous donations from Wayne Enterprises.

"There you are," Martha said to Thomas. "I was looking all over for you."

God knew, Thomas had made some mistakes in his life, yet he'd made some good decisions along the way as well—and the best had been marrying this amazing woman. They'd met in their early twenties—set up by mutual friends. Martha didn't come from money, but Thomas knew from the get-go that she wasn't a gold digger. Her honesty, integrity, and overall down-to-earthiness had been some of her most enchanting qualities. Oh, and it didn't hurt that she was gorgeous. She became a great mother to Bruce and had raised him without the help of a full-time nanny. They had talked about having more children, but Martha felt she wanted to focus on raising Bruce and her charity work in Gotham. He respected her decision.

She came over, kissed Thomas.

"I can't find the keys to the Bentley," she said. "Do you have them?"

"Yes, they're inside," Thomas said.

"And how are you this morning, Bruce?" Martha asked, smiling.

"Fine," Bruce said. "Just doing some schoolwork."

"Don't forget, you have your tennis lesson this afternoon—Alfred will take you."

"About tennis," Bruce said. "I enjoy the sport, but can I possibly take boxing lessons instead? There's a gym downtown, and it has a great reputation. Many professional boxers have trained there."

"Absolutely not," Martha said. "Boxing is a brutal sport. Boxers get hurt, wind up with awful head injuries that affect them for the rest of their lives."

"I don't mind the pain," Bruce said.

Thomas smiled, but Martha remained serious.

"No, en-oh," Martha said to Bruce. "You're not a fighter, so just get that out of your head."

"Dad, what do you think?" Bruce asked.

While Thomas thought that a boxing class would be good for Bruce—toughen him up—he knew it was important for parents to put up a unified front, and he didn't want to be disrespectful to Martha.

"I think you just got your answer from your mother," he said.

Bruce seemed disappointed, but he was a smart kid—he knew that Thomas wouldn't bend, and it would be a waste of time to try to manipulate him. He had taken it as far as it was going to go.

"I understand, Mom," he said. Then he said to his father, "There's a big fight on TV tonight. Can we watch it together?"

"Right, the Williams-Sanchez bout," Thomas said. "I forgot that's tonight. I'd love to." Then he noticed Martha's disapproving expression, but tried to avoid it.

"Great," Bruce said, and he returned to reading his book.

As Thomas and Martha walked side by side through the garden back toward Wayne Manor, Martha spoke.

"Sometimes I worry about Bruce," she said.

"It's just a fight on the television," he replied. "The whole country will be watching it."

"No, it's not that," Martha said. "I just feel like he's looking for trouble." A frown wrinkled her perfect features.

"I think it's age appropriate," Thomas said. "He's not looking for trouble, per se. He's just looking for a little adventure."

"Well, I think there's a way to achieve adventurousness without getting your head bashed in," she persisted. "If he wants adventure, he can go hiking, or take a trip to Africa, or read spy thrillers. People who look for fights wind up getting killed."

"But there are situations when he might need to defend himself," Thomas said. "Last night for example. Those men were armed and dangerous. What if they'd come upstairs?"

"He would've tried to fight them, and they would've shot him," Martha said. "My point exactly."

Judging from her tone, Thomas knew there would be no way to win this argument. When she got stuck on an opinion she rarely budged.

"Well, we won't have to worry about head injuries on the tennis court," Thomas said, hoping to put the issue to rest. They entered the house through the back entrance. Construction noise came from Thomas's study—an electric saw, a drill.

"Any word from the police?" Martha asked.

"No, and I doubt we'll hear much," Thomas said.

"Really, why's that?" She looked puzzled. "Detective Bullock said there have been other robberies lately, didn't he? He seemed confident he'd crack the case, even if he'd had a few too many last night."

"That didn't exactly inspire confidence," Thomas said. "I wouldn't count on Detective Bullock, if I were you."

"He's a man's man," Martha argued, "but it seemed to me as if he was sincere. One of the good guys."

"A good guy." Thomas let that linger as they headed

along the wide, lavish hallway. Then he said, "I agree, Bullock *seems* like a good guy, but sometimes I wonder if there are any truly good guys left in law enforcement. The whole system is so corrupt, from the top down, that it's impossible to have confidence in anyone anymore." It was his turn to frown. "Something has to be done about it. Somebody has to come to this town, and clean it all up—but I don't know who that person is, or whether cleaning up GCPD is even possible."

They entered the drawing room.

"Well, I still have faith, and I certainly hope the police find the painting soon," Martha said. "It's not just about the money. I mean that's important, of course, but the Picasso is a masterpiece, and it needs to have an owner who appreciates its value. Great art is like a beloved pet—it deserves a great home with a kind, loving owner."

Thomas opened the drawer of the antique oak armoire, took out a set of car keys and handed them to Martha.

"I swear I looked in there five minutes ago, and didn't see them," she said. "God, I feel so scatterbrained today."

"That's understandable," Thomas said. "We had a wonderful relaxing time in Switzerland, and then we come back to a difficult situation. Still, I guess that's just par for the course in our beloved city, right?"

"Sad," Martha agreed, "but probably true." They left the drawing room. A repairman—an older man with a potbelly, carrying a can of paint—passed by in the hallway on his way to Thomas's study.

"Mr. and Mrs. Wayne," the man said in a friendly, respectful way. They smiled, acknowledging him. When he was out of earshot, though, Martha spoke.

"I think it could've been an inside job," she said, her voice low. "I mean, think about it, people come in and out of Wayne Manor all the time—workers, acquaintances, delivery people. Many seem nice, but how do we know who is and who isn't trustworthy? And how long have we had this new alarm system? Over a year now, right? In all that time, someone could have seen one of us setting the alarm, and memorized the code."

"I guess anything's possible," Thomas said. "We'll change the code, that's for sure, and maybe even upgrade the whole system."

"But if it was an inside job," Martha said, not letting it go, "I still don't understand why they destroyed the walls in your study. What were they looking for? And why in there?" She noticed his expression. "I know, I know, I'm playing detective, but I can't help it. I feel like the answer's obvious, but we just don't know it yet."

Thomas didn't want to tell Martha about his secret office—mainly for her protection. If she didn't know the office existed, no one could extract the information from her. For the same reason, he didn't tell her much about what he did on a day-to-day basis at Wayne Enterprises, and the sordid people with whom he sometimes had to interact.

He wanted to run Wayne Enterprise with honesty

and integrity, but sometimes in Gotham that was simply impossible. He had enemies, including some on his own board of directors. Nevertheless, he didn't intend to be deceitful to Martha in any way—his secretiveness was for her own protection.

The less she knew, the less the danger.

"Look, who knows why they tore up the place?" Thomas said. "Maybe they were trying to disable an alarm—that was my first instinct. Or it's possible they weren't looking for anything at all. Maybe they just did it because they're destructive, mentally unstable, anarchistic, or all of the above. Sometimes people don't need a reason to act crazy. It's just what they do."

"Well, I still think there has to be an explanation," Martha said. "There's something they wanted—in your study. Maybe something they thought was there, in the wall. Something hidden. So that means it had to be somebody who knows you."

"The guy who got shot, the one in the werewolf mask," Thomas said. "I'd never seen him before in my life."

"But somebody may have hired them," Martha said. "Somebody you work with. Somebody who's visited the house before."

"We may never have all the answers," Thomas said, seeking to keep his voice even. "Not every mystery is meant to be solved."

"I suppose you're right," she said, though he knew better than to think she'd let it go entirely. "I'd best be going. The luncheon awaits." She kissed him on the cheek, and walked briskly toward the door.

As Martha left, Thomas began to think.

Maybe she's right. There had been something else behind the home invasion—something they were looking for, and didn't find. Maybe—as Harvey Bullock had suggested—they thought there were treasures in his study, but his private records, which he kept in a safe in his secret basement office, were more valuable by far.

If a business associate was, in fact, behind the robbery, there were far too many suspects to consider, including members of Wayne Enterprise's Board of Directors. And there was one person in particular he needed to rule out. Not a business associate, per se, but someone with whom he had once worked, on a project he regretted every waking hour. A former friend who had become a bitter enemy.

Thomas went upstairs to his bedroom where he could be assured to have privacy, and picked up the phone.

"Frank, there's been a new development," he said. "We need to meet immediately."

FOUR

"Heard we may have a print match on Mr. Werewolf."

Gotham City Police Department Headquarters was already bustling and noisy in the early afternoon, as Amanda Wong approached Harvey Bullock's desk in the center of the cavernous room. Despite the high, arching windows and hanging lights, the steel beams and railings, open holding cells, dark wooden front desk, and concrete walls left shadows in every nook and cranny of the chaotic landscape. Old-fashioned metal desks, piled high with paperwork, seemed vaguely out of place in the Victorian workspace.

"Who is he?" Harvey asked.

"Don't know yet," Amanda said, "but let's go find out."

Harvey stood, grabbed his coffee mug, and followed his partner, weaving through the mob of beat officers, detectives, recently arrested criminals, and then down the long corridor to the Forensics Department. As with the rest of the GCPD, the laboratory seemed like something out of the past, with brick-and-tile walls, cluttered granite countertops, and thick wooden blinds.

The body of the werewolf guy was laid out on a cold metal slab. Edward Nygma, a young lab technician, was peculiarly intent on his examination as they entered, and to Harvey it seemed as if he might be enjoying his work a little *too* much.

"Ohmigod, visitors," Nygma said quickly, as if surprised—and maybe a little annoyed—at being interrupted. "Knocking is *polite*, you know," he added, pushing his glasses up on the narrow bridge of his nose.

"If you want some more time alone with your new friend, we can come back," Harvey replied. Truth be told he, like everybody else at the GCPD, liked to kid around with Nygma, give him a hard time, but the kid was all right. A freak show, yeah, but harmless.

"Well, we *are* getting to know each other." Nygma grinned the way he always did, showing too many teeth. "I always love meeting new people."

Man, this kid was weird, with his nerdy glasses and goofy, toothy smile and all. Then again, anybody who wanted to work with dead bodies all day long, as his freakin' *career*, had to be one taco short of a combination plate.

"So what's the verdict?" Harvey asked. "Who is he?"

"What word of five letters only has one left when two are removed?" Nygma was grinning again.

"Sweet mother of Christ," Harvey said. "I'm barely through my second cup of java here, Ed."

"A stone," Amanda said.

"She's a smart cookie," Nygma said, in his usual smug, know-it-all tone. "Label me impressed."

"So his name's Stone?" Harvey said.

"*Byron* Stone," Nygma said. "He was released from Blackgate Penitentiary two weeks ago, where he'd served twelve years of a twelve-year sentence for manslaughter." He looked down with a look of... admiration? "No time off for good behavior for this bad boy."

Harvey went over to the body on the slab.

"Byron Stone, yeah, now I recognize him," Harvey said. "I didn't connect the dots last night, 'cause he'd been off the board for so long. I was a beat cop when Stone took the manslaughter rap. If I remember correctly, he was a career criminal, hired gun, typical Gotham freelancer. No loyalty to any criminal organization. Worked with Falcone, Maroni, and anybody who had cash money to pay him."

"Basically, he could've been working for anybody," Amanda said.

"Basically," Harvey said.

"So I suppose that puts you back at ground-zero," Nygma said, sounding almost happy about it.

"You need to make some friends, Nygma," Harvey said. "I mean friends who are *alive*." Without another word he turned and headed for the door, one step ahead of his partner. Walking back through the station, he said to Amanda, "Since Stone just got outta lockup, it's unlikely he's connected to the other painting robberies."

"Unless he was a recent hire," Amanda said.

"Good point," Harvey said. "Let's find everybody who's interacted with Stone since he got out of jail—there must be an old cellmate or someone he shot his mouth off to. And let's see if anybody knows who he went to work for. The top two choices are Maroni and Falcone."

"Our first stop should be a visit with Fish Mooney," Amanda said. "She's running that club for Falcone, and you two have a history, don't you?"

That made him stop. He stared her down.

"How the hell do you know about me and Fish?" Harvey asked.

"I saw it on the list."

"What list?"

"The list of worst-kept secrets."

Harvey almost smiled. Yeah, all right, Amanda could be funny—when she wanted to be—but that didn't mean he had to like working with her.

"Well, don't believe everything you hear," he said.

"So you and Mooney *don't* have a past?"

"Oh, we have a past all right," Harvey said. "I said don't believe *everything* you hear, but that don't mean some of it ain't true." They reached his desk. He chugged the rest of his murky coffee, then grabbed his hat and overcoat and together they left the precinct. At the car, Harvey said, "I'm driving this time, so don't even ask."

Amanda frowned and looked him over. "Is this how you are in a relationship?" she asked, then she handed him the keys.

"Relationship?" He grunted a laugh. "I haven't been in a relationship since my high school girlfriend, and that lasted three weeks. I like to get out while the going's good."

On the way to Mooney's Nightclub, Harvey pulled out a flashing light and put on the siren to make better time, weaving through traffic.

"You should avoid Chinatown," Amanda said. "The traffic's terrible this time of day."

"If we go through the theater district, it's even worse," Harvey said.

"See? This is exactly what I'm talking about." she said. "You're so controlling. You'd be the type of guy who always has to hold the remote, and who has all the light switches on his side of the bed."

"I don't see a ring on your finger," Harvey said.

She looked away, out the window. Harvey could tell he'd hit a sore spot.

Finally she said, "I don't have time for a relationship."

"Lonely person's greatest excuse," Harvey said.

"What's that supposed to mean?"

"It means I know your type. You get on the horn with your girlfriends on Saturday night, and complain about how there are no good men in Gotham anymore—everybody's taken. That all the single guys are only out for one thing, or they're too this, or too that. Or when you meet one who seems okay, you try to change him into something he's not, and that blows up in your face. Then you wallow away your sorrow with a big carton of mint chocolate chip ice cream. Meanwhile it's your attitude that's the problem. You know, a chicken-and-the-egg kinda thing."

"First of all, it's vanilla swirl," Amanda said. "Second of all, you don't know what the hell you're talking about."

"I'm talking about *that*," Harvey said. "Perfect example. Your attitude is your own worst enemy. If you could just rein it in, a guy would be able to put up with you, but your loneliness becomes a self-fulfilling prophecy."

"Yeah?" Amanda said. "And what about *your* loneliness? You're not exactly the ideal relationship counselor yourself."

"I ain't lonely," Harvey said. "I'm *alone*. Big difference." He swung a left on State Street, heading toward Chinatown. Then he had to hit the brakes because of bumper-to-bumper traffic.

"What did I tell you?" Amanda asked.

"And what did I tell *you*?" Harvey said. "Attitude issues. I can spot 'em a mile away."

Although they were only about ten blocks from Mooney's, it took them another half hour to get there. Fish had taken over the location ten years earlier, from a Chinese bookie who used to use the place for cockfighting. Harvey had been to the old joint many times, and it was still hard to believe this was the same place.

Fish had done a great job with the renovations—and getting the stench out. When they entered the moody, low-lit club, Harvey had to squint as his eyes adjusted from the brightness outside. It was late night twenty-four hours a day at Fish's. Up ahead, a few sad sacks were sitting alone at tables, looking unemployed, sipping their drinks, gawking at the scantily clad young woman on stage who was singing, appropriately, the blues.

"Been workin' all day… but ain't gettin' no pay…"

"Hey, Harvey, what can I do for you?"

Butch Gilzean, Fish's bulky right-hand man, was sitting at the bar. He was in a suit and tie, sipping a drink. Harvey had never seen Butch kill anybody, but if he was working for Fish Mooney, it was a good bet that the guy had at least broken a neck or two.

"Looking for my lady," Harvey said. He didn't have to glance over to know Amanda was rolling her eyes. "Oh, sorry," he added quickly. "This is my… partner, Amanda." He turned to her and gestured. "Amanda, meet Butch."

"How do you do?" Butch said, checking her out, eyeing her up and down.

"She's single and lookin'," Harvey said. "I mean, if you wanna take her out sometime."

"Oh, yeah?" Butch had seemed half asleep before. Now his interest piqued.

Amanda gave Harvey a vicious look.

"How 'bout some drinks?" Butch asked.

"I'll have water," Amanda said.

"Bourbon," Harvey said. *Why not?* It was afternoon—way past the time for a little hair of the dog.

"Harrrrvey."

And there she was—the goddess herself. She had come out from the back and was strutting toward them, hips swinging in a dress that barely went to mid-thigh. She had a tight body—stronger than most men—but the muscles didn't overwhelm the curves. And the best part, as far as Harvey was concerned? How she smelled. Her natural aroma always sent shock waves through his brain. She was the kind of a woman a blind man could fall for.

Call it love at first scent.

"Hey, Fish, baby."

Harvey kissed her—man, those lips felt good—and then he hugged her and didn't want to let go. What made it so great—he knew she felt exactly the same way about him.

Butch brought the drinks over.

"You shouldn't be drinking on the job," Amanda said, sounding pissed off. He had a feeling it wasn't about the bourbon, either.

"What're you gonna do," Harvey said, "report me?"

"Maybe I should."

"You do that, you're a squealer."

"Now, now," Fish said. "Look at you two, fighting like an unhappy couple."

"We ain't a couple," Harvey said, "just partners."

"Can't you just agree to disagree?" Fish smiled slyly. "That's my motto. You know how much I hate conflict."

"It's the people who say they hate conflict who always seem to wind up in the center of it," Amanda said, and the smile disappeared. Fish glared at Amanda the way she glared at her enemies, like a tiger preparing to strike.

Uh-oh, Harvey thought. *This is going south way too fast.*

"Really?" Fish said. "If I didn't know better, I'd think you were talking about me."

"I'm not trying to be ambiguous," Amanda said. "I *am* talking about you."

Fish tilted her head slightly and squinted. Harvey had seen that look before.

"Hey, come on now," Harvey said. "No need to let the tempers flare, ladies." There was something about Fish that did that to other women.

Fish ignored him, and said, "It *seems* like somebody has already overstayed her welcome, and she just got here."

"Don't worry," Harvey said before Amanda could say anything. "We won't be long. We just need your help on something… a little favor."

"Oh really?" Fish didn't just laugh—she guffawed for a few seconds—and then turned serious again, looking straight at Amanda. "What makes you think I'd do a favor for *you*? I mean, I'm just keeping it real, but you haven't been around long enough to earn favors from me. You've only been a detective now for, what, two and half weeks? Yeah, you were a parole officer for six years, and did two tours in the army, but as far as I'm concerned you're a total novice."

"How do you…?" Amanda asked, and she gaped.

"Honey, I know *everything* that goes on in this town. Why do you think they call me Fish?" With her index fingers she touched one of her own cheeks, right below her eyes, and added, "Cause like a fish I can see in every direction. I can see in front… to the side… even behiiiind me." Then, without looking back, she suddenly shouted, "No cameras!"

Harvey jumped and glanced beyond her. Sure enough, a man in front of the stage had taken out a camera. He was in the process of photographing the blues singer. He almost dropped it, putting it down so fast.

"Wow, that was pretty impressive," Harvey said.

"Butch, escort that gentleman out," Fish barked at her right-hand man.

"Yes, Fish," Butch said, sounding more like a servant than an employee. Harvey knew Fish was probably paying Butch well and all, but the guy took orders like a well-trained dog.

As Butch approached the tables near the stage, the camera guy cowered.

"No… p-please." Too late. Butch grabbed the guy's camera, crushed it with his bare hand.

"Holy Jeez," Harvey said.

Then, with little effort, Butch lifted the guy up over his shoulder like a sack of potatoes and carried him toward the entrance.

"Please!" the guy begged. "P-p-put me down. I'm sorry, Fish—I-I mean, Ms. Mooney. I'll never do it again. I swear."

"Hey," Amanda said, "let him go."

Harvey gritted his teeth. She was getting involved where she had no business. Cop or no cop, it was the biggest mistake you could make in Gotham. Not if—as they said in Ireland—you wanted to live long enough to comb gray hair.

"Leave it alone," he said.

Butch tossed the screaming guy out to the street, then he returned to the bar to finish his drink.

"As you were saying?" Fish cooed.

Amanda gave Harvey a look, as if to say, *Go ahead, you take it*.

"There was a robbery last night at Wayne Manor," Harvey said.

"Yes, I know that," Fish said.

"And a guy named Byron Stone was killed."

"I know that too. Byron was a useful pawn... at times. But pawns, of course, are always expendable."

"Do you know who else is in his crew?" Amanda asked.

"What did I say about favors?" Fish reached over and began caressing Amanda's hand. "You have to *earn* them."

Off guard, Amanda let her do it for a few seconds. Then she yanked her hand away. Harvey had to smile. Amanda was so high on her horse, it was interesting to watch her get taken down a rung or two.

"I wouldn't do a favor for her," Fish said, turning to Harvey. "But for *you*." She leaned in close and kissed his cheek. Man, she smelled good. A bunch of sexy memories flooded back, all at once. He loved it when that happened.

"Roberto Colon," Fish said. "Old cell mate of Byron's from Blackgate. I heard last week they were planning to work together."

"Where can we find him?"

"He's a regular at Angel's, near South Station."

Harvey knew Angel's—a criminal hangout controlled by Don Maroni, but it was hard to make a bust there because it was a "protected location." The owner, Bobby Angel, made regular payments to the GCPD to ensure that they stayed out of his business.

"Thanks, baby," Harvey said.

As he and Amanda got up, Fish grabbed Amanda's right wrist—hard, like a clamp—and pulled her in close. She whispered something into Amanda's ear, so that Harvey couldn't hear. Then she let go.

"*Any* time, Harvey," Fish said.

Amanda was livid, her face red, but she didn't say anything.

Outside they were heading back to the car when a guy approached them. He was youngish, kind of deranged looking, with wild blue eyes and messy black, spiked hair.

"Hello, kind detectives," the man said.

Harvey and Amanda didn't stop, and the man kept walking briskly alongside them.

"Who the hell are you?" Harvey asked.

"I'm a great, great friend of Fish Mooney's," the man said. "One day, with any luck—and, let's face it, the right connections—I'll be a powerful figure in my own right."

"Good for you," Harvey said, thinking, *Is everybody in this city whacked? Am I one of the last of the sane people?* It was a scary thought—even for him.

"I assume you came here for a favor," the man continued. "Why else would detectives come to see Fish Mooney? I mean, let's face it, you didn't come to see a mediocre blues singer." He laughed, cracking himself up, then said, "But I want you to know, that if you ever need a favor, I can be an *extremely* useful source of information myself."

The guy held out a business card and, just to make him go away, Harvey took one. At that the guy stopped walking, and they quickly left him behind. Harvey had more important things on his mind, but he waited until he and Amanda were back in the car, heading toward the South Village.

"What the hell happened back there?" he demanded.

"She grabbed my arm," Amanda said. "Who the hell does that woman think she is?"

"That woman is Fish Mooney, that's who she is," he said. "She's connected to Don Falcone."

"I don't care *who* she's connected to," Amanda protested. "I should've cuffed her, taken her in for assault."

"Yeah, you don't want to know what would happen if you tried," Harvey said. Then he added, "Besides, you started it, trying to analyze her, telling her she's looking for conflict, for chrissake."

"The woman's a known criminal."

"So's half of freakin' Gotham," he replied. "If you want to be a detective in this town, sometimes you gotta do things you're not so proud of. You get into a thing with Fish, Butch or another one of her goons will pay you—or worse, somebody in your family—a visit."

"I'm a police officer," Amanda said, but she seemed to be running low on steam. "I refuse to be intimidated."

"You won't be a cop for long, with that attitude," Harvey said. "You'll be fired, or you'll be a dead cop." He let that sink in, then asked, "So what did she say to you anyway? I mean before she left."

"It had to do with you actually," Amanda said.

"Me?" Harvey was intrigued. "What did she say? Good things, I hope."

"She said, 'Stay away from him. He's mine.'"

Harvey laughed. "My kinda woman." Part of him wasn't sure what to make of it, though.

"I don't know what you see in that thug," Amanda said.

"Yeah, you wouldn't."

At a red light, Harvey looked at the business card.

Oswald Chesterfield Cobblepot

CONSULTANT

"Looney Tunes," he muttered, and he ripped the card into little pieces. When the light turned green, he tossed the pieces out the window like confetti, and sped away.

FIVE

Thomas drove to downtown Gotham City and parked in an indoor parking lot on the corner of Smythe and Wexler. As he was leaving the lot, Rick Allen, the parking attendant, waved to him.

"Hey, Mr. Wayne, how's it going?"

"I'm doing well, Rick, thanks," Thomas said. "How are Deborah and the kids?"

"Deb's great, and the kid are doing well, thanks for asking. Annie's starting high school next year."

"They grow up fast," Thomas said. "Every time I look at Bruce, he looks more and more like a man."

"You gotta live in the moment," Rick said. "Enjoy the time while you've got it, 'cause nobody knows how much time they got."

"So true," Thomas said, and he continued on. "Have a great day."

"You too, Mr. Wayne."

Thomas always enjoyed moments like that. Although he was the wealthiest man in town, he didn't feel the need to live an isolated life. He didn't think he was better than anyone else, or that his life had any greater meaning. He often reminded himself that the only difference between him and the less fortunate was that he'd had some good luck. But just because he'd been dealt a good hand, that didn't mean he'd come out the winner in the end. Any poker player would say the same thing—and Thomas took nothing for granted. He tipped well all the time, especially around the holidays, but that wasn't why most people liked him. They liked him because he was real, because he was genuinely interested in their lives. Thomas had no political ambitions, but if he had wanted to run for mayor of Gotham, he would have won in a landslide.

As long as the past stayed buried, he mused.

He entered the tenement-style building and headed up the steep stairs to the second floor. There were few offices on the floor—a real estate agency, an insurance company, and at the end of the hall, an office with golden letters emblazoned on the frosted glass door.

FRANK COLLINS
PRIVATE INVESTIGATOR

Thomas knocked and a voice grunted, "Come in."

Frank's office couldn't have looked more like the stomping grounds of a stereotypical PI. The messy desk, the old filing cabinets, the dirty windows—and of course Frank himself had a potbelly pushing against a stained button-down shirt with rolled-up sleeves. A cigar smoldered in the ashtray that sat in front of him.

He was at his desk, on the phone, and motioned for his visitor to sit down across from him. Thomas had to move piles of papers and folders from atop the rickety chair, and then he sat.

While Thomas could have afforded any private investigator in the world, he'd kept Frank on a retainer for nearly ten years to handle his personal assignments. In hiring someone, Thomas only cared about two things—the person's work ethic, and their ability to get a job done. Frank was a former GCPD detective who had struck out on his own, and knew Gotham inside out. He was the best PI in Gotham, and he was discreet.

Thomas didn't want the press finding out about his personal affairs, and he didn't want board members to know the details either. Frequently the board itself—especially over the past few years—had been the subject of the investigations. Guys like Frank had "private" in their business titles for a reason, or at least the good ones did.

"Look I know, I… that… Yes, of course…" He had the old-fashioned phone pressed to his ear. "No, that would be a mistake… I… Look, I… I don't suggest doing that. Look, I know you're upset right… I know, but if you do that, you're gonna wind up in Blackgate in an eight-by-ten cell for the rest of your life, and I don't think you want that, do you? I understand… I understand, but is murder really worth it?"

Frank gave Thomas a look as if saying, *Can you believe this crap?*

"I'm sorry? No, no, I'm sorry, but I don't give out referrals, especially not for that. Look, I have someone else in my office, and I have to go now… Yes, I know… Yes, and I'll send you a bill for the balance of your fees, including expenses… All right, okay. Goodbye."

Putting the phone back in its cradle, he gave a deep sigh, then reached out.

"Hey, Tommy, how's it goin'?" Frank might've been the only person in Gotham who'd ever called Thomas "Tommy."

"Good to see you," Thomas said, taking the hand.

Picking up the cigar, Frank took a long drag, blew the smoke across the desk toward Thomas, and responded.

"Can you believe these people? I catch her husband red-handed, cheating on her with four—that's right, *four* different women—and she can take him to the cleaners, wind up with the house, the cars, the boat, the kids, you name it. But that's not enough with her. She wants me to find her a hit man to kill the cheating son of a bitch."

"Sounds like you should refer her to a therapist," Thomas said.

"Or a loony bin," Frank said. "And, lately, I get calls like this all the time. I do what I can, try to talk them down off of the roof, but if somebody wants to do something stupid, there's a limit to what I can do to stop them, you know? I mean, what am I gonna do, turn them into the cops? Go to the GCPD, 'Hey, I got a client, tells me she wants to whack her hubby?' What're they gonna do, arrest the broad for what she *might* do? How many people around the city are plotting to kill somebody, or hurt somebody, right this second? A lot, that's how many. It's like what they say—you can't stop crazy."

"There certainly is a moral crisis in Gotham these days," Thomas said.

"Crisis?" Frank said. "It's a freakin' epidemic." He took another puff on his cigar, then said, "But, hey, who am I to complain? It keeps me in business. If the crime rate in Gotham went down to zero, I'd have to go back to my old job."

"As a GCPD detective?"

"No my *old*, old job," Frank said. "I used to be a house painter, back in the day."

"I didn't know that," Thomas said.

"It's not exactly experience I put on top of my resume," Frank said. "But, speaking of painting, I heard there was a break-in at your place last night. They took a Picasso that's worth a pretty penny."

"News travels fast," Thomas said.

"Hey, I got my finger on the pulse," Frank said. "That's what you pay me for, right?"

"I pay you because I know you're the best at what you do," Thomas said.

"Exactly," Frank said. "I'll get on the case right away. If that painting's in Gotham, I'll find it. If it isn't, I'll find out where it went."

"That's perfect, but I think it may be more complicated than a simple theft," Thomas said. "I think it might be related to Hugo Strange."

With a slight *whoosh* of air, Frank sat back, the cigar clenched between his teeth. He didn't speak, though, and Thomas knew why.

Though it had ended ten years earlier, Thomas's association with Strange had been, by far, the most regrettable mistake of his life. He lived in constant fear that Strange would someday resume his medical experiments. Although Thomas had funded them with good intentions, hoping Strange's genetic research would cure disease, prolong life, and provide the next step in the evolution of mankind, it turned out that Strange was a deranged madman whose procedures had caused deformities such as missing limbs, grotesque malformations, and uncontrollable psychotic behavior.

Thomas managed to stop Strange's experiments by defunding the operation, but this didn't end the horrific human suffering that Pinewood Farms had caused. For years, Thomas had supported many of its victims—giving them housing, money, and medical care. He did it for redemption, and because he knew it was the right thing to do, but Pinewood remained a great burden and, without doubt, was the greatest regret of his life. He'd never been able to fully forgive himself for the damage he'd done.

Over the years, he watched the victims he'd been helping die off, one by one. Many met their demises by natural causes, or by suicide, and some just disappeared. Thomas suspected that Strange and his associates were responsible for some, if not all, of the disappearances, and it added to his frustration that there was nothing he could do to stop Strange, or bring him to justice.

Because Thomas had founded Pinewood Farms with Strange, and had provided all of the financing, he couldn't go public without incriminating himself and damaging, perhaps irrevocably, the reputation of Wayne Enterprises.

"So lemme get this straight," Frank said finally, and then he took another drag on his cigar. After exhaling, he continued. "You think Hugo Strange broke into your house and stole a Picasso?"

"Whoever did it might not have been after the Picasso," Thomas said. "I think it was just a cover. I think Strange was behind it, and that he was after something else."

"Must've been something he wanted pretty badly," Frank said. "I mean, to send three guys in, three *armed* guys… That's quite a risk to take."

"I keep my old records to Pinewood, hidden in my office," Thomas said, being careful not to mention which office he meant. "I think Strange might want them back."

"First question, then," Frank said, "why would he want them back?"

"I'm not sure," Thomas said, "but if he's thinking about resuming experiments, picking up where he left off ten years ago, he might want to make sure I have no information that could incriminate him."

"But Strange is a smart guy," Frank said. "A genius maybe. Why would he think if he found and destroyed some records in your office, then that would be it? That he'd be free and clear? I mean, wouldn't he assume you have them backed up?"

"He knows better," Thomas said. "It would have been too dangerous all these years, keeping multiple sets, running the greater risk that my involvement in Pinewood would be exposed. I have my records and he has his. It's like we've been stuck in a cold war, using nuclear weapons to deter each other. Only in this case it's not nuclear weapons, it's the information that might put either one of us in jail."

"So," Frank said, "I'm assuming he didn't find what he was looking for."

"No," Thomas said with certainty. "No, he did not. As I said, I have them hidden. In a very a secure place."

"Well, then, it sounds like you dodged a bullet last night." Frank peered at Thomas, as if trying to read his mind.

"Literally *and* figuratively," Thomas said, recalling the projectile that had whizzed by his head.

"Okay, I'll look into all of it," Frank said. "I'll ask around, check in with my contacts, see what he's been up to. I haven't heard anything new lately, but it can't hurt to check again. I'll start with the painting."

At the mention of the Picasso, something clicked into place for Thomas.

"Maybe the Picasso was his target after all," Thomas said. Noting Frank's puzzled look, he continued. "If it's true that Strange is looking to restart Pinewood, he might need funding—and it's not as if he can apply for a federal grant. Maybe he stole the Picasso to raise funds to finance the operation."

"Seems like a stretch," Frank said. "I mean, why *your* painting? If it's just about money, why not rob an art gallery? Or a museum?"

"Think of the irony," Thomas said. "Maybe it was personal, to get my attention and send me a message. As if he was basically saying, 'You can cut me off, but one way or another, I'll have my revenge—and you'll be responsible for the new Pinewood.' Strange is a brilliant yet deeply insecure man, so it makes sense that he's been getting antsy. He's been out of the limelight, and would want to do something splashy to make himself the center of attention again.

"The burglars obviously figured out a way into Wayne Manor, and that has Hugo written all over it. Maybe he got help from the guard at the gate, or maybe he hacked into the security system. Either way, now that we've been warned, he won't try it again." Thomas paused, then added, "Look, maybe my hunch is wrong about all of this. Maybe the robbery had nothing to do with Strange, but I think it's something we have to rule out as a possibility. My life, my family, and my future depend on it."

"I agree," Frank said. "Well, lemme see if I can find out what Strange has been up to—" His phone rang. He held up his index finger and mouthed, *One sec*, then said into the phone, "Hey, how's it going? Okay, what's the line now? Yeah, okay, gimme another G on Williams... That's right... and gimme another five hundred on a third-round knockout... Right, okay... Yes, very good... Okay."

Ending the call, he looked back to Thomas. "You think I made a mistake? Third round? Maybe I should've gone with four or five? Nah, third has a good ring to it, and you always gotta go with your instincts, right?"

"Or against them, depending on your superstition," Thomas said. "So you like Williams, do you?"

"Yeah," Frank said. "Sanchez talks a big game, but Williams is prepared. That's what always wins out in the end—preparation. I just hope it ends in the third round. Or maybe you're right, and I should go against my instincts for a change. I mean I've always gone with my gut, and where has that gotten me?" He looked at his belly as if it had betrayed him. "Maybe I should change the bet to the fourth round. Or, better yet, the fifth. Yeah, the fifth."

Frank called his bookie, and changed his bet to a fifth-round knockout.

"Bruce wants to learn how to box," Thomas said after the PI hung up. Frank had never met Bruce or Martha, but Thomas had often talked about them.

"Fighting is a good skill to have in this town," Frank said. "I don't think I'd be alive right now if I didn't know how to fight."

"I agree with you," Thomas said, and he smiled, "but Martha wants him to continue with tennis."

"Tennis?" Frank said. "In Gotham? What's he gonna do if he gets mugged? Beat the guy up with a racket?"

"Exactly my point," Thomas said, and they both laughed. He liked Frank—he was one of the good guys.

"So about the painting…" Frank said.

"First and foremost we have to find out if Strange was involved in the robbery," Thomas said. "We'd love to recover the painting obviously, but if Strange goes away for orchestrating an armed robbery, well, that would solve a big problem for me—I wouldn't have to worry about him starting experiments again, if he was locked up.

"It's also imperative that if Strange is involved, we find out about it before the GCPD. Obviously if they were to dig up anything about Pinewood Farms, it would be a disaster for me, and for Wayne Enterprises. That would send a ripple effect throughout all of Gotham."

"Yeah," Frank said. "I heard Harvey Bullock's working on this case with his new partner. An Asian broad."

"Wow," Thomas said. "You really do stay informed, don't you?"

"I have a new contact feeding me info, guy named Cobblepot," Frank said. "I swear, the guy's like a sponge—he sops up everything. Ambitious kid, too—he's gonna go places. Anyway, Harvey visited Fish Mooney earlier today, so he's probably bearing down on some suspects. The good news is, he's starting from the bottom up and it'll take him some time to get to the top. But you have a legitimate concern. If Strange is involved, you can't have Harvey Bullock stumbling across your involvement in Pinewood."

"Then we have to get there first," Thomas said.

"One thing you should definitely do," Frank said, "is make sure that girl you've been taking care of, Karen Jennings, hasn't heard from Strange lately. If it's true what you're suspecting, and Strange really is back doing experiments, then your records aren't the only loose end. Jennings is a loose end, too."

As far as Thomas knew, Karen Jennings was the only remaining survivor of Pinewood. Over the years, he'd been giving her money, paying her medical expenses, and he'd even moved her to a secluded cabin upstate, just to ensure that she remained safe. They had become close over the years, and Thomas considered her to be a good friend.

"If Karen had heard from Strange," Thomas said, "she'd tell me. Besides, she never knew Strange by name during her time at Pinewood. For her protection I still haven't mentioned his name to her."

"I know you like this girl," Frank said, "and I'm guessing she likes you, too. She also sounds like the type of person who puts other people ahead of herself. What I mean is if she thought it could put you in any danger, most likely she'd keep her mouth shut."

It was true—Karen was one of the most selfless persons Thomas had ever met. In her place, he didn't know if he could ever be so forgiving of his sins.

"Very well," Thomas said. "I'll get in touch with her, just to make sure."

"Aside from you," Frank said, "Karen's the only person Strange knows might incriminate him, right? You haven't told anybody else, have you?"

"Aside for you, not a soul," Thomas said.

"Good," Frank said, "let's keep it that way."

Thomas stood. Frank came around from behind the desk and they shook hands.

"Don't worry," the PI said, "we'll get to the bottom of all of this."

"If anyone can do it, you can."

"Just out of curiosity," Frank said, cocking his head, "how much is that Picasso worth? I mean, gimme a ballpark."

"Hard to say," Thomas said. "Similar paintings have gone for twenty million or more."

"Whoa, Nelly," Frank said, and he whistled. "So let's say whoever stole it tried to resell it. What would they get? Half that?"

"Actually on the black market paintings can go for as little as twenty-five percent, or less, of their market value. It's understandable, as a buyer would be taking a big risk—especially in the case of a Picasso, because it's so recognizable. You can't just take *Le Picador* into a major auction house and sell it after a high-profile robbery."

"Very true," Frank agreed. "Then where do you think it would be sold?"

"Russia has a notorious black market for art," Thomas said. "North Africa as well."

"I'll put out word at the airport and the docks. That

painting will never get out of Gotham, if I have any say in it."

"Amen to that," Thomas said.

Frank walked him out of the office and into the hallway.

"Thank you," Thomas said, as he shook Frank's hand again. They both had strong grips.

"Any time, Tommy," Frank said. "I'll be in touch sooner rather than later, I'm sure."

Later, driving back toward Wayne Manor, Thomas replayed snippets of the conversation in his mind, in particular what he'd suggested about Karen Jennings. Thomas hadn't spoken to Karen in about a week or so. Everything had seemed fine then, but over the years, things had seemed fine with other victims of Pinewood—and then a couple days later, *boom*, they vanished, never to be seen again.

Karen was the last one, his last chance to salvage any redemption for what he'd done. If anything happened to her, he'd never forgive himself. So he tapped his smartphone and called her number. All he got was her voicemail.

Five minutes later, he tried again.

Voicemail.

His anxiety building, he called her a couple more times, with the same maddening result. This wasn't like her. She had no place to go, and normally she picked right up when she saw his number.

To hell with it, he concluded, and he headed for the highway that would take him upstate. The drive would take about an hour and twenty minutes—an hour if he really hit the gas. Seeing her in person would provide him with some peace of mind, and he could inform her about the possible new threat.

As he pulled onto the access road, he made another call, leaving another message.

"Alfred, listen," Thomas said into this cell. "I have some business to attend to this afternoon, and I may not be able to make it to dinner tonight. Can you let Martha know? You know how she gets... And can you please take Bruce to his tennis lesson this afternoon, then pick him up as well? I really appreciate it, you're the best."

He felt lucky to have Alfred to rely on, but felt bad because Karen didn't have anyone, other than Thomas. She led a lonely existence, hiding from her enemies, living like a prisoner. But a prisoner has bars as protection—Karen had no such safety.

He tried her again.

Voicemail.

Veering onto the Gotham Turnpike, he gunned it.

SIX

Angel's was a regular hangout for gangbangers, pimps, hookers, arms dealers, drug dealers, and just about every other kind of degenerate lowlife you could imagine. Instead of "Bar and Club," the sign in front should've been "Halfway House," and there should've been bars on the windows. Everybody in the place was either wanted or had some kind of record, and not the kind that spun on turntables.

Harvey and Amanda had double-parked in front. Before they got out of the car, and even with the windows shut, Harvey could already hear the throbbing death metal beat coming from inside.

"You may want to wait out here," he said. "I mean this isn't exactly the wine and cheese crowd."

Amanda didn't answer or even look at him. She got out of the car.

"Okey dokey," Harvey said.

They entered and the music went from loud as hell to deafening. Although it was the middle of the afternoon, the place was dark—and not just because Harvey and Amanda's eyes hadn't adjusted to the light. Seedy, sweaty men were three or four deep at the bar, shouting over each other for drinks. Harvey recognized at least a few former busts. As word got around that they were there, like a game of telephone on speed, a few guys ducked out the back or side exits.

"Where's Bobby?" Harvey shouted at the thin, grizzled bartender who was covered in prison ink.

The guy didn't answer, just gestured toward the back with his chin as he poured scotch into two glasses at once. The drinks looked good.

Later, he thought, and he glanced at his partner.

As they headed toward the back, the crowd parted, creating an aisle for them. But it didn't feel like they were walking through a bar. It felt like they were in a prison, passing by the angry, raucous cellmates in maximum security. Amanda—Harvey realized—was the only woman in the whole place, and the men were acting like they hadn't seen a real live female in years. Some of them were actually salivating, with their tongues hanging out of their mouths.

He hoped Amanda was smart enough to stay professional this time, and not let any of these jerkoffs get under her skin. Then a guy stepped in their path. He was the size of a bear, had to be way over three hundred pounds, with a thick black beard and—going by the dense hair on his arms, hands, and neck—his whole body was probably covered with it as well.

"She with you?" he said to Harvey. His voice was

deep and hoarse, like he smoked three packs a day. He smelled like a smoldering ashtray. Harvey and Amanda had to stop. The guy was so big there was literally no way to get by.

"She's my partner," Harvey said, "so, yeah, she's with—"

"I'll handle this," Amanda said, stepping in front of him to stand face-to-face with the hulky goon. Or, actually, her face to his stomach.

"No, I'm not *with* anybody," Amanda said, looking up at the guy. "What's it to you?"

Uh-oh, here we go. Now they had an audience— guys in the bar were huddling around—whistling and catcalling. Harvey didn't like the look of it—they were outnumbered and outgunned. He shook his head.

"You couldn't let it go, could you?" he whispered to himself.

"That case, looks like we got somethin' in common then," the guy said to Amanda. "I ain't with nobody neither. How about you let me buy you a drink?"

"Well, that's an offer that's going to be hard to turn down," Amanda said. "I mean, it's one thing to find a guy who's as charming as you are, but to find one who's as handsome, too? God, I feel like I hit the jackpot today."

What the hell? Harvey knew she was stubborn, but this wasn't playing with fire—it was playing with a freaking inferno.

The guy grinned. A few teeth were missing. The rest were yellowed and crooked. Obviously the sarcasm had gone way, way over his head.

"What can I get you?" he asked.

"How about a big, tall glass of no way in hell?"

The crowd jeered. Finally the big guy was catching on, and looking pissed off.

"What did you just say?"

"You heard me, loud and clear."

"Hey, we're not looking to give anybody a hard time, big guy," Harvey said, knowing he was wasting his breath. "We're just here to see Bobby."

"I don't think so," the guy said. "The girl said I could buy her a drink, and I'm gonna buy her a drink."

The crowd began to chant.

"Drink, drink, drink, drink…"

Great, now it was an ego thing, so there was no way in hell the guy would back down.

"Girl?" Amanda said. "I'm not a girl."

"That's right," the guy said. "You're *my* girl." He tried to put his hairy arm around her waist. Harvey had a hand on the handle of his gun, ready to come to Amanda's rescue. Jeez, talk about a headache he didn't need to have…

As the goon reached out to grab her, however, Amanda did some kind of karate move. She grabbed the guy's wrist, twisted it around, and he crumpled to his knees with a grunt of agony. Everybody in the bar froze, stunned and silent—including Harvey. He left his gun right where it still was, in his holster.

The beat of the music continued.

"P-p-please," the guy begged. "L-l-lemme go." He could hardly be heard over the beat.

"I should probably break it," Amanda said loudly. "Just so you can't try to grab the next girl you come across." She twisted his arm a little further. He groaned louder.

"Please."

"I can feel it breaking," she said. "Just a little more, and it'll snap like a wishbone. What do you say? Ready to make a wish?"

Then Harvey heard a familiar voice.

"You wanna see me?"

He looked up and saw that Bobby Angel had come out of his office. He was short, bald, with thick glasses that made one eye look about twice as big as the other. Rarely had anyone been so beautiful as he was at that moment.

"Yeah, Bobby, actually, we do," Harvey said.

"My office," Bobby said.

Amanda held the big guy for another second or two, then let go. He remained on the floor, writhing. Harvey shot her a look that said, *What the hell?* Amanda ignored him. They followed Bobby to the back of the bar, to his cramped, windowless office.

No wonder the guy's so pasty, Harvey mused, *living in here like a rat*.

After Bobby shut the door, he turned toward them, barely-contained fury on his face.

"The *hell* was that all about?" he bellowed. "I pay you good money every month to keep you and your pigs out of my bar, then you show up and start fighting with my customers?"

"With all due respect," Harvey said, "we didn't start that fight."

"You still shouldn't even be in here—*ever*."

"I'm sorry, Bobby," Harvey said.

"Wait, you're taking *kickbacks* from this guy?" Amanda glared at Harvey.

"Guess you and your partner don't communicate too well, huh Harvey?" Bobby drawled. Then he said to Amanda, "Yeah, he gets kickbacks—two G's a month to keep my bar a cop-free zone."

"Is this true?" she demanded.

Harvey didn't bother answering her.

"Look, you're right, and I'm sorry," Harvey said to the club owner. "It won't happen again. I just needed to ask you how I can find a guy named Roberto Colon."

"Never heard of him," Bobby said. Harvey knew he was lying.

"According to a reliable source he hangs out here."

"Reliable source, eh." Bobby smirked. "You mean Fish Mooney?" The smirk morphed into a laugh. Then he added, "You cops're so arrogant. You really think you're the only ones with ears on the street?"

Harvey remembered that weirdo who'd given him the business card. What was his name? Hobblepot? Something like that.

"How many years we go back?" Harvey said to Bobby, keeping his expression serious.

"Ten, maybe twelve," Bobby said.

"That's a good stretch," the detective said. "Hate to play hardball with you, I mean, given our long, amicable history and all. But if you don't cooperate I'm gonna tell Don Maroni I found out you've been skimming off the top at this joint, ripping his ass off for years."

"Why would he believe you?"

"Why would he believe *you*?" Harvey countered. "It would be a 'he said, he said,' and Maroni respects me, knows I'm a straight shooter. Maroni's known to kill his own people who steal from him. So the question is, how much faith do you have in your relationship with the Don?"

Bobby's hesitation spoke volumes. "Me and Maroni are good friends," he said, like he was trying to believe it himself.

"Hope you're right about that," Harvey said, "because if you're wrong, you're gonna be fish food in the Gotham River before midnight." Then he turned to leave, knowing what was gonna happen next. If they could just get there before Amanda said something stupid.

"Wait, you bastard."

Man, Harvey thought, *I love being right*. It always gave him a rush.

"Okay, Colon was here before," Bobby said, "but he must've took off when you two came in."

"Where'd he go?" Amanda asked.

"I dunno, but I know he's staying in this SRO on Caldwell near Walker, above the liquor store. You better not tell him I tipped you off." He gave them as close as he could to an angry glare, what with the glasses.

"Give me a break, Bobby," Harvey said. "Don't act like you're some kinda virgin. You've ratted out plenty of perps over the years, and nobody's killed you. Well, yet." When the club owner didn't reply, Harvey led the way out of the bar, with Amanda close behind.

This time nobody bothered them, or even looked at them, including the big guy, who was at the bar with a bag of ice against his wrist. After they left the bar, Harvey asked a question that was becoming far too familiar.

"What was that about in there?" he demanded.

"You tell me," Amanda said. "You didn't tell me you were protecting this place."

"I didn't think that was… pertinent information."

"I'm your partner. *Everything* is pertinent information."

"You coulda got us killed," he persisted. "What if that guy in there had a friend who got trigger happy? Did you even think about the danger you were putting me in, when you put that guy onto the floor with some fancy move you learned in a police self-defense class."

"Actually, I'm a third degree black belt," she said.

Harvey didn't think she was lying.

"Good for you," Harvey said. "So you can chop and kick, but I'll tell you one thing—I never saw karate win a gun fight." She didn't respond.

They got into the car, Harvey driving. The stony silence persisted, and Harvey turned on the radio, tuning in his favorite oldies station.

"Taking kickbacks is against the law," Amanda said finally.

"Really?" Harvey deadpanned. "I had no idea." Then he added, "So, what're you gonna do, report me, *partner*?"

"Maybe I should."

Crap, that again.

"Go ahead," he growled, and he half meant it. "Rats have a long life expectancy at the GCPD, I'm sure." He rolled his eyes for emphasis.

"I don't get it," Amanda said. "I mean, I get why other cops get dirty, but why Harvey Bullock? I mean, I know you have a moral center in there somewhere. I've watched you do your job, and you're pretty good at it, at least when you're sober."

"It's called earning a living," Harvey said. "You think I can live on a cop's salary? Nobody can. Kickbacks are like a performance bonus."

"How much do you get?" she asked.

"Why? You want a piece of the action?"

"It doesn't have to be this way. Corruption in Gotham is part of the problem. I should report all of this. You'd go on desk duty or, better yet, you'll get suspended. Either way, you'd be off the street, and part of the problem would go away."

"A suspension would be great right about now," Harvey said. "I could use the beach time."

"Gotham could use it, too," she said. "One less dirty cop."

Harvey yanked on the steering wheel, pulled over to the curb, and hit the brakes. Amanda, not wearing a seatbelt, had her hands on the dash to protect herself from putting her head through the windshield.

"Are you *crazy*?" she said.

"You have no idea who or what I am, lady," Harvey said. "I dedicate my life to my job, I put scumbags in jail every day. Another priority of mine? Staying alive. It's survival of the fittest in this town. So, yeah, I know how take care of A-Number-One. Me."

"What the hell does that mean?" Amanda said.

"It means if you wanna be a cop in Gotham, you gotta know how to play the game," he said. "People who don't play the game end up with worms in their brains. Now get out."

"I'm not going anywhere," Amanda said.

"You sure as hell aren't—not with me," he said. "I can handle the personality issues. I mean, I can deal with a pain in the ass and all, criticizing me all the time, acting like you're holier than thou, but you want to talk about partners? You almost got into a fight by shooting your mouth off to Fish Mooney, then when you get into an actual fight—one we could've avoided—you threaten to turn rat on me. But then, worst of all, you have the balls to tell me how to do my job. There's a solution for having a partner like you—it's called a divorce."

"If I have a problem with the way you're doing your job, I have the right to speak up," she countered. "You can't…" She searched for the words. "You can't fire me."

"No, I can't," Harvey said, "but I can make you get out of my goddamn car."

She didn't budge.

He took out his gun and aimed at her face.

"I said get out."

Maybe she didn't believe Harvey would actually shoot her, but the threat worked because something made her get out. Harvey reached across the front seat and slammed the door shut.

Amanda stepped back and stared through the open window.

"Wow, and I thought you were one of the good guys."

"Wake up," Harvey said. "This is Gotham. There are no good guys."

He sped away, leaving her on the curb. When he got a couple of blocks away, he looked in the rear-view mirror and saw that she was still standing there, hands on her hips, stubborn as all hell.

SEVEN

Traffic was heavy at times, and Thomas made it upstate in about two hours. He was eager to get to Karen's retreat to make sure she was okay, but he stopped at a supermarket in the closest town to where she lived—about twenty miles away—and bought as many groceries as he could fit into his trunk and the back seat of his car. He also bought lots of toilet paper, paper towels, soap, shampoo and conditioner, light bulbs, and other necessities.

If she was going to remain safe, then it would be best that he minimize his visits, and she would need enough supplies to keep her for an extended stretch.

Leaving the main roads, Thomas drove along a winding, secluded stretch for about ten minutes, then turned on to another even more secluded lane. Finally he turned onto a nameless rocky dirt road that went through dense woods. Anyone who wasn't looking for it would miss it.

He continued along the road for about a mile, until

he reached the cabin by a small lake. It was where Karen had lived for the past ten years. In the beginning Thomas had considered putting her up at an apartment in Gotham, where it would have been easier to watch her, but as other Pinewood victims went missing— some of them in the city—he knew he needed another option. He'd considered an armed guard, but was concerned that it would draw unwanted attention, and guards couldn't necessarily be trusted.

Anyone could turn, for the right price.

Parking near the house, he got out of the car. He took a deep breath of the country air, which always felt invigorating after the smog in Gotham. He pulled a couple of bags of the groceries out of the trunk and went up the rickety steps which led to a screened-in porch, leaning in at an awkward angle and knocking a few times.

She didn't come to the door, and he didn't hear any movement from inside. During the ride up, he'd tried to call her again, and had gotten her voicemail. There was no cell service out here and she didn't even have a cell phone—just a landline.

He'd managed to assuage his fears that something was wrong, that something had happened, telling himself that she was probably napping, hiking in the woods, or maybe she'd gone out on her row boat. She'd told him how much she enjoyed rowing alone on the lake, how the solitude made her feel safe.

He banged on the screen door, which was hook-locked on the inside.

"Karen? Are you home?" he said, nervous to speak so loudly. "Karen?"

No answer. He shook the door and was able to jiggle the lock open. Once on the porch, he peered in through the window. Nothing looked out of the ordinary, but he didn't see her.

He banged on the door a few times with the side of his fist.

"Karen? Are you in there? Hello? *Hello*?"

"Thomas."

The sound jarred him. He spun around and saw Karen standing there, outside the cabin. She was young—in her early thirties—with wavy brown hair. If she hadn't been a victim of Pinewood, she could have been leading a simple, happy life—had a career, a husband, a couple of kids, a great future. Thomas had no idea what Strange had done to her, or what he'd been trying to achieve. He hadn't been privy to the details of his experiments though he knew, in general, that the experiments had involved merging animal DNA with human DNA.

Most likely Karen had been given materials taken from some reptile, which was how she'd received the huge, monstrous claw where her right arm should have been. Knowing Hugo Strange and his twisted ways, though, he might have introduced dinosaur DNA into her system.

Nothing was off-limits for that madman.

"You scared the hell out of me," Thomas said.

"Who else were you expecting?" Karen asked. She

had cut off all ties with anyone she had known before Pinewood—friends and relatives alike. Many assumed she had died years ago. Thomas was the only human being she had encountered in years.

"Good point," Thomas said. "But I tried to call you before and, well, I was getting worried."

"I was just out walking," she replied, "but thanks for worrying."

Taking a deep breath, he forced himself to relax. Thomas had gotten to know Karen well. She had become not only like a daughter to him, but also a friend. They talked about pretty much everything. Although she'd never met Bruce and Martha, he'd told her all about them. When Bruce had an issue with a teacher or a classmate at school, Karen offered good advice. When Thomas had to make a big decision about something going on at Wayne Industries, he talked things through with her, getting her input.

She was smart and insightful. She told him about the trauma of her childhood, and he tried to help her, but not like a therapist—he was an ear for her, a sounding board. Having been involved in so much of her pain, he wanted to do whatever he could to make her life a little better. He'd brought her books to read, and they spent hours talking about them. She had never travelled, so he told her about his times in Europe, Asia, and other places.

Although she was free to do whatever she wanted, with no car or money of her own, she was essentially a prisoner. While a cabin in a serene area wasn't exactly like being in Blackgate or Arkham, solitude could seem like the worst punishment of all. She'd had mental health issues in her past—which was part of why she had been selected for the Pinewood experiments—and sometimes Thomas wondered how the aloneness out here didn't drive her over the edge.

Karen helped Thomas take the rest of the shopping bags out of the car. She could only use one hand, because her claw was so sharp it would slice right through the plastic and containers inside. Quite some time ago, in a fit of rage and despair, she had tried to cut the claw off with a saw. She'd almost bled to death, but then something worse had occurred—the claw had regenerated. It had returned a little longer and more pronounced than it had been before.

Since then she had become resigned that there was no escape—the claw would remain a part of her for the rest of her life.

When he was away, Thomas allowed denial to comfort him. As always, however, when he saw Karen, the pain pushed it aside, until it was replaced by shock, shame, and disgust at the gruesome memories of deformed victims and their horrific fates. He hated knowing that he was responsible for this poor woman's misery. As monstrous as the claw appeared, he tried to remind himself that the situation could have been much worse.

Many patients had died during the procedures, unable to withstand the lethal dosages of the concoctions that Strange injected into them. Others wound up with extra limbs, missing eyes, and brain disorders—yet they had survived! Despite occasional fits of rage, Karen was at least an intelligent, functional human being.

At times like this one, it was hard for Thomas to believe that he'd become involved with Hugo Strange at all. They had been good friends once, played at the same polo club, celebrated holidays together, and enjoyed some good laughs. While there had always been a dark side to Strange, it had seemed to manifest in a fierce, sardonic wit—not in a willingness to hurt people. He enjoyed the witty insult, the occasional practical joke, but it was always under the guise of camaraderie. Sometimes people even commented, *"Oh, Hugo, he's harmless."*

If only they had known.

Although Hugo had seemed to have a thick skin, perhaps that had added to whatever drove him as he was dismissed, ridiculed by others. Because something in him changed. The dark side that he'd managed or concealed for years finally had taken over.

Ultimately Strange was responsible for the horrors that had occurred. Thomas had been misinformed, deceived, a victim himself in some respect, yet this realization had never been enough. Although Thomas had become involved with Strange with good intentions—to cure disease, to prolong life—the onus was on him for trusting Strange without question, for not realizing sooner that something was amiss.

That pain was his alone.

To continue to function, Thomas tried to detach himself from all of the horrors of his past, much as others detached themselves from the horrors of war. Compartmentalization was his coping mechanism. Sometimes his past didn't even feel real. It seemed like a nightmare, and not even his own—someone else's nightmare, one that he was watching unfold like a movie or television show.

That wasn't me, he wanted to tell himself. *That was somebody else.*

Yet he knew better.

He'd made attempts to redeem himself. He did good things for Gotham, supported initiatives in which he believed. He'd never be able to undo the mistakes of his past, or heal the wounds of the victims whose lives he'd ruined, but he could do some good. He could help the people of his city, enable them to lead happier and healthier lives, and help create a better world in which Bruce would grow up.

At Wayne Enterprises, he had developed technology and health initiatives that improved people's lives. On his own, he'd supported many of the Pinewood Farms victims, paid their housing and medical bills. Aside from Karen, none of the victims ever knew that Thomas had been involved in their horror. They'd assumed that his support was entirely humanitarian. He was discreet about his efforts—even Strange was unaware of what had occurred after the closing—and so the victims didn't go public.

Strange probably lived in fear that Thomas would,

at some point, blow the whistle on him, and that likely had ensured his own silence. For years, as far as Thomas knew, Strange had dropped entirely out of sight. They encountered each other on random occasions, had awkward yet amicable conversations, but that was all. Neither of them discussed the past and, as far as Thomas was concerned, that dark period of his life had ended.

What if that had all changed?

What if Strange had come out of the shadows?

If they were caught, Thomas could lose his entire company, his fortune, and perhaps spend the rest of his life in prison. While he couldn't undo the mistakes he'd made, he could prevent future tragedies. He feared there might be new victims, new subjects for Strange's hideous experiments. He couldn't let anyone else experience what Karen and the others had gone through.

In the cabin, after they had brought all the bags inside, Karen and Thomas sat in the living room, sipping wine and nibbling on cheese and crackers.

"It's good to see you," Karen said. "I wasn't expecting to see you for at least another week."

"I just got nervous when I couldn't reach you, so I figured I'd come today."

"Nervous?" Karen was confused. "Why? Phone service sucks up here. You haven't been able to reach me before, and you didn't get nervous."

Thomas didn't want to frighten her by telling her about the robbery at Wayne Manor, and about his suspicions that Strange could have been involved. At least not yet. So he tried to keep the mood light.

"Oh, you know how I get," he joked. "I'm like an overprotective father." Then his eyes shifted toward the end table, landing on the music box he'd bought her last Christmas. She followed his gaze.

"Thank you, again, for the gift—I love it," she said. "I listen to the music all the time. Especially at night, when I find it very comforting." Then she hesitated. "Wait, is that weird?"

"No, it's charming," Thomas said, but he decided to shift the topic. "How are you fixed for clothes?"

"I'm okay," she said. "Not much use for formalwear out here."

"You sure?" he pressed. "Winter's coming. Supposed to be a cold one this year according to the almanac. I'll get you a warm coat—wool or down."

Whenever Thomas brought Karen shirts, blouses, or coats he cut off most of the right sleeve, so she could get them on and leave her claw exposed. It didn't seem nearly as sensitive to temperature extremes as the rest of her body.

"It's very generous of you," she said. She glanced at the floor then, and continued. "You know, I'm glad you're here, because I've been thinking a lot about this, well, situation. And you don't have to keep coming here, you know. I mean, Bruce is getting older now, and you work awfully long hours. I'm sure you'd rather spend time with your family than with me."

"Don't be ridiculous," Thomas said. "I enjoy coming here. And you *are* family to me."

"I believe you… and I don't believe you," Karen said. "I know you care about me, and you're a good man—if my own father were like you, then my life would've been so much different."

She took a sip of tea, then looked away. When her gaze shifted back toward Thomas, her eyes were glassy, as if she was holding back tears. That was strange—she never cried.

"I can feel it whenever you come here," she said. "I can see the pain in your expression when you look at me. Even when you're smiling or laughing, it's always there, in the background."

"That isn't true," Thomas said.

"It is. I see it right know," Karen said. "I know what it's like to feel shame and self-hatred, so I'm pretty good at spotting it in others." She snickered a little, holding one hand up to her nose. "Others. Like there are any others. I mean in *you*. I can spot it in you."

Thomas reached out to hold her hand. When he realized he was about to grab her claw, he pulled it back instinctively.

"I… I'm sorry," he said.

"It's okay," she said. "I don't blame you. Whenever I see it in the mirror I get freaked out, too."

"Look, I understand how you feel," Thomas said, "at least I think I do, and I'm not going to lie and say it will always be as it is now, but I really do love spending time with you. I think you're funny, and smart, and wise and—I know this will sound corny, but you've taught me a lot about how to live my life. Your fearlessness and dignity in the face of adversity are nothing short of remarkable."

"You're sweet, Thomas, and thank you for saying that." She got up, walked to the window and stared out. "I appreciate all you've done for me and I don't blame you for anything that happened to me, but I know you. You'd be happier without me in your life, without this obligation."

"I'll never abandon you," Thomas said.

"It's okay—I've lived a lot longer than I expected to when they were… treating me at Pinewood. Ha, *treating* me, like I had a medical condition that needed curing. I think their brainwashing is still affecting me, all these years later…" She cut herself off, and was silent for a couple of seconds and then said, "Oh my God."

She still had her back to Thomas, still staring outside.

"What is it?" Thomas asked.

"I… I just saw someone," she said. "Oh my God, he was behind that tree, and now he's—"

A gun fired, and then glass in front of Karen shattered. Thomas darted across the room, grabbed her by the waist, and tackled her to the side as another bullet shattered the rest of the window where she had been standing a second earlier.

He held her down on the floor.

"Did you see who it was?" Thomas asked.

"No," she said.

"Where's the gun I bought you?"

"In the bedroom. In the top drawer of my dresser."

"Stay down here, you understand me? Don't move."

"I won't," Karen said.

Thomas crawled, as fast as he could, into the bedroom. He passed other windows and feared that if he stood above the level of the sill he'd be killed. He had no idea who had shot at Karen, but he knew it was no coincidence—he'd been followed.

In the bedroom he came to his knees, reached up, and opened the top dresser drawer. He knew he didn't have much time. Fumbling around he felt undergarments—panties, something silky, maybe a slip.

Damn it, where is it?

She said the top drawer, didn't she? He tossed the undergarments onto the floor, reached further inside, but nothing was there. Becoming more frantic, he opened the other drawers, flung clothes onto the floor, but couldn't find the gun.

Then he heard noise—a screen door opening, a creaking footstep. Someone was on the porch. He checked the bottom drawer, the only drawer he hadn't checked yet, but the gun wasn't there either. He got up and looked in the drawer of the night table, on the small bookshelf, in the closet, but time was running out.

The front doorknob rattled.

He looked for another weapon—the table light with a heavy base was the best he could find. He removed the shade and held the lamp upside down, over his shoulder like a club. Then he heard a loud *bang* and realized that the intruder had broken down the front door.

Thomas hoped Karen hadn't listened to him after all. Hopefully she'd gotten away—maybe climbed out of the broken window and run into the woods. He moved to the door, stood with his back against the wall, and listened carefully. He heard creaking footsteps, but no more gunshots—a good sign, because if Karen had been in clear view the person would have shot again.

Suddenly there was a man's voice.

"Okay, come on, let's make this easier for all of us," the man said. "I mean, it's all over now anyway, so what's the point of the hide-and-go-seek crap? I'm gonna find both of you anyway, so you might as well make it quick." The harsh, gravelly voice sounded unfamiliar. Thomas remained still as the man's footsteps grew louder.

"Come on, you freak show, where are you?" the man said. "Come on, lemme put you out of your misery. I'll put a bullet in your head, right between your pretty eyes. You won't know what hit you. You, too, Mr. Billionaire Wayne. It's time to go bye-bye."

Then the man stopped walking. All Thomas could hear was his own breathing, then maybe the intruder's breathing too, unless he was imagining it. He kept a strong grip on the lamp, ready to swing.

Maybe ten seconds passed. It seemed much longer.

Then the footsteps resumed. As the guy entered the bedroom, everything seemed as if it was in slow motion. Thomas saw the tip of the gun, then the whole gun, then the guy's arm.

He made his move—swinging the lamp like a club. He'd hoped to hit the man in the face, to knock him out or at least stun him, but the intruder was much taller than he had expected—maybe a foot taller than Thomas. The lamp's brass base hit the guy's upper chest.

Still, the force of the blow knocked him off balance. Thomas dropped the lamp and grabbed the guy's arm, the one with the gun. As they struggled, his assailant managed to squeeze off a couple of shots. They went into the ceiling.

"You shoulda let me make it easy," the guy said.

Thomas was overmatched physically, but he had learned some self-defense moves from Alfred. He kneed the guy in the gut, and when he bent over, Thomas head-butted him. Stunned, the man dropped the gun to the floor. Thomas went for it, but just when he was about to grab it, the guy grabbed him by the hair and pulled him back.

"You had your shot and you blew it," the intruder said. He lifted Thomas up and tossed him, head-first, against the dresser. Sparks blocked his vision—he felt as if he might pass out, but he knew if he lost consciousness he'd never wake up again. So he garnered the strength to wheel around and charge at the guy—who wasn't expecting any more resistance.

Thomas wanted to tackle him, but the guy was too strong. He couldn't budge him, and the man easily grabbed him and pushed him back up against the wall. He must've retrieved his gun while Thomas was dazed, because he had it in his hand again and he pressed the tip of the barrel against Thomas's forehead, between his eyes.

"Sayonara, billionaire," the guy said. "Too bad you can't take your money with you, huh?" He had scars on his face, a few teeth were missing, and his breath was foul. "But don't worry, this is the painless part."

Thomas stared straight ahead, at the guy's thick neck, ready for the permanent darkness of death, and then he saw an image of Bruce, on the veranda overlooking the gardens at Wayne Manor, reading *Beowulf*. Bruce had a content, peaceful, Buddha-like smile. He was so young, but wiser than his years and had so much potential. Would he ever realize it? Was he strong enough to survive in Gotham without his father?

Then something odd happened. The image of Bruce vanished, but no gunshot was fired, and darkness didn't set in. Thomas was still staring at the man's neck, but something had pierced the center of it, maybe a blade, and then blood spurted like water from a garden hose. It came from the guy's mouth, and Thomas's face was warm and wet.

Then he realized it wasn't a blade—it was one of Karen's claws, and as she yanked the claw out of the guy's neck, he crumpled to the ground and lay still.

Blood stung Thomas's eyes. He could barely see, and the salty, metallic taste on his lips disgusted him. Then he wiped his eyes with the back of his hand and saw that Karen had remained standing there, mesmerized and horrified, staring at her bloody appendage.

"It's true," she said. "It's all true."

Thomas had no idea what she was talking about. After his close encounter with death, he was still in shock himself.

"What's true?" he asked.

"What people have always said about me," she said. "Strange and Pinewood didn't turn me into a monster—I've *always* been a monster. That's what people used to say about me, after I killed my parents. In newspapers, on television, people on the street. 'Karen Jennings is evil, she's a monster, she deserves everything she gets.'

"I used to think they were wrong, that they didn't understand who I really was. I was abused, I did it in self-defense. I told them *I* was the victim, not them. But no—they were right, and I was wrong all along. This is who I really am. This is the real me." She looked frantic, but still she refused to cry.

"You're not a monster," Thomas said, "you're a hero. You just saved my life, for God's sake. Of course, I could've handled it myself if the gun I gave you had been in your dresser."

She looked startled at the mention, and it seemed to calm her down, as he'd hoped it would.

"Oh, that's right," Karen said. "I got nervous the other night, and put it under my bed. Who knows? Maybe I was having a premonition." Then her eyes widened, looking to Thomas's left. "Thomas, watch out!"

Thomas turned and saw that the man, with the gushing wound in his neck, had managed to get ahold of the gun and, with his weak, unsteady hand, had aimed it again.

Thomas dove toward the man and wrestled him for the weapon. He couldn't get the gun away, but managed to twist it, so that it was aimed upward, at the man's own face. He had a demented smile, blood dripping from his lips.

"The carnival always ends," he said.

Then the guy, most likely delirious from blood loss, probably unaware of where he was, or even *who* he was, pulled the trigger and a bullet ripped through his own head, splattering his brains on the wall behind him.

There was sudden, absolute silence in the room.

"The man in charge of Pinewood…" Karen looked terrified. "The man with the weird beard and the tinted glasses. He… he's behind this, isn't he?"

She seemed incapable of moving, and Thomas couldn't either.

Hugo Strange.

Thomas's greatest fear had come to pass. It had to be him—he had to be responsible. He'd hired people to break into Wayne Manor, and now had hired someone to follow Thomas, to find out what he knew. To locate the last, irrefutable evidence of his crimes.

Still, Thomas didn't want to frighten Karen. Though she didn't know Strange by name, she'd seen him many times. The poor young woman, she'd been through so much—he didn't want her to feel any more pain. He stared at the mess on the wall—blood and brains dripping in a seemingly coordinated way, like a macabre work of modern art.

"Looks like we have our work cut out for us," he said. "How are you fixed for sponges?"

EIGHT

A bunch of degenerates were hanging out in front of the liquor store on Caldwell Street and one of them recognized Harvey.

"Hey, look who it is." The guy's voice boomed. "Harvey Bullock. GCPD's finest."

The dude seemed sort of familiar. He had stringy long hair, over the shoulders, and looked like he hadn't had a bath in weeks. He was drinking from a bottle of Scotch, without even bothering to put a paper bag over it.

Heading into the building to question Roberto Colon, Harvey nodded, vaguely acknowledging the seedy speaker. Then the guy broke away from his friends and came over to him.

"You don't remember me, do ya, Harvey?" the guy said.

"Your face looks kinda familiar, but not the rest of you." He looked the guy over, and made a half-hearted attempt not to show his disgust.

"I grew it out in Arkham."

Harvey stopped, facing the guy. He took a closer look. "You really don't remember me, huh?"

"I don't," Harvey admitted.

"Ryan... Ryan Maxwell. You arrested me. They said I wasn't fit to stand trial, and they were right—I wasn't."

Harvey was a quick draw, but he put his hand a little closer to his piece just in case. When an ex-con you locked up met you on the street, it rarely led to anything positive.

"Name rings a bell now," Harvey said. "What did I arrest you for? Armed robbery? Rape?"

"I strangled my wife."

Suddenly Harvey remembered the case. The wife hadn't shown up for work for a few days. When Harvey and one of his ex-partners arrived at the apartment, Maxwell was sitting at the dining room table, having dinner, across from his dead wife. The body had been decomposing, but Maxwell didn't seem to notice or care. The guy was a real freakin' whack job.

"Shouldn't you *still* be in Arkham?" Harvey asked.

"They let me out last week," the guy said. "Get this. They said I was cured."

Harvey wasn't surprised. Because of overcrowding, Arkham had a revolving door these days and often let dangerous people out too soon—people who remained a threat to themselves and to society. You couldn't blame the asylum for the problem, though. It was a numbers game—too many crazy people in Gotham versus too few beds in which to put them.

"Good for you," Harvey said, and he gave Maxwell a thumbs up. "Well, it was great catching up." Before he could move, however, Maxwell got in front of him, wouldn't let him go into the building. Man, the guy reeked, like he'd doused himself with a new cologne called Back of a Gotham Taxi.

"Trust me, Ryan," Harvey said, "you don't want to do this. I've already been having a messed up day, and you don't want to deal with Harvey Bullock on a messed up day."

"But you can't go yet," Maxwell said. "I mean you didn't give me a chance to thank you."

Harvey tried to breathe through his mouth to avoid the stench.

"Look," he said, "I'm gonna give you and your hygiene issues one chance to get out of my face, and then I'm gonna have to cuff you and run you in. Next time they send you to Arkham, they'll throw away the key." He was bluffing, but the guy didn't look like the brightest bulb in the chandelier.

"That's *exactly* what I want." Maxwell's eyes widened with excitement. "Cuff me, *please*. You did such a great thing when you arrested me, Mr. Bullock. I'll do *anything* to go back to Arkham."

What the hell…

Harvey didn't know how the shrinks tested people to find out if they're crazy, but if one of the questions was, *"Do you want to go back to Arkham?"* and the person answered, *"Yes,"* then it was a safe bet the guy was a full-blown whacko.

"Maybe you have short-term memory loss," Harvey said, "but Arkham ain't exactly a country club. People would kill to get *out* of Arkham. A lot of them have."

"No, no—I loved it there," Maxwell insisted. "It was the happiest time of my life, really it was. I had three meals a day, and the occasional maggot in my grits didn't bother me. I was busy all the time, had free medical care, lots of chances to socialize with talkative, eccentric people. Sounds sort of like a luxury cruise, doesn't it?"

This can't be real, Harvey thought. The guy continued.

"The bed wasn't the most comfortable in the world, but I got used to it. One downside was that it was hard to get booze, but not impossible. It's kind of like a mini-Gotham in there—it's all about connections. If you know the right people, and do the right favors for the right people, you can get whatever you want. Out here… well, it sucks."

"You're really gonna have to get out of my way now, Ryan," Harvey said, "but I'll give you a piece of free advice. Consider yourself lucky."

"Lucky?" Maxwell said. "Lucky how?"

"Let's put it this way," Harvey said. "You're not gonna be the next mega lottery winner, but most guys who whack their wives never see the light of day again. But like a cat, somehow you wound up landing on your feet. So don't piss this opportunity away. Kick the booze, get a job, *stay* on your feet, find Jesus—anything that works. If you take another fall, you won't get back up."

"But it's not safe for me to be out," Maxwell said. "I

was safe inside—*everybody* was safe. I told them that, but they didn't listen. They sent me to a counselor. The guy wanted me to find a job, become a normal citizen. He told me, 'People can change,' but the truth is that people never change. If you're evil, you stay evil forever. I don't know what it's like to be good, but I guess it's the same way."

"To each his own," Harvey said.

Finally Maxwell stood aside and let him pass.

"I don't need you to take me," the man said, his tone angry, defiant. "I'll wind up back in Arkham somehow. You'll see!"

Shrugging it off, Harvey entered the building. The vestibule smelled like piss, but after breathing in Ryan's stench, it was like a breath of fresh spring air. People were hanging out in the hallway, the kind of crowd you'd expect to find at a cheap S.R.O. on this side of town—pimps, hookers, drug dealers, drug addicts, and ex-cons.

"Lookin' for a date?" a hooker asked Harvey.

She wasn't bad looking—long straight blonde hair in a kinda sexy black leather getup, like something Fish Mooney might wear. At a hornier time and place, Harvey may have taken her up on her offer.

"You know where Roberto is?" he asked.

A moment of hesitation, then she shook her head. Harvey knew what that meant. He held out a twenty.

"Do you know where Roberto is?"

She grabbed the money faster than a seagull snatching a dead fish on the beach.

"Fourth floor, room at the end of the hallway."

Harvey headed up, passing more deadbeats and hookers. It was like a convention. A wide range of music blasted from the rooms—salsa, reggae, hip-hop, metal. Even so, a lot of voices could be heard over the music. People arguing about the usual topics—sex, drugs, and money.

By the fourth floor, Harvey had his gun out. He banged on the door twice.

"Come in."

Harvey opened the door. A scruffy guy about Harvey's age was sitting in a chair facing him. Somehow Harvey felt like an expected visitor, rather than a surprise guest.

"Harvey Bullock, Detective GCPD." He flashed his badge.

"A detective?" The guy acted surprised. "What can I do for you?"

"You Roberto Colon?"

"Either that was a great first guess, or you're a psychic. Either one would be extremely impressive. Though I've met psychics, and you don't have the right soul for it. I can tell that and we just met, what, twenty seconds ago?"

"A talker, huh?" Harvey said. "Great, just what I needed today. Why did you take off from Angel's?"

"Angel's? What's Angel's?"

"You wanna be a wise guy, huh? I'll run you in, and we can talk all you want downtown."

"You're making a big assumption there, Detective."

"Yeah?" Harvey said. "How's that?"

"Well, to take me in you'll have to be alive."

Two guys Harvey hadn't seen, hiding on either side of the door, grabbed him—each one taking an arm. Both of them were big. Then one of the gorillas kicked the door shut. Colon pulled out a gun and aimed it at Harvey.

"This is what I believe is called a turn of events," Colon said. "Drop it, Detective, or I'll kill you right now."

Harvey dropped his gun.

"Well, talk about role reversal," Colon said. "Maybe I should call you Roberto, and you should call me Detective. Or do you prefer Harvey?" He laughed. One of the guys holding Harvey laughed, too. Well, more like gurgled.

"If you're looking for a career in stand-up," Harvey said, "you better work on your material."

Colon got up and approached. "Aw, he doesn't think I'm funny," he said in a mocking voice. "I'm so hurt." Leaning in closer, he added, "You know when you're a guest, you should always laugh at your host's jokes."

Using his free hand Colon lashed out with a blow to the gut. It was a good shot, took Harvey's breath away, and he keeled over as much as he could with the two goons holding him up. The bust had officially gone from bad to worse.

"Now we're clear about the new power dynamics," Colon said, "how about you tell me why you're looking for me?"

"S-son of a bitch," Harvey managed to say.

"True, my mother was quite a bitch," Colon said. "She neglected me, beat me, and pretty much tortured me on a daily basis. So I'm one of the rare guys who don't mind it when you insult my mother. But getting back to the matter at hand—" He lifted Harvey's face with one hand. "—the purpose of your visit."

"A friend of yours was killed at Wayne Manor last night," Harvey said. "A painting was stolen. A Picasso."

"Well, well, I'm impressed with your sleuthing, Detective. It's been, what, twelve hours since the robbery, and you've practically solved the case. Emphasis on *practically*. Which is good news for me, bad news for you."

"So you admit you broke into Wayne Manor?"

"There you go, asking questions again. I thought we discussed that." He unloaded another fist into Harvey's gut, leaving Harvey gasping like he had a bad case of asthma.

"Well, as much fun as this has been," Colon said, "I have business to attend to, so I'm going to have to cut our visit short." He aimed the gun at Harvey's face.

Was this really how he was going to check out? Killed by some loudmouth punk? Harvey glanced at his gun on the floor, a couple feet away, but he couldn't reach for it with the goons holding his arms.

"W-w-wait," he said. "How will you get rid of my body? Too many people know where to find you. People saw me come up, too. You've been sloppy." He was stalling for time, trying to figure a way out.

"You think anybody cares what goes on in this place?" Colon asked, but he lowered the gun. "There are shootings here every day. As for your body, that's where a chainsaw and some trash bags come in handy. This time tomorrow, you'll be sinking to the bottom of the Gotham River with God knows whoever else is down there. Then you'll be fish food. Are there still fish in the Gotham River? You don't have to answer that. Sayonara, Detective Bullock."

He aimed the gun again.

Someone knocked on the door.

"Hello, I have money."

A girl. It sounded like one of the pros.

Another knock.

"Hello, I have money for you," she said. "Open up."

"Who the hell is that?" Colon demanded of his thugs.

They just shrugged.

"Get rid of her," Colon said.

One guy went to the door, while the other one held Harvey. He tried to edge toward his gun, but the gorilla had an iron grip.

The thug who'd let go opened the door. "The hell do you—?"

Wham! The door slammed into his face, so hard that it knocked him off-balance, and he stumbled backward, bellowing in pain. Judging from the blood, something was broken, maybe his nose.

Then Amanda stepped into the room, her gun up so that it was aimed at Colon. She stood with her legs apart and her knees flexed.

"Drop it!" she said.

The thug holding Harvey went for his own piece, which gave Harvey enough slack to break free. The goon swung his pistol up toward Amanda, but he beat him to it, shooting him twice in the chest.

The other guy recovered enough to charge, and Amanda whacked him in the head with the side of her pistol, managing to connect his nose again. He went down without a sound this time, and stayed there. Meanwhile, Harvey grabbed his gun from the floor. He looked over and caught a glimpse of Colon climbing through the window, out to the fire escape.

"He's getting away!"

Colon fired at him, missing. Harvey was about to fire back, but Colon ducked out of sight. Harvey rushed to the window, leaned out, and pulled the trigger, bullets pinging off the fire escape's iron railing. He was so pissed that he expended his whole clip.

"Goddamit!" Harvey yelled. "He got away."

"That was Colon, I'm assuming," Amanda said. "Was he in on the robbery?"

"Sounds like it." He glanced around the room, and walked over to a dresser in the corner, picking up a mass of hair and rubber. It was a gorilla mask. "Make that definitely." He threw it to the floor with a curse.

"Well, now that we know who he is, we'll get him," Amanda said. "Let's put an APB out. I mean, if you think that's the appropriate thing to do. You're the boss." She looked strange. Like she was… *sorry*. "I owe you an apology, Harvey."

Holy crap, he thought.

"For what?" he said aloud. "Bursting in here and saving my fat Irish ass?"

"I'm sure you would've wound up on top, with or without me."

Okay, that's stretching it, Harvey thought, but he didn't want to admit that he'd been prepared to meet his maker.

"Yeah," he said. "That's probably true."

The thug who was still breathing was struggling, getting to his feet.

"It's not easy for me to admit I'm wrong," Amanda said. "I mean, if you haven't picked up on that by now. But I was out of line before." As she spoke, she delivered a well-aimed kick to the back of the thug's head, making it look effortless, knocking him out again. Harvey reassessed the wisdom of pissing her off.

"I'm the rookie and you've been doing this for years," she continued. "It was wrong of me to question your judgment, and to threaten you with a report. I can learn a lot by working with you, I'm sure."

She sounded sincere, though Harvey wasn't sure if he bought what she was saying. Maybe not a hundred percent. Maybe she was afraid he'd spread word around the GCPD that she was a rat, and that it could cost her job—or maybe her life. Whatever the truth, whether it was sincere or bullshit, he was glad she'd shown up when she did. Or he'd probably be checking into heaven right now. Well, if he was lucky.

"No harm, no foul," Harvey said. "By the way,

I liked the hooker routine. If you did that next time with a schoolgirl skirt, I might really enjoy myself." He paused to see how she'd react.

"Hey, watch it," Amanda said, playing along. "You don't want me reporting you for harassment, do you?"

"Jeez, how many complaints are you gonna file?" He chuckled, and looked around the room—searching under the bed, in the closet, behind the furniture. "I mean talk about a laundry list. I take kickbacks, I harass you, I drink. What else you got on me?"

"I'm sure you have other endearing qualities I have yet to discover," she said, and she smiled a little. He thought she might finally be getting with the program.

"Well, no Picasso here," Harvey said. "Nothing to tell us where it might be—no business card, no phone number, no treasure map. So maybe the third robber has it. The zombie." He glanced at the bodies on the floor. The one with the bullet wounds in his chest was very dead, his wide-open eyes staring at infinity. The other one was stirring again.

"Or maybe this Neanderthal knows something," Harvey said.

"Hey, come on, Homo erectus." Amanda knelt next to the thug and slapped him in the face a couple of times. "Wake up! Get it together." The guy's eyes opened and then, remembering what had happened, panic kicked in.

"P-please," he said. "D-don't hurt me again."

"If you answer my questions, maybe I won't," Amanda said. "Where were you last night? Were you at Wayne Manor?"

"N-no, I swear I wasn't." He looked around, saw the body, and his eyes went wide. "Roberto—he gave us money, hundred bucks each, to be his muscle, that's all. I met him for the first time, like ten minutes before you came in."

"Did he say anything about a Picasso?" Amanda asked. "That's a painting."

"No, I swear, I don't know nothing about a painting." The guy actually looked like he was going to cry. "I-I have a daughter. I w-wanna see my daughter again. Please."

"He's probably telling the truth," Harvey said. "But let's take him downtown and beat the crap out of him just to make sure."

Amanda started to laugh, then stifled it.

"Wait, you're not kidding, are you?"

Harvey grinned.

"Better add police brutality to my list."

NINE

"Well, this wasn't exactly how I'd planned to spend my Saturday," Thomas said.

He and Karen had just spent three hours digging a hole in the woods behind the house, burying the body. According to the ID found in the dead man's wallet, his name was Scott Wallace. Thomas had buried the wallet with him, along with Scotty's cell phone. A thorough search of both didn't turn up any connection between Wallace and Hugo Strange.

Next, Thomas and Karen had cleaned up the blood in the bedroom, scrubbing the walls and the floors, and Thomas had swept up the broken glass in the front of the cabin, taping cardboard over the gaping hole. He would bring her a new window the next time he visited.

"You can't go home in those clothes," Karen said.

She was right, of course. His shirt and pants were covered in mud and blood, and he couldn't let Martha, Bruce, Alfred, or anyone else find out about his expedition.

"I have a T-shirt in my trunk," Thomas said, "from the last Wayne company picnic. My pants are a bigger problem, though."

"I can wash them for you," Karen said.

"But how can you dry them? The sun is going down soon and you don't have a clothes dryer here."

"True, but I do have a hair dryer."

He finally relented, and while Karen washed and dried the slacks, Thomas wore a towel around his waist, and a T-shirt which read, "WAYNE ENTERPRISES: THE FUTURE IS NOW." He cleaned the blood from his shoes, as well. He was driven purely by adrenaline, focused on getting rid of any trace of what had occurred. It hadn't fully set in what he'd done.

I killed a man, in cold blood.

This wasn't actually true, he told himself—he had killed Wallace in self-defense. Technically, Wallace had killed himself, yet regardless of the specifics, Thomas had been involved in the death of a human being, and now he was trying to hide the evidence.

The devil is in the details.

A short time later he was dressed again in his cleaned clothes, having tea with Karen. They were seated across from each other in the living area—Karen on the couch, Thomas in the chair.

"I feel like the harder I try to dig out of the trouble of my past, the deeper I fall into it," he commented. "I mean, I drove out here to make sure you were safe, and I wound up killing a man, snuffing out his life, then burying his body. A man who wouldn't have been here had it not been for me."

"Stop saying that," Karen protested. "He was trying to kill you, and me, and you had no choice but to bury the body."

"I used to be a decent, honorable man."

"You still are a decent, honorable man."

"The whole situation feels so surreal," Thomas said. "How did I sink to this level?"

"Surely you've seen killing before," Karen said. "Weren't you in the army?"

"No," Thomas said. "I was in college during the draft. Was involved with a private army several years ago, but I had a hands-off role."

"That explains it," Karen said. "So this is the first time you've been this close to death, isn't it? The first time you were actively involved in the violence."

Thomas nodded.

"Trust me," Karen said, "killing is like diving into a swimming pool for the first time. After you've done it once, it gets easier."

"Who did you kill besides your parents?" Thomas asked.

Karen cringed for a moment, obviously the effect of some dark memory.

"In prison, there were situations where I had to defend myself," Karen said, "but because I felt justified, I felt no guilt afterward. That made it easier, too."

"I don't exactly feel any guilt," Thomas said, remembering how Wallace had tried to shoot him. "I'm not sure *what* I feel, but that isn't it. Burying the evidence makes me feel vaguely ghoulish, though."

"It was necessary," Karen asserted. "What else could we have done? Call the police and tell them that someone from Pinewood sent a man to kill me, one of their former patients, and you as well?"

"We don't know for certain that Scotty Wallace was connected to Pinewood."

"Oh, come on, what other explanation could there be? In all the years I've been in this cabin, no other person has ever shown up, *ever*, and suddenly one shows up right after you arrive. It's too convenient."

They were skirting too close to the truth, to what Thomas had suspected since the break-in. This woman had just helped him bury a dead man. How could he not open up to her, and tell her everything?

"Okay, you're right," he relented. "This must be Pinewood related." Thomas paused, then decided that the direct approach was best. "I think the man in charge may be starting experiments again."

"What's his name?" Karen asked.

"You know I can't tell you that," Thomas said. "It's for your—"

"—own protection. I know." Karen stared at him for a few seconds, not blinking at all. He didn't think he saw fear in her eyes, but there was… anger?

Then she said, "If you knew this the entire time, why didn't you tell me?"

"Because I *didn't* know, not until yesterday," Thomas said. "And I still don't know—not for certain. I'm just speculating."

"Yesterday?" Karen asked. "What happened yesterday?"

Thomas told her about the robbery at Wayne Manor, and his suspicion that the man in charge of Pinewood had orchestrated it. He told her about the Picasso, the damage to his study, and the documents that connected him and Karen to Pinewood.

"Why are you assuming that Pinewood people robbed your house?" Karen asked. "That painting is worth a fortune. It could've been anyone."

"Professional art thieves wouldn't have done the damage they did, wouldn't have risked being caught in the act," Thomas said. "There had to be something else they expected to find. I think they expected to locate the files."

"In your walls?"

"They might've suspected that I had them hidden there."

"Where do you have them hidden?"

While Thomas felt close with Karen, and trusted her enough to share secrets with her, he couldn't tell her about his secret office. He had too many secrets down there. Absolutely no one could know of its existence, or about its contents.

"Let's just say they're in a safe place," Thomas said, "but the fact that I was followed here today, just a day after the robbery, makes it clear that no place is entirely safe. The man in charge—he's fishing, trying to find out what I might possess that I could hold against him. Survivors would be the greatest threat to him, the ultimate proof of his past sins, if he was planning to restart the program."

"So he hired a hit man to kill me," Karen said.

"Maybe not specifically you," Thomas said. "That depends on whether or not he knows what happened to all of the rest. He may not even know that you're still alive—he may have thought this was where I kept the evidence. Wallace's instructions may have been to eliminate me, and anyone he found with me. Until he saw you, he may not have been aware..." He almost said, *"Of your deformity,"* but stopped himself in time.

"Do the police know about any of this?"

"No, the police think it's all about a robbery, that's it... They have no idea about anything related to me, you, or Pinewood, and I intend to keep it that way... No one, not a soul, other than me knows anything about your connection to any of this." Thomas realized this last part wasn't true.

"Well, except one person."

Her eyes went wide and accusing.

"There's a private investigator, by the name of Frank Collins," Thomas said. "He's a man I trust, who's worked for me for years."

"And he knows about Pinewood?"

"Only what he needs to know." Thomas hesitated. "But he knows about you."

"What did you tell him?" Karen sounded panicky.

"Don't worry, he doesn't know any specifics," Thomas said. "He just knows there's someone from my past whom I've been protecting. But he doesn't know where the cabin is, or any details about your past."

"Does he know my name?"

"Yes."

"For God's sake, Thomas." With her non-clawed hand, Karen picked up the music box, the Christmas present Thomas had given her, and cocked her arm as if preparing to throw it.

"Don't!" Thomas yelled.

She stopped herself and placed the music box back on the end table.

"How dare you," Karen said. "My safety is at stake. You shouldn't have told anyone—not without asking me first. I don't know anything about this man, but he knows enough that I could be killed."

"Frank is one hundred percent trustworthy," Thomas said. "Seriously, the man used to be a Gotham City Police Detective, and is the best there is. I *had* to hire him, to find the painting, and find out if the robbery was related to Pinewood. It's doubtful the police are trying very hard, but they still might stumble upon something that could lead them where we don't want them to go. It's imperative that we get there first, and cover our tracks."

"It's true," she said. "If the police find out about Pinewood, it could ruin you, and Wayne Enterprises would go down with you."

"You're right," Thomas said. "It would."

"See, then, this isn't really about me." Karen stood, glaring down at Thomas. "It's never been about me, has it? Who am I? Some ex-con, some mistake you made that you need to hide. You treat me like you got me an abortion or something. You hide me away, pay my expenses, and it's all fine as long as I stay a secret. As long as I remain silent."

"You know that's not true."

"Do I?" she said. "And how do I know that? Because you come visit me once in a while, throw me a bone, act like you enjoy these visits. When I can see it in your eyes—the regret, the shame, the guilt. None of this is about me. It's about you, and your company, and your reputation."

"No, it's not… it's about *all* of those things," Thomas said. "Of course I care about Wayne Enterprises, and the jobs that would be lost, and lives that would be affected if something happened to the company. But I'm also doing all of this to protect you."

"Well, judging from today, you're doing a great job of it." She crossed her arms, placing the normal one awkwardly over the claw, and looked away.

"Can you sit down, please?" Thomas said. "You're making me nervous."

"*You're* nervous?" Karen remained standing. "How do you know your private investigator isn't in on it?"

"There's no way Frank would—"

"You said he knows about Pinewood."

"Yes," Thomas said, "but he doesn't know the details."

This wasn't true—Frank knew just about everything.

"You told him about the robbery, about a possible connection to Pinewood, and then you were followed here. You don't think that's a coincidence, do you?"

Thomas considered this—for a moment. Could Frank have betrayed him? No, the only guy in Gotham whom Thomas trusted more than Frank was Alfred.

"I understand the way you feel," he said. "Someone tried to kill you today, so of course you're nervous, but you have to trust me on this."

Karen began pacing.

"Okay, so whether your PI is on it or not," Karen said, "this is just this beginning. Wallace followed you here. He could've called someone, told them I'm here, and—"

"I don't think we have to worry about that," Thomas said. "I checked Wallace's phone, and he hadn't contacted anyone for more than an hour before he died. Service is so bad up here he couldn't have contacted anyone, even if he'd wanted to. What I'm trying to say is you're safe, Karen. I'm confident that no one knows you're here, except me, and it'll stay that way."

"So what do you expect me to do now?" she said. "Pretend this never happened? Go on with my wonderful life in the great outdoors?"

"Well, there *is* a bright side to all of this," Thomas said.

"Oh, really?" Karen said. "Do tell."

"If Frank can find evidence that links Pinewood

to the robbery, and we keep the details about the experiments out of it, then whoever's responsible could get a long prison sentence. That means you wouldn't have to hide here any longer."

"Oh, that sounds wonderful," Karen said. "Maybe I could get a steady job... at a *circus*. Or, better yet, at a freak show."

Karen went into the kitchen. Thomas followed her. He knew her well. She wasn't crying—she'd never cried around him, but he often wondered if the tough girl act was just for show, if she cried all the time when she was alone.

"It doesn't have to be that way," he said.

She had her back to him.

"I'd help you get through it," he said. "I'd get you counseling, I'd get you any help you need."

"You've paid your penance, Thomas." Her voice was harsh. "I formally absolve you of any responsibility you've had, relating to everything that went on at Pinewood. You can go on with your life, you can stop coming here."

"Come on, Karen, you know I'd never stop—"

"You almost get killed today," she continued. "You need to protect your family, not me."

"But you *are*... you know how I feel about—"

"Your *real* family. I don't have a family. I killed my family, remember?" Her voice rose until she was shouting. "Now just go—leave me the hell alone!"

Thomas didn't want to leave her like this, when she was so upset.

"Come on, Karen. Let's just go back into the other room and—"

She turned around and raised her clawed hand, as if about to slash him with it.

"Get the hell out! Now!"

Thomas didn't think Karen would attack him, but something in him refused to make him sure. She looked so... vicious. She had killed before, after all. Maybe her parents hadn't thought she was capable of murder, either.

Thomas backed away.

"Fine, I'm going, I'm going."

She remained with her claw raised, looking just as dangerous, perhaps exhibiting the traits of whatever reptile DNA Strange had introduced into her system.

"I'll check in with you tomorrow," Thomas said. "Get some rest if you can, you've had a difficult day. And I just want you to know—I care about you very much, and my feelings are genuine."

No response.

Thomas left the cabin. Dusk had set in, but he had no trouble finding his way to his car. Somehow the country air didn't feel as refreshing as it had earlier. He was looking forward to returning to the bustle of Gotham and, most importantly, seeing Martha and Bruce.

Usually when Thomas left, Karen came out to the screened-in porch and waved goodbye until he disappeared from view. This time she didn't come out.

"See you soon, Karen," he said to himself, and he waved goodbye to her anyway.

TEN

Later in the evening, Alfred Pennyworth met Thomas at the front door. From the road, Thomas had called home and said he would be "leaving the office soon," and that his "day ran late."

"Good evening, sir," Alfred said.

He glanced at Thomas's T-shirt. As a former Royal Marine, he recognized when something seemed amiss. As a butler, he recognized when to keep his mouth shut.

"How did your business go today?" he continued. "I hope it was a fruitful day for you?" He feared that his tone leaked subtle sarcasm, but he maintained his professional demeanor.

"It went well, thank you," Thomas said. "It'll be nice to have a more relaxing Sunday."

"It's supposed to be a sunny day tomorrow, so that should get the week off to a good start at least." He gestured toward the study. "The repair work's done, do you want to have a look?"

"Yes, let's see how it turned out," Thomas said. He followed Alfred through the door.

"Impressive," he said, giving a low whistle. "If I didn't know what had happened here, it would be almost impossible to tell."

"Yes, except for one major exception," Alfred said, glancing at the spot where the Picasso had been.

"Hopefully we'll have *Le Picador* back, as well, very soon," Thomas said.

"The police haven't had any luck, I presume?"

"Haven't heard anything as of yet."

"I visited Nigel at Gotham General today. He thanked you for the get well package you sorted for him." He made sure to keep his expression neutral, but doubted his employer was buying it.

"I'm sure I made great selections," Thomas said. "How's Nigel doing?"

"He's had better days, I reckon. Lost several teeth, can't open his eyes. He said he doesn't have the foggiest idea who attacked him, doesn't even remember most of it. It's a nigh miracle he remembers his bloody name. I know you have your doubts, Mr. Wayne, but I don't. I'm certain he's telling the truth."

"I know you have great instincts, Alfred," Thomas said. "One of the main reasons I hired you—aside from the way Bruce feels about you—is that you're great at reading situations. So if you vouch for Nigel, I'm with you. The question remains, though, how did the thieves breach the security system?"

"The most obvious answer is that they got the

information from the horse's mouth itself, so to speak," Alfred said. "Someone at Wayne Enterprises."

"I guess I didn't want to go there," Thomas said, "hoping it wasn't true. But it looks like I may have a rat to sniff out."

"Did you hurt yourself, sir?" Alfred was looking at Thomas's neck.

"What?" Thomas asked. "Why?" Then he glanced in the antique oak-framed mirror to his right, and saw the blood that was there. There was no way around it. Alfred knew blood when he saw it.

"I must've cut myself shaving," Thomas said.

"What a shame," Alfred said, but he didn't believe it for a minute. Thomas Wayne paid him well not to ask too many questions, though. Nevertheless, it was bothersome.

"Well, if there isn't anything else you'll be needing, I'm going to turn in," he said, giving a quick nod and heading toward the door.

"One thing," Thomas said.

"Yes?" Alfred stopped. "What's that?"

Thomas seemed to struggle to find the right words, then said, "If anything ever happens to me or, God forbid, me and Martha, I want your word that you'll be Bruce's guardian until he's an adult." He paused, and then added, "You'll receive generous compensation of course."

Alfred didn't know quite what to say. This was quite out of the blue. After a moment he decided it was better to say little, and listen carefully.

"This is in your wills already, isn't it?" He knew it was.

"Yes, but to hell with wills," Thomas said, and he seemed quite intent. "I want your word, Alfred."

"Did something happen at... work today? Something that I should know about, sir?" He watched Thomas intently, waiting for an answer.

"No, it was just, well, business as usual," Thomas said, but he still seemed to be grasping. "This is just something that's been in the back of my mind, gnawing at me for a while, and I suppose the break-in last night got me thinking about it again. We're living in a dangerous world, here in Gotham, and things don't always work out as planned. I mean, the carnival always ends, right?"

"Yes, indeed," Alfred said. "Unfortunately that is always the case."

"Well, I just want to be prepared for the unforeseen," Thomas said. "As you know, after Bruce was born, I didn't hire you to clean house and handle our lunch appointments. I could've hired any butler in Gotham for that. I hired you because you connected with Bruce the moment you met each other, and because of your, well, unique set of skills.

"I'm not a fool, Alfred," he added. "I was aware of the direction this city was heading and I knew that, unlike the Waynes of previous generations, Bruce would have to rely on far more than his name and fortune. He'll be a target someday—people are going to come gunning for him—and he has to learn how to fight. Both literally and figuratively. You're my secret weapon, Alfred. Martha and I are depending on you. So is Bruce."

"Well, I'm flattered, Mr. Wayne, and honored," Alfred said. "Let's hope the carnival lasts for a very long time indeed, but I promise you that I'll look after the boy, and respect all of your wishes. You have my word."

"That's all I needed to hear," Thomas said.

After Thomas rinsed the remaining blood off his neck in the kitchen, he went up the winding stairwell. He was about to pass Bruce's room when he caught a glimpse of his son standing in front of the mirror, shadowboxing.

Thomas stopped and watched him for several moments, admiring the boy's determination and focus. Then Bruce saw Thomas watching him, and stopped punching the air.

"Don't stop, Bruce," Thomas said, "you're on a roll."

"I don't really know what I'm doing," Bruce said. "Just imitating what I saw on TV tonight. Alfred and I watched the fight."

Abruptly Thomas remembered that he'd promised to watch the Williams-Sanchez fight with him.

"I'm so sorry, Bruce," he said quickly. "My meetings ran late at the office and I couldn't get home in time." He hated lying, especially to his son, but in this case he had no choice. Bruce could never know about Karen.

"It's okay, Alfred told me you'd be late," Bruce said. "It was a great fight. Williams knocked out Sanchez."

Thomas recalled that Frank had bet on a fifth-round knockout.

"What round?" Thomas asked.

"Third," Bruce said.

Ouch. Thomas chuckled, thinking, *Well, maybe going against your instincts wasn't such a great idea after all.*

"What's so funny?" Bruce asked.

"I have a friend who was hoping for a fifth-round ending."

"Why does it matter?" Bruce said. "I mean Williams is still the champion, isn't he?"

"It only matters to the gamblers," Thomas said. "Did you have your tennis lesson today?"

"Yes." Bruce couldn't have sounded less enthused.

"I'll have another talk with your mom," Thomas said, "see what we can do about boxing lessons, if you're still interested."

"Oh, I'm still interested," Bruce said. "That would be awesome." He gave his father a hug, and they said goodnight to each other. As Thomas left the room, the sounds he heard coming from behind said that Bruce had returned to shadowboxing.

He continued along the wide hallway, with its lavish red and maroon Oriental carpeting, coming to the master bedroom. Martha was in bed, reading from a book on the fall of ancient Rome. When Thomas entered, her quick glance told him she was angry with him. She didn't need words.

"I'm sorry I ran so late today, honey," Thomas said. He leaned between her and the book and kissed her, wincing from a muscle he'd pulled when digging the hole for Scotty Wallace's body.

She remained staring at the book.

"Didn't Alfred tell you I'd be late?" he asked.

"Yes, he told me," she said.

More silence as she continued reading, or pretended to read to avoid looking at him. After the day he'd had, the last thing Thomas needed was tension with his wife.

"Please stop playing these games," Thomas said.

Martha put down the book. "Games?" she said, and her voice was terse. "What games do you think I'm playing?" She still didn't look at him.

"Even that," Thomas said, "asking me what games you're playing. If you're angry at me, just come out and say it."

"Fine," Martha said, "I'm angry at you. Is that better?"

"Much." It wasn't. "I apologized for being late. I don't know what more to say."

"I called your office. The service said you weren't there at all today."

Uh-oh…

Thomas needed to think fast. He didn't want to lie, but thanks to Pinewood, it seemed as if that was all he did. The pattern felt endless, with no way to escape.

"Well, I don't know what to tell you," he said. "I was in my office all day. Whomever you spoke to must have been unaware of it."

He waited to see how she would respond.

"I called you on your cell phone, as well," Martha persisted, "but the calls kept going to voicemail."

"The end of the quarter is coming up," he said. "I was in meetings." Then he decided to take a different approach. "What's this all about anyway? Why do you sound so accusing?"

"Your behavior's been… odd, Tom."

"Odd? What in God's name are you talking about?" He wished he could take that one back. The *in God's name* was too much, sounded entirely like a lie. So he added, "We just had a lovely time in Switzerland, and I know it's been stressful for both of us, what with the robbery and all, but—"

"I'm not talking about the damn *robbery*." Her voice was getting louder. "I'm talking about how you've been disappearing for years, taking trips upstate, saying that you 'just need to clear your head.'"

He noticed that she'd clenched her fists.

"I told you, I was in the office today." He wished he *had* said that he'd gone upstate, and done so from the get-go, but was stuck. It was like jumping from an airplane—once you started, there was no turning back. "I do need to clear my head sometimes," he admitted, "but today wasn't one of those days."

Martha looked right at him, for the first time since he'd entered the room.

"Why are you wearing that T-shirt?" she asked.

"T-shirt?" He put his chin to his chest, as if noticing it himself for the first time. Could his acting be any worse? "Oh, the T-shirt, it's just for office solidarity. Morale has been low for a while now, so we're trying to do little things to lift people's spirits."

"It was chilly today," Martha said. "It hasn't been T-shirt weather in weeks. And you weren't wearing that T-shirt this morning."

"I changed," Thomas said.

He'd left his bloodied shirt at the cabin, and hoped Martha didn't ask to see it.

"Why did you change?"

Change? He needed to change the subject.

"What's this all about anyway?" he asked. "What's with the sudden interrogation? I was late from work, alright, but it's not like I murdered someone." Another quick response he wished he could take back.

"Fine, then how about you be honest with me," Martha said, "instead of giving me all of these convoluted explanations? Just tell me the truth."

"How am I not—"

"Are you having an affair?"

He paused as her words sunk in. He should have seen it coming.

"What?" He did his best to sound incredulous. "Do you honestly believe that I'd ever do that to you? *Or* to Bruce?" To his own surprise, some of the shock was real.

"I know you so well, Tom," Martha said. "I can always tell when you're lying."

"Well, I'm not lying to you now," Thomas said. "I am not having an affair."

Martha glared. "If there is someone else, I'd appreciate it if you came out and told me."

"There isn't anyone else," Thomas said gently. "I swear." He was sure he sounded believable. It helped that he was telling the truth… for a change.

"Fine," she said. After a long moment, she added, "I believe you." She, too, sounded sincere, and he relaxed a bit.

"Look, it's late," Thomas said. "I don't know where this is coming from. We just had a wonderful time in Europe, and I think we've been closer than ever lately. So let's just drop this line of discussion, okay?"

"Maybe I don't want to drop it," Martha said.

Damn.

"Okay fine, then go ahead." His words grew louder. "Go on—keep going. Make more accusations. Tell me I'm cheating on you, ruining our lives, when actually it's the opposite. Everything I'm doing is to *help* our lives, and Bruce's life!"

He was losing control a little, but he couldn't help it. All the stress of the day had built up, and the tension needed to come out somehow. But not now…

"Please keep your voice down?" Martha said. "Bruce can hear us."

"That's another thing," Thomas said. "Bruce isn't a child anymore. He's fourteen years old—he'll be a man soon. Hearing his parents having an argument won't be the most traumatic event in his life. You can't just shelter him from the real world. Not forever."

"Does this have to do with boxing again?" Martha

asked. "Because there's no way I'm allowing it."

"Well, I have a say as well," Thomas said, "and I think it would do him some good."

"What good?" she countered. "A concussion or two? Lose a few teeth?"

"He'll learn how to defend himself."

"We have resources, remember? We can hire bodyguards. He won't *need* to defend himself, ever."

"It's about inner strength," Thomas pressed, "not just physical strength."

"He's fine," Martha said. "He's a nice boy. He should stay that way."

"You can't get by on nice in Gotham," Thomas said.

"No boxing—period," Martha said. She got out of bed, went into the bathroom, and shut the door.

Thomas stood there on the opposite side of the bed, and remained angry for a couple of minutes. Then the guilt set in. He hated fighting with Martha—they had vowed never to go to sleep angry at each other. And she had every reason to be angry with him. She just didn't know the reasons.

Thomas undressed, put on a robe, and stood beside the bed. Then he waited a few more minutes, for Martha to come out of the bathroom. Finally she did, and he stopped her before she got back into bed.

"I'm sorry," he said, and he meant it.

"It's okay," she said, her manner subdued.

"No, it's not okay," he said. "I lashed out at you because I had a stressful day, and that's never the right thing to do. No matter what the stresses are before I come home. And I just want you to know, I'd never do anything to hurt you or Bruce."

With his arms holding her hips, he kissed her.

"I'm sorry, too," Martha said. "I get so worried, I build up scenarios in my head, and I couldn't help it. I've been on edge all day, and when you came home so late I guess it sent me *over* the edge. You're right, I'm sure you are—it is related to the break-in. I know they were after the painting, and didn't come here to harm us, but there were armed, violent criminals in our home. They *shot* at you. It's hard not to feel like a target, like people are out to get us."

He pulled her closer, until their faces were about an inch apart.

"I have Frank on the case," Thomas said. "He's the best there is. He'll find out who's responsible, and this will all be in the past before you know it."

"I wish we were still in Switzerland," Martha said. "We were so happy there, and Bruce was so happy there too. And we didn't have to worry about break-ins and the constant threat of crime in this damned city."

"I know how upset you are," Thomas said. "I'm upset as well, but this too shall pass. Besides, Switzerland is always a wonderful getaway, but Gotham's where our roots are, going back for centuries. Gotham is our home."

"Things are getting worse and worse," she protested. "It's a dying city."

"That's why this city needs us, more than ever," Thomas said. "We have the power to create change.

We're doing great things through Wayne Enterprises, and through the charities we support. But sometimes change takes time."

"You sound like you're running for office."

"Who knows? Maybe I *will* run for Mayor of Gotham someday." He smiled at her. "We can do whatever we want. We have choices, possibilities, options."

"I'm scared," Martha said. "What if this is just the beginning? What if things in Gotham never get better? What if they get worse and worse? Do you really want Bruce growing up in a world like this?"

"Brighter days are ahead," Thomas said.

"I wish I could believe you," Martha said. "I *want* to believe you, but I'm still afraid. I'm afraid something awful is about to happen."

Thomas saw a flash of Karen's claw, jutting through Scotty Wallace's neck.

About to?

"Everything's going to be just fine, I promise." Thomas kissed her again. "Let's just get some rest."

ELEVEN

Frank Collins paid top coin to sit ringside. When you had a bet on a fight, he said, why sweat the cost of a ticket? As the old gamblers' saying went, *You just build it into the price.* So he put an extra hundred on Williams to win in a fifth-round knockout, figuring those winnings would cover the ticket.

Simple, right?

He was sitting on top of the world. He'd done some checking around, and by this time tomorrow Tommy Wayne should have his painting back, or be damned close. Frank would be out of debt, and together they'd have a drink to celebrate.

Nothing cheap—just the good stuff.

Things looked great for a while. Williams came to fight, you could see it in his eyes. In the first and second rounds, Sanchez landed a jab here and there, but Williams had several powerful flurries. One right hook to the head dazed Sanchez, but not enough to knock him down. All of the judges ruled the first two rounds in Williams's favor, but Sanchez's legs looked strong enough to make it another few rounds.

During the break between the second and third, Sanchez's trainer got in his face and gave him hell. Whatever he said to his fighter had an effect, because when the bell sounded, Sanchez came out swinging. He connected with a hook, a jab, and then an uppercut that knocked out Williams's mouthpiece and sent him back hard against the ropes.

At that point, Frank feared that Williams was in danger of getting knocked down, as he didn't even have the energy to move around and protect himself. He might as well have had a hook poked onto his head, because he was as ineffective as a punching bag out there.

Then Sanchez took a gamble and tried to finish his opponent off with a powerful right. Williams saw it coming, though, and shifted his head to the left an instant before the punch would have landed. As Sanchez stumbled a little off balance, Williams seized the opportunity to attack.

A right, a left, another right all connected.

Suddenly Sanchez was looking dazed again. Then, after Williams connected with a powerful right to Sanchez's head, Sanchez's legs buckled and he went down.

"Get up!" Frank, on his feet, screamed, "Get up, you bastard! Get the hell up!" He needed Sanchez to get knocked out, but two rounds from now.

As the ref did the countdown, Frank continued to

scream, maybe louder than he'd ever screamed before. At "five" Sanchez got up on his elbows.

Okay, this could work out perfect, Frank thought. *Sanchez gets back up, lasts through the round, and the next round and then in the fifth,* boom, *Williams finishes him off.* If that happened, Frank would win over one hundred grand—enough to pay off most of his debts, and at least quiet down the bookies who'd been threatening to kill him lately.

Wait. What the hell…

Sanchez collapsed again, and the ref grabbed Williams's arm, lifting it and declaring him the winner. This wasn't happening—this *couldn't* be happening. Sanchez was getting up. Frank saw it, so vividly. How could he still be lying there? How could the fight be *over*?

Then it kicked in—what a moron he was. His original bet had been a third-round knockout, but when Tommy Wayne had been in his office, Frank had changed the bet to the fifth round. Did God have something against him, or what? Just when he stopped trusting his instincts, they turned out to be right.

Frank left the arena as dazed as Sanchez. He felt like he had gotten the crap beaten out of him, too, and in a way he had. Actually he was in worse shape, because at least Sanchez had money. Frank still couldn't believe he wasn't back in his seat, ready to celebrate a fifth-round knockout.

His cell chimed—his bookie's number glowing on the screen. Well, *one* of his bookies. He had been in debt up to his lungs with the four best bookies in Gotham, even *before* he'd made the big bet. Now the shit was really gonna hit the fan. Two of the bookies had threatened to kill him if he didn't make a payment soon, and the others had threatened to break limbs.

It wasn't a matter of *if* some goon would come after him, it was a matter of *when*, and which one. He couldn't even borrow money on the street, because he'd burned bridges with every loan shark in Gotham.

Frank had always gambled, but it hadn't become a serious problem until a few years ago, after his third marriage fell apart. Since then he gambled seven days a week—horses, poker, blackjack, sports, you name it. His clients—like Tommy Wayne—had always known that he loved the action, so they didn't think anything unusual was going on. Besides, Frank was great at compartmentalizing.

His clients liked this because it meant he was great at keeping secrets, but it also meant he was great at hiding his own problems. While working he was always locked in, focused, and great at what he did— solving the difficult cases. But when he was gambling, another side of his personality came out. He was wild, reckless, needed new and bigger rushes and, as with any addiction, he could never get enough.

Lost in his obsessive thoughts, Frank drifted from the bustling streets around the arena toward the seedy area by the docks. He passed street kids, prostitutes, drunks, bums, and drug dealers. He heard gunshots, sirens, crying, fighting, and screams for help. Nobody looked at him or even seemed to notice him—he felt like a ghost. Frank wished he was a ghost, dead already. That would be easier. He had no destination— he wasn't even thinking about where to head.

He just wanted to move, get away, disappear.

At some point he bought a bottle of whiskey with the last money he had. Well, that wasn't true—he still had the change in his pocket and maybe he could scrounge up ten bucks.

With the whiskey came darker thoughts. He didn't have enough for a last meal, so he might as well get it over with tonight. Yep, killing himself seemed like the best way out of this mess. It would be much quicker and less painful than if he let the bookie's goons whack him. There were a couple of bridges within walking distance—but given that he was afraid of heights *and* of drowning, that seemed like a rough way to check out.

Looking back on the cases he'd handled as a GCPD detective, and later as a PI, he searched for a better way to go. Preferably something that involved as little pain as possible. Getting drunker, he stumbled in the general direction of his apartment, actually becoming excited about his upcoming demise. Maybe death wasn't exactly a future, but it was something to look forward to. Not living anymore, not having to deal with all the crap, it felt very freeing.

Not that he actually *wanted* to die. If there were two doors—life and death—he'd choose life. He liked living, liked his work, and, okay, he liked gambling. That might be his main reason for wanting to live—to have a chance to win his money back—but that ship had sailed when Sanchez stayed down on the mat. He had no more options.

There were two doors and both doors led to death.

Heading through a defunct train yard, he glanced at the wall of an abandoned building, covered with colorful graffiti, and a different line of thinking began to take hold.

Maybe there is a way out…

A few years ago, the idea of ripping off Tommy Wayne never would have occurred to Frank. After all, he liked Tommy—they were pals, had history, and Wayne's trust in him meant something… but that was then.

A lot had happened. Something in Frank had changed. His moral center had eroded. He'd lost trust in everybody, even himself. He was out of control—couldn't get back on the straight and narrow, even if he wanted to.

New Frank only cared about one thing—money.

Tommy Wayne had money.

How many millions was that Picasso worth, he wondered? With that kind of money, Tommy could pay off all his debts, quit the PI business, leave Gotham, move to a little island off the coast of Mexico. He'd be set up for life.

Frank had done some digging. He'd found out that a guy named Roberto Colon had stolen the painting. Word on the street was that the cops had tried to bust

Colon at Angel's, but Colon took off. So now all Frank had to do was find Colon before the cops did, and get his hands on the Picasso. He'd find a ship heading to Europe—nothing fancy, something below the radar—then he'd sell it on the black market.

Lurching, Frank sat down hard on a stack of tires, rats scurrying away. He finished the last of the whiskey and tossed the bottle over his shoulder, hearing it splash. Then he pulled out his cell and made a call.

"Hey, C-cobblepot," Frank slurred. "It's Frankie… Frankie Collins."

"Who?" Cobblepot asked.

There was loud noise in the background—music, people yelling.

"Frankie Collins," Frank yelled.

"Oh, Mr. Collins," Cobblepot said. Frank heard shuffling, and the noise receded. The guy must've found a private place to continue the conversation. "How may I assist you?"

"I've got a proposition for you," Frank said, glancing around to make sure no one could hear him. There was no one there but the rats. "I'll pay you five grand if you can track down a guy named Roberto Colon, and do so before the cops find him."

"I can do *anything* faster than the police," Cobblepot said. "It's the advantage of being a one-man operation—no red tape."

"I like the way you think, Cobblepot," Frank said. "Maybe you can be a PI yourself someday." Silently, he added, *you creepy little freak.*

153

"Over my dead body."

"What?"

"I said that's very unlikely, Mr. Collins," Cobblepot replied. "I accept. I'll find Colon, and I'll do it expeditiously, but I will require ten thousand dollars for my services."

"All right, you got it," Frank said. "Ten grand. No problem. Way I see it, you're worth every penny." Not that Frank had ten grand to pay him, but by the time the kid figured it out, Frank and the painting would be out on the high seas. It wouldn't be the last time the kid got ripped off in Gotham, either. Someday he'd look back at this as a learning experience.

"Thank you, Mr. Collins, for being so generous," Cobblepot said. "So much so that I confess to being suspicious. Mr. Colon must possess something quite valuable, indeed, if you're willing to pay ten thousand dollars for it. May I ask, is it property, or is it information?"

Oh, shit. The last thing Frank needed was Cobblepot finding out about the Picasso. *Better nip this in the bud.*

"Just find out where Colon is," Frank said. "That's all that matters, and that's all I'm paying you to do. Call me as soon as you have results."

There was a moment of silence, and he wondered if the kid had cut him off.

"Of course, sir," Cobblepot said. "I understand. You're the customer, and as they say—the customer is always right."

Without another word Frank ended the call.

His instincts screamed at him that there was something off about Cobblepot, but the creep had delivered in the past, and he'd kept his mouth shut, too. There was no reason to think he'd act any different this time, and by the time he figured out he was being screwed, Frank would be long gone. Maybe Cobblepot and Tommy would have that drink, to commiserate. Frank started to chuckle at the thought, then tried to belch, but instead he threw up all over himself.

"Oh, hell," he said.

Then he passed out.

TWELVE

At the breakfast table, Bruce sat alone, reading the article in the Gotham *Herald* about the Williams-Sanchez fight. He was reading it for the third time when Alfred entered.

"Can I get you something else, Master Bruce?" the butler asked. "Some more scrambled eggs, perhaps?" Absorbed in his reading, Bruce didn't answer right away. He peered at the photograph of the referee holding up Williams's arm in victory.

"Why do you think Sanchez stayed down for the count last night, Alfred?"

"Well, I don't think he had much of a choice," Alfred said.

"But it was only the third round, and he's a fighter," Bruce said. "He shouldn't have quit so easily."

"There could've been a number of factors contributing to it, I suppose," Alfred said. "Faulty conditioning is one possibility. Boxers need to be focused on their craft, eliminate the distractions, and some are better equipped at doing so than others. Another possibility is that he's lost his edge. Having the desire to win is almost as important as having the ability to win. It's called having killer instinct."

"When you were boxing, did you have a killer instinct?"

"I was hardly *boxing*, mate," Alfred said. "When I was a teenager in the East End, we had illegal fights in basements and bars, and punters would bet on us. We didn't know what we were doing, really—didn't have any form to speak of."

"Then you must've relied entirely on your killer instinct," Bruce suggested, "the way animals do."

"Well, you're just full of compliments this morning, aren't you?"

But Bruce didn't notice his friend's sarcasm. He imagined that he was Alfred, boxing in the back of a smoky bar, pummeling the other fighter. What must have been akin to adrenaline caused him to shiver.

"It must've felt great," he said.

"What did?" Alfred asked, pouring himself a glass of orange juice.

"To strike somebody," Bruce said. "Cause them pain. To feel so strong."

Alfred stopped pouring, put the pitcher down, and leaned in close to Bruce, staring with a serious expression. Instinctively Bruce leaned against the back of the chair, and his eyes went wide.

"Never," Alfred said sharply, then he added, "It's *never* right to take joy from someone else's suffering,

Bruce, no matter what the situation. The desire to win is for yourself, and you alone. It's not right to feel good about pain, not at the expense of someone else."

Bruce absorbed what Alfred had said, but he couldn't resist the opportunity for a philosophical argument.

"Even if the person's evil?" he countered. "A thief, a murderer, or a rapist? What about the robbers who broke in here? Didn't you feel good when you shot one of them? Didn't that give you a sense of accomplishment?"

"Not at all," Alfred said. "I felt justified, but I didn't feel satisfied."

"Well, I'd feel satisfied if I killed a bad person," Bruce said.

"That's how vigilantes feel," Alfred said.

"Then I guess I'm a vigilante."

"Well, when you get older, hopefully you'll sort this out," Alfred said. "I don't think your parents would want you to grow up to become a man who hunts down criminals—whether for justice or for money. I'd hazard to guess they'd consider that a right nightmare."

Bruce frowned, and was silent. Then he glanced again at the newspaper.

"Last night, before Sanchez went down, he hit Williams with that big uppercut," Bruce said. "How do you do that?"

"Do you really want to know?" Alfred finished the glass of juice.

"Yes, Alfred. Please show me."

The butler stood there for a long moment, leaning

against the counter, looking at him. Studying him. Bruce couldn't tell what he was thinking, and began to feel uncomfortable. Abruptly Alfred straightened, and stepped toward him.

"All right then," he said. "Stand up."

Bruce stood and faced him.

"You start with your fists in front of you, in your ready, protective position." Alfred demonstrated and Bruce mimicked him. "Now what you want to do," Alfred continued, "is wind your arm back like a crank, see?" Bruce began the movement.

"Can I have a word with you, Alfred?"

Bruce's mother stepped into the room behind Alfred.

"I'm sorry, madam," Alfred said. "We were just—"

"Right now, please."

Alfred nodded, and Bruce's mother turned. Together they left the room. Bruce recognized the look on her face, and wouldn't have traded places with Alfred for anything. He just hoped he wasn't next.

He felt bad for getting Alfred in trouble, but maybe it would turn out for the best. Bruce wanted to learn to fight more than anything. Maybe Alfred could convince her that in Gotham, learning to fight was a necessity.

Pulling his arm back, he tried to duplicate what Alfred had shown him, tacking it onto his memory of the fight the night before. He knew his form was off, and he felt awkward and clumsy, but still he imagined he was Sanchez. In his mind's eye he connected, and then Williams followed with his furious assault.

Like Sanchez, Bruce let his knees buckle, and he

went down. But unlike the real Sanchez, as the ref counted, Bruce refused to quit. He got back to his feet.

The crowd cheered him on.

THIRTEEN

Alfred was ready to catch hell.

"What were you just doing in there?"

And, sure enough, there it was.

They were in the drawing room, out of earshot of Bruce.

"It's not how it appeared," Alfred said, though he knew it was *exactly* as it appeared. "You see—"

"I've made it very clear to you and to Thomas that I don't want Bruce learning how to fight," Martha said tersely. "This idea, that he needs to learn to defend himself, is ridiculous. People who know how to fight find themselves in fights. It's like four-wheel drive."

"I'm afraid I'm not following," Alfred said.

"Four-wheel drive for cars," Martha said. "The people who have it start looking for situations where they can use it. They start trying to drive through snow, and water, or up mountains, and they wind up killing themselves. Bruce has all the advantages in life. He should be focusing on his education, getting ready for college and medical school. Not squandering his efforts on useless and dangerous pastimes."

"Medical school?" Alfred said. "That's the first I've heard of this. Bruce fancies being a doctor, does he?"

"Well, it makes sense," Martha said. "He loves science, and got the best grade in his class in biology last semester." She paused, as if flustered, then continued. "My point is he can do whatever he wants in life, and that's what he should be focusing on, not some barbaric sport."

Alfred held his tongue. He loved boxing, saw it as beautiful and graceful—an art form—but knew saying so to Martha wouldn't accomplish anything. Well, except fueling her anger.

"I understand your wishes," he said instead. "Rest assured, I won't teach Bruce how to box, or instruct him in any self-defense skills, not without the explicit permission of you and Mr. Wayne."

She didn't reply at first, as if letting that sink in. Then…

"Can you make a promise to me, Alfred?"

Alfred had a feeling where this was headed.

"Yes," he said. "Of course."

"If something ever happens to me and Thomas, as you know, you'll become Bruce's guardian." Her voice quieted, as if she didn't want her words to be heard.

"Yes, I'm quite aware of that," Alfred said, wondering if she and Thomas had chatted about this.

"Can you promise me that, if a worst-case scenario happens, you'll still respect my wishes? That you'll make sure Bruce continues with his education. Keep him away from violence, no matter what you have to do to accomplish it? Promise me, please."

"Does Thomas know you're having this conversation with me?" Alfred asked.

"No," Martha said. "Why?"

"Just curious," Alfred said. Then he added, "Yes, I give you my word."

He didn't know how he'd do it—keep both promises, so very different from each other. But for the problem to arise, both of the elder Waynes would have to have died. Though the world in which they lived was violent indeed, such a likelihood seemed far from likely.

"Thank you, Alfred." She sounded firm again. "That makes me feel so much better, and I'm sorry if I sounded too harsh. I didn't mean to force you to defend yourself. It's just something that's... that's *very* important to me, something I think about a lot. I guess I'm just afraid lately. Afraid for Bruce, afraid of a lot of things."

"If there's anything I can do to help, Madam, please let me know."

Martha nodded, turned, and went to the hallway. She looked to her left and right, as if to make sure no one was eavesdropping, and then returned to the drawing room and shut the door.

Almost whispering, she asked, "Has Thomas confided in you, told you anything about what he's been up to lately?"

"No," Alfred said. "He hasn't."

She peered at him, as if wrestling with a thought.

"I know you wouldn't tell me even if you did know," Martha said, "but for weeks, even months now, his behavior has been odd, and lately it's getting even more so."

"What sort of behavior do you mean?"

"He goes into his office and locks the door for hours on end," Martha said. "He won't let anyone in there, and won't tell me what he's doing. He says he's 'working,' but that's so ambiguous. What does 'working' mean? What is he working on, and why does he have to be so mysterious about it?"

"That's hardly new, Madam," Alfred said. "He's been doing it for years."

"But he does it more frequently now, it seems," Martha insisted, "and he's more mysterious about it. He takes these strange day trips upstate, to clear his head, he says. Yet he never tells us where exactly he goes, what exactly he does.

"I want to respect his privacy, give him his space," she added. "I mean, I understand his work is very stressful, especially lately, and sometimes he needs some alone time. I'm the same way—but I go to spas, for long walks, and I don't feel like I'm being evasive or elusive. That's my problem right there. He's acting evasive and elusive, and it has me concerned, that's all. I hate secrets."

Alfred didn't quite know how to respond.

"I understand," he said after a moment, "but I'm sure it's exactly how it seems—that he just likes to get away for a bit." Now he just had to convince himself that it was true.

"So he hasn't told you where he goes?"

"No, I'm afraid he hasn't, madam."

"I believe you," Martha said, "even though I'm still not sure you'd tell me if you did know. You always respect Thomas's privacy, and that's the right thing to do—as our butler and as his friend. But I consider you my friend, as well. I mean, don't you feel the same way?"

Alfred didn't like where this was heading.

"I admire you, Thomas, and Bruce, all very much," he replied.

"So as *my* friend, the right thing to do would be to tell me what you know," Martha said. "Don't you think?"

"It's as I told you," Alfred said. "I don't know anything at all."

"So Thomas hasn't mentioned a woman to you?"

"Never," Alfred said, "and, to be quite honest, I don't think he ever would have an affair. He's not the type, and he adores you."

"Is there really an affair type, though?" Martha asked.

"Well, yes, I think there is actually. I mean, some blokes I knew in London, used to go 'round the local, chatting up the birds, with their wedding bands in their shirt pockets, hoping the tan lines went unnoticed."

"Those are the obvious cheaters," Martha said. "Anyone can spot *them*. But what about the more subtle ones? The ones you never suspect? I'm talking about the secret-keepers. The ones who on the surface seem like the family men, the providers. Their friends say, 'Bob? Bob would never cheat. He's a good guy.' What about the Bobs? What about the good guys?"

"I can't speak for what secrets Thomas may or may not be keeping," Alfred said. "And I can't say whether he's one of the Bobs you're referring to either, but I would be shocked if there were another woman. It just doesn't feel right, in my gut."

"Believe me," Martha said, "I don't want to be the woman who gets paranoid, jumps to conclusions, thinks her husband is fooling around behind her back. But his behavior is odd, he's been elusive, so what am I supposed to think?"

Alfred recalled the blood on Thomas's neck. He'd claimed it was from shaving, though there didn't seem to be any cut on his face whatsoever. Just the blood. Odd, indeed.

"Thomas is a complicated man," Alfred said. "Always has been, always will be. But there is one thing I'm absolutely certain of—he would never do anything to hurt you or Bruce, or to put you in harm's way."

"Why harm's way?"

Oh, crikey, Alfred wished he could take that one back.

"It's just a figure of speech, Madam. I meant he wouldn't want to get you into a dangerous situation."

Martha looked as Alfred as if she were trying to see through him.

"What sort of dangerous situation?"

Worse and worse…

"Why do I feel as though I'm climbing out of a hole?" Alfred said. "I just meant a hypothetical situation. I know security is a major concern to Mr. Wayne. That's why the break-in rattled him, and if I'm guessing, I think it's related to why he was home late yesterday. He's been concerned over how the security system was breached, so he's trying to sort things out at his company."

Silence.

"I think you know something," she said. "Something you're not telling me."

"You're a clairvoyant now, are you?" he said, trying to lighten the mood.

"No, but I know you well, Alfred. Sometimes I feel like I know you better than I know Thomas himself. If he did tell you something, and told you not to tell me—if it's a man's code or something, I promise I'd never put you in an awkward position."

"I really have nothing more I can share with you on this matter, Madam," he replied, trying to sound reassuring. "If there was, I would speak up—for you, for Thomas, and for Master Bruce."

"I'm sorry, Alfred. I know you're just doing your job, and I didn't mean to make you uncomfortable. Thank God you were here the other night, or we could've all been killed."

"Don't be silly," Alfred said, "I was just doing my duty."

"No, you went well beyond your duty. Any other

butler who heard gunshots would have hidden in his room until the danger was over. But not you, Alfred. You ran *toward* the danger—that's what heroes do. And that's precisely why there's no need for Bruce to learn how to fight. As long as he has you to protect him, he'll be safe."

Alfred was well into his fifties and had lived a hard life—recovering from countless injuries, grieving dead lovers and fallen mates. He'd be lucky if he lived another twenty years himself.

He couldn't protect Bruce forever.

"I don't think I'm a permanent insurance policy," he said, "but I appreciate the sentiment."

Martha reached out and—to his surprise—hugged him, clinging to him.

"Thank you so much, Alfred," she said, her voice low. "It feels good to know I can count on you."

The hug felt a bit *too* good. Awkward. Alfred wriggled free.

"Well then, right," he said, "I should be heading off. I think I left some water boiling on the stove."

She nodded, and he rushed away down the hall to the kitchen.

FOURTEEN

Alas, no water was boiling, though there was some cleaning up to do. Bruce, always a thoughtful boy, had cleaned the table and placed his dirty dishes in the dishwasher. Alfred still had to scrub the pan and straighten up the countertop.

As he did, his mind was awhirl.

While Alfred was technically just the Waynes' butler, he had taken on other, well, duties over the years, including driving and cooking. When he'd started working for the Waynes, when Bruce was a young lad, the Waynes had employed a chef called Howard. When Howard retired, Alfred volunteered to step in and take over the culinary duties. He'd been a cook for a time with the royal army, and his fellow soldiers loved eating at "Al's Kitchen," which had caught on as a nickname for the mess hall.

As he enjoyed cooking, he didn't consider it work at all. Over the years, Alfred had perfected his specialties, which included Italian, Spanish, French, and yes, British cuisine. Anyone who thought that "British cuisine" was an oxymoron hadn't had Alfred Pennyworth prepare them a meal.

Yet there was far more on his mind than food.

When the kitchen was all clean, Alfred headed upstairs to his room, figuring he'd read for a bit perhaps, maybe try to catch a football match. West Ham United, the team he'd grown up supporting, was playing Liverpool. They'd probably get their arses handed to them, as the Americans liked to say, but it was always nice to keep up with what was happening across the pond.

He was relieved he'd made it to his room without running into Martha again. He had never gotten a vibe before that she fancied him in any way, so the tight hug and her strange tone had caught him off guard. He didn't think she actually meant anything by it— she was just upset, "in a bad place." Alfred had no romantic interest in her, of course, but he had to make sure things didn't escalate. He hoped that she and Thomas sorted things out straight away.

The truth, of course, was that he *did* suspect that Thomas was up to something. The blood on Thomas's neck had been odd, to say the least. If he were to put his detective's hat on—which he had no intention of doing—he would probably conclude that the blood had come from someone else. Had Mr. Wayne been in a tussle at work? Unlikely.

Which meant he had lied about his whereabouts yesterday. As for Martha's suspicions that he was off gallivanting with another lady—this seemed doubtful, no matter what the appearances. Thomas just wasn't the cheating sort. Yet Martha's instincts were correct—something was amiss.

It wasn't Alfred's place to speculate, but if he *were* speculating, he might guess that it had to do with the break-in. The intruders seemed to be searching for something other than the Picasso, or they wouldn't have chopped up the walls the way they had.

Perhaps it *did* have something to do with Wayne Enterprises. At times Alfred's duties took him to Thomas's office. In recent months, he had overheard Thomas having a number of heated discussions, sometimes with Lucius Fox, or with other personnel. More often than not it seemed to relate to the board of directors. There seemed to be a concern that the board might try to oust Thomas from his position of CEO.

Despite any concerns he might have, Alfred's job title was "butler," not detective, and his duties didn't include solving mysteries, especially mysteries involving the behavior of his employer. If Thomas requested his help in any matter, he would provide it, without question, and he'd go to any means necessary to protect the entire Wayne family. Thomas had hired him for a reason, because he had a unique set of skills that perhaps no other butler in the world possessed. That said, for the time being he planned to mind his own business and remain neutral, like Switzerland itself.

* * *

Lo and behold, miracle of all miracles, West Ham was beating Liverpool—four to nil and the match was well into the second half. Hearing the chants from the punters at the Stadium at Queen Elizabeth Olympic Park, Alfred felt a bit homesick. He knew the feeling would pass, though. While there were many things he missed about London—in particular drinking at the local with his mates, watching football, snooker, and rugby—he never regretted his decision to leave the United Kingdom and come to work for the Waynes.

In fact, the decision may have saved his life.

At the time he accepted the position, Alfred had possessed zero experience as a butler, nor had he ever contemplated such a career. He'd had a long, celebrated time in the Royal Marines, had secured a Military Cross, and saved an entire regiment on a mission in Kazakhstan. After a couple of years at Scotland Yard, he'd worked for a stretch at MI3 where, yes, he'd received a license to kill. He worked as an operative on numerous classified missions, where he'd inevitably gained many enemies.

On two occasions assassins had targeted him, and each time he had narrowly escaped. In an attempt to have a calmer life, he took a position working for a private army in the Middle East, which protected interests of multinational corporations. During an assignment in Libya, he met Thomas Wayne, one of the army's financiers. Although they came from very different backgrounds, Alfred and Thomas quickly became friends. Over the next few years, they stayed in touch.

Alfred was thrilled when he learned that Thomas and Martha had brought a baby boy into the world.

A couple of years later, during a Wayne family vacation to England, Alfred drove to the countryside and met Martha and Bruce for the first time. Although Bruce was nigh two years old, he already had a presence, an aura about him that Alfred found remarkable. Bruce seemed to get on with Alfred as well—smiling and wanting to play with him all the time. Martha and Thomas thought it was unusual, because Bruce usually acted shy and distrusting around strangers.

Thomas knew Alfred had enemies who were continuing to target him. Later, over pints at the local pub, he offered Alfred the opportunity to get away from it all and come to Gotham to work as his "butler." While Alfred had no suitable experience, Thomas said that the job "wasn't rocket science," and he fancied the idea of having Bruce growing up influenced by Alfred's skill set.

The offer intrigued Alfred, but he politely declined. It seemed like too dramatic a change of life for him. In addition, he had a love affair going for many years with a former French espionage agent, a blonde sprightly bird named Gabrielle Brument. Gabrielle had relatives in Paris, and Alfred knew she wouldn't want to move across to America.

Then, a few weeks later, Alfred and Gabrielle were dining at a modest Thai restaurant in Finsbury Park when two men entered. As always, Alfred had taken a seat facing the door. With his inherent ability to assess danger, he knew the men hadn't come to dine. He reached for his gun, but the men had already opened fire. He shot and killed both of them, but a bullet from one of their weapons struck Gabrielle in the head, killing her instantly.

Alfred emerged physically unscathed, but emotionally devastated. Gabrielle had been the love of his life, and he'd lost her. Worse, her death had been his responsibility, as his past had come back to bite him on the arse.

He got a taste of revenge, hunting down and killing the Russian man who had ordered the hit—the brother of a man whom Alfred had taken out several years earlier. Even so, he knew the cycle of violence wouldn't end. His enemies would target him again, and if he didn't wind up dead, another innocent person could get caught in the crossfire.

Besides, living in England had become nigh unbearable. It seemed as if every park, every street corner, every tube station sparked a memory of Gabrielle. So Alfred phoned Thomas and asked him if the butler position was still available.

"When can you start?" Thomas asked.

Thus Alfred became ensconced in Gotham, learning his way about town as well as a native, and aside from the occasional bout of homesickness related to his old mates and football, he *felt* like a native most of the time. He enjoyed his work, particularly helping to raise Bruce, who had already turned into such an extraordinary young man. Nevertheless, he thought about Gabrielle every day. He carried a photo of her in his wallet, which used to cause pangs of sorrow whenever he looked at, but now brought pure joy. He had been in love once, he had experienced what it felt like. Some people died young, or never met their soul mate.

The way he looked at it, he was one of the lucky ones.

Alfred turned off the television, confident that even West Ham couldn't lose with a four-goal advantage.

Then he glanced out the window and saw Thomas, wearing a determined expression, leaving through a back entrance of Wayne Manor, heading toward the gardens. He checked back over his shoulder, as if to make sure no one was watching him. Alfred shifted out of view behind the curtains, but could still see Thomas heading into the maze of English-style shrubbery.

Presuming he was out of view, Thomas took out his mobile and made a call. His expression remained serious, as if he were discussing some grave matter. Alfred recalled the blood on Thomas's neck, the odd conversation regarding Bruce's guardianship, and how Thomas had snapped at him during the repair work in his study. If Alfred had his detective's hat on, he would have considered these clues.

Instead he just pulled the curtains together, and went about his day.

FIFTEEN

At first, Bruno Walsh, the thug Harvey and Amanda had picked up from Roberto Colon's room at the SRO, wouldn't talk at all. Harvey didn't know if it was because Walsh didn't know anything, or he just wasn't spilling.

Well, one way to find out.

With Amanda watching through the one-way glass, Harvey went to the old stand-by—his favorite pair of brass knuckles. When Walsh, with his jaw broken and a few of his teeth on the floor, still claimed that he and his dead friend were hired guns, and he had no idea where Colon went or anything about the stolen Picasso, Harvey finally believed him.

He left the interrogation room and instructed a uniformed cop to clean up the mess and book Walsh for attempted manslaughter.

"You got it, Harv," the cop said.

Amanda approached Harvey.

"Did you have to work him over so hard?" she asked.

"Look who's talking," Harvey said, "my ninja sidekick."

"Touché," Amanda said.

At seven, it was time to call it a day. The captain had assigned a couple of other detectives to pursue Colon and, assuming there wasn't a middle-of-the-night bust, Harvey and Amanda would resume the hunt *manana*.

Harvey went to his apartment, did two of the three S's—no need for a bearded man to shave—then hit Old City, his favorite watering hole just around the corner from his apartment building. Old City was a classic art deco Gotham bar, with high tiled ceilings and classy booths to sit in, not these mosh pit style bars they were building nowadays. Once upon a time, when he was at the police academy, he used to moonlight, bartending at Old City.

Jesus H on a popsicle stick, that was a long time ago.

Sidling up to his regular seat at the end of the bar, Harvey had Smitty, his favorite bartender, pour him a pint of bitter and a double of Jameson, straight up. He downed the Jameson like a man, taking it straight down his throat, not even moving a muscle to swallow it, and then chased it with the bitter. Finally, after a long-ass day, he'd gotten his hair of the dog.

The infusion of alcohol livened him up and numbed the pain in his ribs from the beating he'd taken, and the pain in his wrists from the beating he'd doled out. On the bar's TV, he watched the Williams-Sanchez fight. He was pulling for Sanchez only because Williams was cocky as hell, and Harvey hated cockiness. If you could walk the walk, you didn't have to talk the talk, and he had more respect for guys like Sanchez who buckled up, shut their traps, and got the job done.

Other than that, he really didn't give a damn.

Sanchez went down in the third. "Goes to show ya," Harvey said to Smitty, "boxing's like life—the jerkoffs always seem to come out on top."

He took it easy, drinking wise—only had a couple more brewskies—then hit the road. He had energy still, didn't feel like hitting the hay… well, not alone anyway. So he got on the horn—*Well, if you consider a cell phone a horn*—and gave a shout to Lacey White, the TV reporter he'd run into at Wayne Manor the other night.

"Lace, guess who?"

"I'd recognize that voice anywhere," Lacey said. "How are you, Mr. Nygma?"

Harvey's brain was slow to react. "Wait, who?"

"Kidding," Lacey said. "I'd recognize your voice anywhere, Harvey."

"Oh. Ha, ha," Harvey said, remembering that Lacey had met Nygma at the station a couple of times. She really knew how to hurt a guy.

"So, let me guess," Lacey said, "it's around ten on a Saturday night, and you decide to give me a call. That could only mean one thing—"

"You know me too well," Harvey said. "So what do you say, baby? Old time's sake?"

"I'd love to, Harv, but actually I have someone here right now."

"Oh, I didn't mean to interrupt." Harvey was

disappointed as hell, but tried not to let it show. "I hope he's a good guy."

"*She's* great," Lacey said, "but I only met her about ten minutes ago, when she came to fix my sink. There's something so sexy about female plumbers."

"You can fool me once any day," Harvey said, "but never twice, my darling."

"No, I'm serious," Lacey whispered. "She's in the bathroom right now, and I don't want her to hear me."

Wait, was she for real? Since when did Lacey White swing from the other side of the plate?

"Really?" Harvey asked.

"Well, I guess you were wrong—I *can* fool you twice." She laughed. "Just goes to show you that man will always believe what he wants to believe."

"Yeah, what I believe right now," Harvey said, "is that you want me in your bed."

"Give the man a prize," Lacey said. "How fast can you get here?"

"As fast as humanly possible," Harvey said, with his hand up, already hailing a cab. One pulled over to the curb and Harvey climbed in. He showed the cabbie his badge, then told him Lacey's address and said, "Get there as fast as you can." He put it back in his pocket. "Forget the lights."

Seven minutes later he was dashing into Lacey's building. She did well in the reporting biz. It was a classy high-rise—a guy wearing white gloves held open the door for him. Then Harvey approached the concierge at the desk.

"Harvey Bullock to see Lacey White."

Did the concierge smirk a little before he announced him?

Harvey heard Lacey's muffled voice. "Send him right up." The concierge gestured, and gave Harvey a knowing glance.

"Have fun tonight."

Okay, so Harvey wasn't exactly Lacey's only dance partner, but that didn't matter to him. He liked a woman who didn't need an instruction manual.

On the nineteenth floor, he buzzed her apartment, already feeling ravenous. Then the door opened and she lassoed him, tight as hell, so he couldn't move his arms.

Freakin' A—

She was dressed in a latex cowgirl getup that covered maybe five percent of her curvy body. With her three-inch heels, she towered over him.

"Yee-ha," he said.

She lassoed his chest, then yanked on the rope so hard it probably stopped circulation. Harvey groaned, but he loved it.

"You won't speak until I tell you to speak," she said. "Do you understand me, Detective?"

"Yes, Lace—" Harvey said. "Oops, sorry."

"What did I just tell you?" she said.

He braced himself.

Man, he loved disobeying.

* * *

"Is it true you once dated Fish Mooney?"

They were lying in bed, and Harvey jumped a little.

"You still like to ask questions even when the camera's not running, don't ya?" Harvey asked. He couldn't decide whether or not to be annoyed.

"And you like to avoid my questions," she countered. "I'm not going to have to teach you another lesson, am I?"

As appealing as it sounded, Harvey wasn't ready for that. He still hadn't recovered from the last education.

"Dated isn't really the way to describe it," Harvey said. "Let's just say I didn't take her to a movie and an ice cream shop."

"I've interviewed her a couple of times." Lacey was twirling Harvey's chest hair with her index finger. "She's, well, pretty far out there. What did you see in her?"

"She knows how to have a good time," Harvey said, "and knows what she wants. Those are two of my favorite qualities in a lady. Case in point." But she didn't take the bait.

"You didn't mind that she's a criminal?"

"I don't do background checks before I start something new," Harvey said. "Takes all the fun out of it."

Finally she let it drop, and rolled over to plant a passionate kiss. That gave Harvey a new surge of energy, and he decided it was okay to resume his curriculum.

At some point, they fell asleep. Then something woke Harvey up—the sun stinging his eyes.

His cell was ringing.

"Yeah," he said, without checking the display.

"Harvey, there you are." It was Captain Essen. "You weren't answering your home phone."

"That's cause I'm not home," he said, wincing when he tried to move his right arm.

"You have to come in right away," she said.

"Is it Colon?"

"Who?" Essen asked.

"Roberto Colon, one of the art thieves we're looking for."

Lacey stirred, muttering, "Did I give you permission to make that call?"

"Forget the art robbery, this is way bigger. Two cops were killed last night. Set on fire in their squad car."

Harvey sat up, ignoring all his pains.

"Cops?" he asked. "Who?"

"Warren and Lewis," Essen said.

"Goddamnit." Harvey didn't know Lewis, a rookie, too well, but he and Warren broke in together. "I'll be there A-S-A-P." He ended the call and started getting dressed, pulling on his pants.

"Where you going?" Lacey asked, fully awake now.

"Somebody set a couple of cops on fire."

"Oh, crap," she said. Then she added, "I'll probably get called in, too."

"Maybe I'll see you down there."

"What if I don't?"

"Then I guess I'll see you around somewhere." Harvey put his shirt on, and grabbed his socks and shoes.

"That how you want this to play out?" Lacey said, an edge appearing in her voice. "Just see if you happen to run into me again? So you can call me, drunk from a bar, and see if I want to have a good time?"

Harvey thought about it for a beat, pulling on both socks.

"Yeah, pretty much."

"That's what I love about you, Harvey," she said, the edge gone again. "Your honesty."

"It's nice to know I have *one* endearing quality."

Both shoes were on.

"I wish I was more like you," Lacey said.

"No, you don't," Harvey said.

"You're right, I don't."

"Till we meet again."

Harvey left the apartment.

SIXTEEN

"Are you okay?"

Thomas went out to the gardens to call Karen. He knew calling her from home was a bad idea, especially with Martha getting suspicious, but he needed to make sure she was okay.

"Yes, everything's just *awesome*," she said.

Ignoring the sarcasm, Thomas said, "Seriously. Has anyone else showed up?"

"Yes, five more guys with guns, but don't worry I killed all of them."

"I'll take that as a no," Thomas said. He glanced back at Wayne Manor. Did he see movement upstairs, in Alfred's room? It looked like the curtains had jostled, but it might have been the wind.

"It will be fine, I promise," Thomas said. "I'll come back in a few days, or as soon as I can, to check on you. You should have plenty of food, and I took measurements on your broken window. I'll get that all fixed."

"There's no rush," she said. "Come whenever you feel like it."

She sounded oddly calm, and Thomas couldn't tell whether she was really doing okay, or if depression had set in. He often worried that she might sink into a deep depression, and attempt suicide. She had already suffered so much, she didn't deserve to any more.

He wasn't sure he could handle it.

The world was random, and there was no such thing as justice, as far as he could tell. If there was justice, Hugo Strange would be the one to get depressed and commit suicide. That would solve a lot of problems.

"Hang in there," Thomas said. "Brighter days are ahead." After he ended the call, though, he realized that had probably been the worst possible thing he could say to a depressed person, especially when he didn't believe it himself.

He glanced back at Wayne Manor—no sign of Alfred or anyone else watching—and then he called Frank.

"How are things looking?" Thomas asked.

"Great," Frank said, "coming along." His voice sounded deeper than usual, and a little hoarse.

"Did I wake you?" Thomas asked.

"No, no, I've been up for a while," Frank said. "So, um, yeah, I think I have a couple of leads on the painting."

"Any link to you-know-who?" Thomas had gotten in the habit of not mentioning Strange's name over the phone, as wiretapping was always a possibility. It was probably a futile gesture, but he'd take reassurance anywhere he could get it.

"What?" Frank seemed lost for a beat, then he said, "Oh, oh him—no, nothing yet." He coughed, or maybe cleared his throat. "But I have ears on the ground, and I'm sure I'll call you later with an update." He coughed, definitely coughed, again.

"Very good," Thomas said, still thinking that something about Frank seemed odd today. Maybe he was just imagining it.

"Oh, did you check in with Karen?" Frank asked.

"Yes," Thomas said. "And I think you may have been right in your suspicions."

"Why? She told you something? Has he been in touch with her?"

In person, Thomas would've told Frank about the person he'd killed, Scotty Wallace, and the fear that Hugo had sent him, but he didn't want to get into the gory details, or any of the details really, over the phone.

"Let's just say I'm more concerned than I was yesterday," Thomas said.

"Gotcha," Frank said. "Hey, I need to get going, but I'll be in touch with you later, okay?"

"Okay," Thomas said, and he ended the call.

Walking back toward the house, he felt again that Frank definitely hadn't sounded like himself. He sounded distracted, as if there was something he wasn't saying. Thomas had never doubted his trust in Frank before, but he began to wonder if Karen had been right. Had it been a mistake to tell Frank about Pinewood Farms?

"Stop it," he said out loud to himself. Frank was an

old friend, and a pro.

Entering through the back door, Thomas saw Bruce coming downstairs the way kids do—almost skipping. He stopped at the bottom stair.

"Hey, good morning," Thomas said.

"Good morning," his son said. "Mom's looking for you."

"Where is she?"

"I'm right here." Thomas jumped a little and looked behind him. Martha was there.

"You look very pretty today," he said.

While she did look pretty, she didn't look any prettier than usual. Yet after all the tension, Thomas wanted to get the new day off to a good start.

"Thank you," Martha said, "that's sweet." Then she said to Bruce, "Have you finished all of your homework?"

"Yes, Mom. I finished my *Beowulf* paper as well."

"In that case," she said, "I think we should all do something as a family today. How about a movie?"

"The circus is in town," Bruce said. "I haven't seen the circus since I was seven years old. Can we go?"

"That sounds like a great idea," Martha said. "What do you think, Thomas?"

Thomas agreed the family time would be nice, but after being followed to Karen's, he was concerned about taking his family out in public without some sort of protection, at least until he had a better sense of what was going on.

"Sounds fun," Thomas said, "but how about we

have Alfred come along as well?"

"Great idea," Martha said. "Should I ask him?"

"I'll ask him," Bruce said. "I'm so excited." He dashed upstairs, taking the stairs two steps at a time. About a minute later, he shouted from the top of the landing, "Alfred said yes. Yes!"

Thomas felt much better going around town with Alfred, his secret weapon, in tow.

A short time later, Alfred drove them in the Bentley to the old fairgrounds on the outskirts of Gotham.

The massive tent where the main performances took place towered over smaller tents and trailers where the performers lived while the circus was in town. They pulled up by the main entrance to the grounds, a valet parked the car, and then the Waynes and Alfred headed into the central area. Thousands of Gothamites had come out on the sunny Sunday afternoon to enjoy the festivities. Some recognized the Waynes and waved or said hi to them.

"This is wonderful," Martha said. "What a great idea to come here today."

"Look," Bruce said, "it says he's the strongest in the world."

Sure enough, in front of a tent hung a sign,

STRONGEST MAN IN THE WORLD

A man, maybe seven feet tall, with massive muscles,

lifted a barbell stacked with weights over his head.

"You wouldn't want to meet him in a dark alley," Alfred said.

But Bruce had already moved on, and was staring at another sign.

THE SIAMESE SINGERS

Two young women, apparently conjoined at their hips, were singing some song in the baroque style, *a cappella*. They had surprisingly good voices, and a crowd had formed around them to listen while a grown man with a head no bigger than a cantaloupe went around and collected money in his tiny baseball cap. The spectacle reminded Thomas of the comment Karen had made about winding up in a freak show.

The morose thought must have showed in Thomas's expression.

"Are you okay?" Martha asked.

"Yes, I'm fine," Thomas insisted. Abruptly someone knocked into him, hard, and Thomas stumbled and almost fell backward, but Alfred grabbed hold of him.

"Mate, are you alright?" Alfred asked.

"Fine," Thomas said. Then he looked over at the young man—really a teenager—who had knocked into him. The boy had an odd, sinister smile.

"Watch it, jerkoff," the boy said to him.

"You should watch where you're going," Martha said.

"Screw you."

"Hey, that language isn't necessary," Martha said.

"She's right, mate," Alfred said. "And an apology is in order, as well."

The boy didn't say anything, just kept smiling.

"Being rude isn't funny," Bruce said to him.

"Says who?" the boy said. "Just because you're Bruce Wayne, you think the whole world has to be polite to you?" Despite his ominous words, his grin seemed to grow even larger. Then an older woman, wearing a long flowing shawl with bright colors and shiny bangles, came over to the boy and slapped him hard on the back of his head.

"Come along, Jerome," the old woman said, then she grabbed him by the hand and pulled him away into a trailer.

The trailer had a sign:

SNAKE CHARMER

"She may do well with snakes," Alfred commented, "but her way with people leaves something to be desired."

"That boy is creepy," Bruce said.

"Well, we are at a circus," Alfred said. "Attracts all sorts, I suppose."

"It's all right," Thomas said, brushing himself off. "Let's enjoy our day."

While the circus was one of the hottest tickets in Gotham, as benefactors who helped to sponsor the event, the Waynes had access to the best seats in the house. At the circus, this meant front row. One act after another paraded past, often within feet of them, including the trapeze artists, acrobats, a tap-dancing elephant, a man swallowing fire, and of course, clowns.

Bruce soaked it all in, alternating between awe and glee. When Thomas was younger, he cherished the days when his parents—now both dead—had taken him to events like shows and circuses, and on family trips. Similarly, Thomas knew that someday Bruce would look back at days like these, and savor the memories. While he felt fortunate that he'd grown up with a privileged lifestyle, and was happy that he'd provided the same for Bruce, he also knew that, in the end, memories were far more valuable than money.

He had brought his camera and, afterward, he took photos of Bruce with the circus performers. Then, outside of the tents, he had Alfred take a family photo of the three of them with their arms around one another. It would make a great family portrait, and might work as this year's Christmas card, as well.

SEVENTEEN

After the circus, they went out to dinner at one of their favorite French restaurants. Thomas and Bruce had the mussels, while Alfred and Martha both tried the duck. The adults shared a twelve-year-old bottle of delicate Bordeaux that had been well paired by the sommelier.

The drive back to Wayne Manor was uneventful, and Bruce struggled not to fall asleep in the back seat— and failed. When they finally arrived at Wayne Manor, he woke, and instantly broke out in a smile.

"This was one of the best days of my life."

That comment made Thomas's day.

"I'm glad you enjoyed it, Bruce," he said.

"We had a great time, too," Martha added.

Still grinning, Bruce headed up to his room, and was followed shortly thereafter by Alfred. Martha looped her arm in her husband's, and gave a small yawn.

"I'm exhausted," she said to Thomas, "and tomorrow's a busy day. Coming to bed soon?"

"In a bit," Thomas replied. "I have some work to take care of."

"On a Sunday night?" Martha asked. Her contented look was replaced by a small frown.

"I have a big week ahead of me," Thomas said, "and a lot of meetings to prepare for. Unfortunately, Monday morning comes far too quickly."

"I understand," she said, though she sounded as if she didn't quite buy his explanation. Nevertheless, she kissed him—a quick peck on the lips—and then headed upstairs.

The undercurrent of his talk with Martha still lingered, despite the fun day they'd had, and she still harbored her suspicions. Martha was nobody's fool. Perhaps she suspected that when he went into his office alone, late at night, it was to have secret conversations with a lover. That would be a natural assumption.

Ironically, the truth was exactly the opposite. He had never cheated on Martha, and had no interest in seeking any sort of relationship outside of his marriage. He went into his office for solitude, to escape from the world. He was a public figure in Gotham, always under scrutiny for something, and sometimes he needed his alone time, to isolate himself, in order to function. Only then could he properly provide for his family.

He would have reassured Martha, but without disclosing details he simply couldn't share, there was little he could say that would ring true. He might be able to placate her later, but what would happen the next time he disappeared upstate for an afternoon, to see Karen? The suspicion would return, and the only remedy would be to tell her the truth.

Yet he couldn't tell her the truth, without also telling her about Pinewood Farms. If Strange suspected that Martha knew anything, he'd probably try to eliminate her, as well. A methodical man, Hugo would seek to tie off all loose ends. No, the way Thomas looked at it, if the mistakes of his past led to his demise, then so be it—but he intended to do everything in his power not to drag Martha down with him, even if it meant allowing her fears to perpetuate.

He shut the door to the study and locked it. Instantly he felt more relaxed. To keep the mood going, he put on some soft classical music—a Tchaikovsky violin concerto—and smoked a good Cuban cigar. This was how he wound down—his form of yoga and meditation. With every exhale of cigar smoke, he felt less stressed and more focused.

Confidence returned, the feeling that somehow all his problems would work themselves out. Strange would back off, or wind up in jail for orchestrating an armed robbery, Karen could lead a normal—or at least semi-normal—life. The board members who had been trying to oust him from his position as president and CEO would back down. The corruption that had infested Gotham in every dark shadow finally would taper off.

Bruce would grow up in a safer, more peaceful city. His mood bolstered, Thomas called Frank, but got his voicemail. Although Frank had told Thomas he'd called to check in, Thomas wasn't concerned. Frank was one of the good guys. He worked in mysterious ways, at his own pace, but always got the job done in the end.

Any doubts Thomas had harbored went up in smoke.

Thomas finished most of the cigar, then smothered the stub out in the ashtray on his desk. He left the music on—the way he always did, to make it seem to everyone else in the house that he was still working in the study—and then he flicked a switch. The fireplace parted, and the entrance to the basement appeared. He entered the stairwell, shutting the fireplace entrance behind him. Downstairs, he tapped B-R-U-C-E into the control panel on the steel door and, *voila*, he was in his secret office.

He looked around warily. Nothing seemed out of the ordinary—not that he expected anything to be. Unless someone hacked the password—he'd have to change it to something more complicated when he had a chance— the only way in would be to blow up the door.

Before that, someone would have to find out about the office's very existence, and the only people who had access to any of this information were several trusted security people at Wayne Security, the subsidiary of Wayne Enterprises, who had designed and helped install the security features, including the steel door. Was it possible that someone at Wayne Security could have leaked this information, perhaps to Hugo Strange?

As of a couple of days ago, Thomas had felt there was little chance of this happening, but the break-in proved that he was more vulnerable than he'd thought he was. People were capable of crossing any line for a good payday. If a corrupt board member at Wayne Enterprises, or some other rogue employee, wanted to access information that hurt Thomas, they could do so, and there was little Thomas could do to prevent it.

"Every king is vulnerable to a coop." Thomas had said that to Lucius Fox, one of the few people he trusted implicitly. Someone didn't have to turn rogue on their own—there could be a web of deceit. For example, one of the workers who had installed the steel door in the basement could have told a friend about it, and that friend could have told another friend. Was this likely? Who knows? It was impossible to defend against everything.

As Thomas logged onto his computer desktop, he reminded himself that the worst-case scenario hadn't yet occurred. If the intruders knew about the exact location of the office, they would have found a way in. While someone might have leaked the codes to the main security system at Wayne Manor, now new codes had been set up, and tighter security, so Thomas's secrets were as safe as they could possibly be.

One intruder was dead, and with any luck the other two would be captured soon. If there were some larger conspiracy or plan in the works, he would find out about it soon enough.

A squeaking bat darted past overhead while

Thomas scrolled though the files on Pinewood Farms. All of the files, listing patients in the program, as well as observations that Strange and his staff had made during the course of the experiments. In retrospect, some of it seemed so benign, reports of positive reactions to the various DNA-altering "therapy." The documentation purposefully excluded the dark stuff, about the patients who had been systematically transformed into virtual monsters.

Thomas had only been privy to the whitewashed version of the program, which Strange had provided to him. But now, if the police—or any decent investigator, for that matter—got hold of these files, they could deconstruct all of the horror that had been engineered. All someone needed to do was search for the old "patients" of Dr. Hugo Strange, to discover that they were all dead or had disappeared under mysterious circumstances.

With one exception, of course.

Thomas pulled up Karen's information, which detailed the steps in her therapy from the day she entered the program to her final treatments. It had been no easy task, acquiring the full report. The file included photos of Karen taken throughout her time at Pinewood. Somehow the "before" photos were more disturbing than the "after" ones. Thomas had gotten used to the monstrous version of Karen whom he had seen for years now.

But the "before" version of her—where she seemed younger, hopeful, and without the reptilian extremity—

was more shocking. It pounded home what she'd been through, how the experiments had destroyed her life, and the lives of so many others. Yes, Karen and many of the others had been convicted felons, but that didn't mean that Strange had the right to do what he'd done to them—to use their bodies as a virtual playground for his perverse experiments.

Karen had been told that if she participated in the research, it would reduce her prison sentence, as well as help repay her debt to society by aiding in the search for cures for deadly diseases—even death itself. Would she or anyone have agreed, if she'd known the risks involved? That there were no cures on the horizon, especially not for the patients themselves?

If Thomas was right, and Strange wanted to destroy all of the evidence in order to have a clean slate and restart the program, he would need to eliminate Thomas as a threat. So as he had so many times before, he checked the files for any signs of intrusion.

Everything was there, encrypted and password-protected. The password was a series of seemingly random letters, numbers, and symbols that he had memorized with painstaking precision. So if something happened to him, no one would ever locate the files.

Thomas would take the information to his grave.

This last thought made Thomas shudder. Was it possible that the break-in was just part *one* of Strange's plan? Maybe he had sent a crew of criminals on a sort of "search and destroy" mission, in the guise of a robbery, to locate the data, purge it, and then take out Thomas himself. All that would leave would be Karen, and they would have a road map that would lead directly to her.

With that thought, he stood and began to pace.

That Strange could try to kill him had occurred to Thomas before. The man was unhinged, capable of anything. In the early days, right after Pinewood shut down, Thomas assuaged his fears by hiring bodyguards for his whole family. He'd never told them the real reason for the protection, of course. He'd made up a story that some Wayne Enterprises employees had received death threats, and that the amped up security was just a precaution.

As time passed, Thomas began to feel secure that the threat had waned, that Strange had indeed moved on. But now, especially with what had happened at the cabin, the danger reared its ugly head once again.

Thomas was nervous, pacing, as a bat zipped and swirled overhead.

He wondered if he should get bodyguards again. Martha was already suspicious, and if Thomas announced that the family needed more protection, she'd demand to know what was going on. If she found out about the secrets he'd been keeping for all these years, there was no telling what she might do.

Best-case scenario, she would demand a divorce.

Worst-case scenario—if Strange found that Martha knew about Pinewood, he might identify her as a threat, as well.

At times like this, Thomas wished he wasn't in this

alone. He wished he had a confidant, someone with whom he could discuss all of this, to help him make the right decisions. Over the years, Karen had been that person, but those times seemed to have come to an end. He had told Frank about Strange, and Pinewood, but Frank only knew the essentials, and Thomas didn't want to let him into his secrets any more than he already had.

His pacing slowed, and Thomas arrived at a decision. As difficult as it would be, he had to wait. He had to be one-hundred-percent sure that Strange was responsible for the break-in, and was planning to resume his genetic research, before making any major decisions.

Thomas sat again at his desk and lit another cigar. He felt better, here in his hidden sanctum, where he always felt safe. This was his man-cave, after all—it was just him and the bats down here. Over the years, humans had betrayed him so many times, but the bats had provided some much needed consistency in his life. When things were going rough, he could come down to his office, escape from the human world, and listen to the screeching and scratching of the bats. Weird, maybe, but everyone had their quirks.

In a dark and dangerous world, the bats always provided him comfort, or maybe even hope.

EIGHTEEN

Harvey smelled. He wore the clothes he'd worn yesterday, and arrived at the crime scene downtown. A burnt-out car still smoldered in front of a defunct warehouse. He assumed it was a GCPD patrol car, a black-and-white, though it was impossible to tell for sure. EMS workers and forensics were working, gathering evidence. The medical examiner stood to one side.

Captain Essen was there, talking to some cops. The Captain didn't come out to most crime scenes, only the major ones. And when cops were killed, that made it major.

"Where're the bodies?" Harvey asked a young officer.

"You're looking at 'em," the cop said, gesturing.

"Mother of Christ," Harvey said. Closer now, he could make out the charred skeletons. On first glance they'd seemed to be part of the car.

"The M.E. said they went fast at least," the cop said,

"didn't feel much pain. But I don't know about that. Getting burned alive sounds pretty damn painful to me."

"I'm with you on that," Harvey said. "How'd it happen?"

"Somebody snuck up on 'em, doused 'em with gasoline, and tossed a match in the car," the kid said. That made Harvey squirm a little.

"Well, I'll tell ya one thing," he said. "Whoever did this is gonna burn somewhere for a lot longer than these cops did."

Captain Essen came over, walking briskly.

"I don't know what's going on lately," she said. "This city's going to hell."

"Going?" Harvey said. "Where've you been lately? It's long gone, Cap."

"I had a long conversation with Officer Warren yesterday," Essen said. "Told me how he was looking forward to going on a camping trip next month with his family."

"Son of a bitch owed me two hundred bucks from a poker game last month," Harvey said. "Maybe this was his way out."

"That isn't funny," Essen said.

"I wasn't trying to be *funny* funny," Harvey said. "Gallows humor. Haven't you heard of that?"

Essen just glared.

Jesus, Harvey thought, *am I the last cop with a sense of humor?* As he thought about it, though, he kind of understood.

"We need all available resources on this case," Essen said. "We've got to contain it, not lose more good officers. That means every available detective at the GCPD, including you and Detective Wong."

"I want to help out," Harvey said, "but we're closing in on finding the Picasso thieves. So technically, we're not available."

Now the glare turned into a sneer.

"Dead cops are our priority now, Detective Bullock. Not some rich guy's stolen painting."

"Obviously this case is the priority," Harvey agreed, "but somebody got killed when that painting was stolen. And me and Detective Wong got shot at yesterday. Damn near killed. I think it's a priority to get those guys off the street, too."

"The man who was killed in the Wayne robbery was a four-time loser," Essen said. "Are you seriously comparing that animal to two of GCPD's finest?"

Harvey knew she was right. It was just frustrating to have to let Colon go, after they'd come so close to nailing the son of a bitch. Without them, he'd be free in an hour. He could get on a ship headed out of the country, maybe as quick as today, and it would be sayonara to him and maybe the painting, too.

"I got it," Harvey said. "The painting case goes on the back burner."

"Good, I'm glad we're on the same page about this," Essen said. "Now I want an arrest in this case by the end of the day, at the latest."

Why don't you ask for world peace, while you're at it?

But Harvey didn't say it. He went over to check in with Pete Shaw, a GCPD cop who had been one of the first responders. Shaw explained that there had been no witnesses to the attack, nor were there any security cameras in the area.

"But get this," he said, "a security camera a few blocks away picks up a dark blue sedan leaving the area. We get the plate number, track down the driver across town. Turns out it was unrelated to this incident, but the driver had been wanted for whacking his mother two days ago. You try to solve one crime, you stumble onto the solution to another one. Only in Gotham, right?"

"Only in Gotham," Harvey agreed.

Then he saw Amanda approaching. She looked good in jeans, sneakers, and a black T-shirt, swinging her hips a little.

"Hey, partner," she said.

"Hey, yourself," Harvey said, and he smiled. "Lookin' good." At that very moment Captain Essen looked over, and gave him the evil eye again. His smile disappeared.

"Great," Harvey said. "Now the Captain thinks I'm treating this like it's a game."

"You're welcome," Amanda said. "Well, this is the suckiest Sunday morning ever, isn't it? I was at my local farmers' market, buying a cup of Joe, when I got the call." She looked over at the car. "Any idea which psycho did this? Or what the motive could've been?"

"Nada and nada," Harvey said.

Then with a serious tone, Amanda said, "I know you were friends with Officer Warren. I'm sorry for your loss."

"Appreciated," Harvey said. "Well, looks like this is going to be our priority for the foreseeable future. So this is the best news ever for Roberto Colon, and whoever the hell he was working with."

Harvey caught Amanda giving him the once over, looking him up and down. She gave a little sniff, and wrinkled her nose.

"What's wrong?" Harvey said with his chin to his shirt, thinking maybe he'd spilled something.

"So you're taking the walk of shame this morning, huh?" Amanda was smirking.

"Maybe I just have two of the same sport jacket," Harvey said. He didn't know why he didn't just tell her straight-out that he'd had a wild sexy night with Lacey White. He was an adult, a free agent. It wasn't like he had anything to hide. If he wanted to have a fun night with an old flame, he didn't have to beat around the bush about it.

"Sure, doesn't everybody?" Amanda said. "Well, I hope you got some sleep at least. Looks like it's gonna be a long day."

As if on cue, Harvey saw a Gotham News van pull up, with Lacey riding shotgun.

"Time to rock 'n' roll," he said.

"Where to?" Amanda asked. "Shouldn't we wait to see if forensics find any leads?"

"In these ashes?" Harvey said. "What do you think

they'll find? A fingerprint? Nah, waste of time." The van came to a stop. "Let's check out every known arsonist in town, and see who doesn't have an alibi for last night."

"All right," Amanda said. "How about I follow you in my car, then I drop it back at the station."

Lacey got out of the van, along with a cameraman.

"Sounds like a plan," Harvey said. He wanted to avoid an awkward situation, get the hell out of Dodge, but Amanda must have seen him looking at the news truck.

"Aren't you going to say hi to your friend?"

"Friend?" Harvey said. "What friend?"

Then he looked over and saw Lacey coming toward him, smiling. *Ah, crap.*

"Harvey, baby, I'm glad I caught you here." Lacey pulled Harvey's watch out of her purse. "I think you forgot something this morning."

He didn't look at Amanda, but he could imagine her expression.

"Thanks," he said.

"I don't believe we've actually met," Lacey said to Amanda. "I'm Lacey White."

"Amanda Wong."

They shook hands.

"I've heard a lot about you," Amanda said.

"Good things, I hope," Lacey said, smiling.

"Oh, the best," Amanda said. "You've gotten some great reviews."

"Oh, really?" The smile disappeared, and she glared at Harvey.

"She's kidding," Harvey said.

"Oh, really?" Lacey said. "So I *didn't* get a great review?" Then she added, "You're gonna pay for that next time, Harvey boy." Spinning, she sashayed away, back toward the truck.

"Two of the same sport jacket, huh?" Amanda smirked.

"Shut the hell up," Harvey said.

"Watch that attitude," Amanda said, "or else, Harvey boy." Amanda laughed, but he had to admit, the way she'd said it had been kind of hot. He couldn't help chuckling a little.

Captain Essen saw the laughing and shot him another look.

"Officially not my day," Harvey said.

NINETEEN

Frank had been in the middle of the best dream ever. He was on the beach, maybe an island, walking hand in hand with Michelle O'Reilley.

Michelle O'Reilley had been the wife of Don O'Reilley, a successful real estate entrepreneur in Gotham. Several months back, Don had come to Frank, suspecting that Michelle was cheating on him. Talk about dead-on instincts—oh, boy, was she cheating on him, with at least three different guys.

Frank followed her around town for a while, accumulating evidence. He got some nude shots of her through the windows of the various apartments and hotel rooms. It was easy to see why she was so popular with guys. She was drop-dead gorgeous—wavy red hair, great curves, a smile that could cure depression. It was also easy to figure out why she was straying. Her husband Don was a class-A prick. He was controlling, abusive—physically and psychologically—and her affairs were a cry out for help.

Frank wanted to save her, but that wasn't his job. He was working for Don, not her, sort of the way a defense attorney might know his client is guilty, but he has to do his job anyway. So he gave Don the evidence and two weeks later, Michelle wound up whacked, her body found in pieces in a dumpster. Did Don whack her or hire somebody to whack her? Yeah, probably, but the cops couldn't find evidence that he had, and Don got off Scott Free. Frank usually kept his emotions and his work separate, but the Michelle O'Reilley job ate away at him.

So in the dream Frank and Michelle were walking hand in hand along the beach on some tropical island. Warm water was splashing at their feet and, as always, she had that spectacular smile. Then they were lying down, starting to make love. Yeah, this wasn't a sex dream, this was a *making love* dream. It felt good, knowing he had whisked her away from Gotham, her smarmy husband, and all those other guys who were just using her for one thing. As she pinned him down onto the sand, he looked at her eyes.

"Thank you for saving me, Frank."

"Any time, baby."

Then he opened his eyes and realized he wasn't on a tropical island with a beautiful woman. He was by the railroad tracks in the old train yard in the seediest part of Gotham, looking up at the eyes of a large gray rat.

"Goddamnit," he said.

He flung the rat off him and tried to get up. He was disoriented, wasn't sure how he had wound up here.

As he tried to get up he stumbled on some garbage and fell again, and cut his arm on a piece of broken glass. Well, at least he was wide awake now.

Who needs coffee?

As the dream faded into vague forgetfulness, he remembered key details from last night—the knockout in the wrong round of the Sanchez-Williams fight, and then wandering around Gotham, getting smashed, wondering how he was going to avoid becoming fish food in the Gotham river when the loan sharks cracked down.

And then finally, the plan.

Ah, the plan, the sweet plan! That's why the dream had taken place on a tropical island, because that's where he was headed as soon as he found Tommy Wayne's Picasso. This was Frank's endgame, his big out. He'd put in years of hard work, helping others solve their problems. Now it was time to put himself first. What was the alternative? Do the moral thing? Stay in Gotham, give Tommy Wayne his painting back? That was a surefire way of winding up dead. To hell with morality. He'd been moral his whole life, more or less.

It was time to play on the other side of the fence.

Frank made it back to his apartment. It was a decent place—a good-sized one bedroom, but that's all he'd ever needed. He'd had girlfriends over the years, but none of them had ever stuck because he'd always put his job first. Well, that would change when he was living it up in the tropics. He'd get any woman he wanted, and he'd have plenty of time to spend with her—to roll around in the sand and sip drinks with little umbrellas in them.

The phone rang, and he almost jumped out of his skin.

It was Tommy Wayne, wanting an update about the case. Frank assured Tommy that he had some good leads, and then got him off the phone as fast as he could. He was about to get into the shower when someone started banging on the door. Who the hell could it be, at around nine o'clock on a Sunday morning? Maybe it was the super, or a neighbor returning from a night of partying, trying to get into the wrong apartment. That happened sometimes.

Frank put on his robe, then went to the door. Just in case, he picked up his gun.

"Who's there?"

"Oswald Chesterfield Cobblepot, Mr. Collins."

Oh, right, Cobblepot. But this early?

Frank opened the door and saw Cobblepot standing there, grinning like a hyena. He was well dressed—in a suit and tie, and recently shined shoes. As a PI, Frank never missed the details.

"How did you find out where I lived?" Frank asked. His home address wasn't listed, and he didn't give it out to many people.

"I have a knack for figuring things out," Cobblepot said. "But you know that, don't you—that's why you hired me." Cobblepot laughed in an odd, demented way. Frank remembered how last night, when he was drunk, he had regretted getting involved with the guy, and now that he was sobering up, his opinion hadn't changed.

"Come in," Frank said.

Cobblepot entered the apartment and Frank shut the door.

"My apologies for the unannounced visit," Cobblepot said. "I would have called, but I was in the neighborhood, and I had a feeling you wouldn't be in church."

"Yeah?" Frank said. "And why did you assume that?"

Cobblepot laughed again. Had Frank missed the joke?

"Well," Cobblepot said, "let's just say that a man of your—well, let's just say—*habits*, isn't consistent with the behavior of your typical churchgoer. I mean, am I right or am I right, Mr. Collins?"

Cobblepot's eyes were so wide that Frank could see the whites under the bright blue irises—always a sign of a loon. Frank used to be good at spotting psychos— he'd always avoided doing business with them—but, somehow Cobblepot had slipped between the cracks, perhaps another indication that it was time for Frank to shut down his PI biz and hit the hammock full-time.

"Habits?" Frank asked. "What habits are those?"

"You're a drinker and a gambler, to name two," Cobblepot said, "and you're a bad gambler at that.

Betting on a third-round knockout last night? Not a good idea."

Good lord, this nut did seem to know everything that was going on in Gotham. Or he'd been stalking Frank. Not that the two were mutually exclusive.

"Okay, I'll bite," Frank said, "how did you know that?"

"Call me a natural observer," Cobblepot said. "From a young age I've watched my mother, the most wonderful woman in the world. I've worshipped her, studying all of her habits, all of her mannerisms, until I grew up to know her perhaps better than she knows herself. And then I began to branch out, leave the nest so to speak." He laughed. "Now I apply my observation skills to criminals, mainly—it's not difficult to find a lot of subjects in Gotham." He laughed again. "I find criminal behavior to be just fascinating. I guess I could've been a great psychotherapist. But healing people? Not my thing, Mr. Collins."

"You didn't answer my question," Frank said.

"I think you'll be more interested in discussing the matter at hand," Cobblepot said. "The location of Roberto Colon."

"You found him?"

"Yes, indeed I have."

"So okay? Where is he?"

"There's a small detail first," Cobblepot said. "The ten thousand dollars you promised me."

"Don't worry, I'll give it to you," Frank said, "but after your info checks out."

"Please don't be insulted, Mr. Collins." Cobblepot sat on the sofa and crossed his legs, even though Frank hadn't invited him to sit. "I'd love to be able to accept your good word," he said, "but I'm afraid you're not a good risk."

Frank had hypertension. His blood pressure was usually around 160 over 90. Now the top number had to be 200, easy.

"*I'm* a bad risk?" Frank said. "Who are you? Some guy on the street. Some nobody. I'm Frank Collins, ex-GCPD detective, now a respected PI."

"Yeah, well, you're a respected PI who's also in deep trouble," Cobblepot spewed, his voice taking on a suddenly vicious tone. "I'm worried about your financial stability, Mr. Collins. Or instability, I should say. I know all about your debts to two bookmakers connected to Don Falcone, and where there's one roach there's more roaches. God knows how much debt you have right now, yet you promised me ten thousand dollars.

"That means you're lying, and planning to rip me off, or you're planning to make so much money through Roberto Colon that you actually intend to pay me the ten thousand. In that case, the information I hold must be valuable indeed—far more so than you're letting on."

Frank began to get really steamed. He didn't know how Cobblepot had found out about his debts, but he was sick of this no-name kid trying to push him around.

"It's *twenty* grand, after I find out if the info is real," Frank said. "That's the deal. Take it or leave it."

"Agreed, the deal is now twenty grand," Cobblepot said. "And I want the money now—up front, unless you have some collateral. In that case, I'll take diamonds or gold, but I won't take an IOU."

"I'm sorry you're taking this position." Frank pulled the handgun out of the pocket of his robe, and aimed it at Cobblepot. "If there's one thing I hate, it's a guy who goes back on his word."

Cobblepot laughed.

"Having a gun pointed at your face is a joke to you?" Frank asked.

"Funniest joke ever." Cobblepot laughed some more. "You would never kill me."

"I wouldn't, huh?"

"If you killed me, it would be murder. You're a known gambler and a known drinker, Mr. Collins, but you're not a murderer. Second of all, if you kill me ,you'll never find out where Roberto Colon is."

"Eh, I'll find him," Frank said, "with or without you. Nobody's indispensable, Cobblepot." Frank fired. He was a great shot, hit the bull's-eye every time at the range. If the bullet had missed Cobblepot's left ear by a half an inch, that would've been a generous estimate.

Showing his true spineless nature, Cobblepot fell backward and cowered, shaking with fear. His eyes were wider than ever.

"What are you doing!"

"See?" Frank said. "You think you know everything,

but you don't. I have a feeling I'd be doing Gotham a favor if I took you off the board right now. Guy like you is gonna get himself into a lot of trouble someday, and drag a lot of people down with him."

"You almost shot my ear off!" Cobblepot began to recover, and sounded more offended than angry.

"Yeah, guess my aim was a little off." He fired another shot, aiming for strands of Cobblepot's spiky hair. *Bingo.*

Cobblepot's bravado evaporated, and he shivered with terror.

"This is your last chance to tell me where Colon is, and stick to our original deal," Frank said, "or I have a feeling the third time won't be a charm, at least as far as your life expectancy is concerned."

"What happened to you?" Cobblepot asked.

"Huh?" Frank said.

"You're not one of the good guys anymore. You switched teams. Something must have caused this tectonic shift in your psyche. What was it?"

"I thought you didn't want to be a therapist," Frank said.

"I'm a great observer," Cobblepot said, "and something in you changed."

"You're right, I *have* changed," Frank said. "A couple of years ago I never would've considered aiming a gun at you. Couple of months ago, I wouldn't have considered shooting at you. Couple of days ago, I wouldn't have considered killing you. So do you really want to push me any farther, Cobblepot?"

He didn't. "Okay, fine," he said. "Roberto Colon is staying at the Star Bright Motel, just outside of town. He checked in there last night under a fake name—Duncan."

Frank knew the Star Bright Motel—had been there many times over the years. It was a favorite spot for cheating husbands and wives.

"You better not be wasting my time, Cobblepot. If I get up there and find out you lied to me, I'll find you, and the next shot's going to go into your head."

"Understood," Cobblepot said.

Frank lowered the gun. Cobblepot got up from the couch.

"Well, this has been an enjoyable visit," Cobblepot said. "You should have me over again sometime. Maybe we can bring lady friends next time. Double date."

"Get the hell out of here," Frank said.

"When will I get my money?" Cobblepot asked.

"I'll find you," Frank said. "Don't worry about it."

Cobblepot nodded and headed out of the apartment; opened the door. Then he stopped and turned back.

"Speaking of gambling, Mr. Collins, I'm betting you're going to need me again someday. I'm going to be big—bigger than you can imagine. Someday I'll be the king of Gotham. Everybody who wants to get somewhere in life needs friends in high places, Mr. Collins, and I just want you to know that I won't hold your behavior today against you." He gathered himself, and brushed off his jacket. "I'm a forgive-

and-forget kind of guy. I'll be your friend when you need me, I'll do favors for you—and in exchange you'll do favors for me. Life in Gotham is like a maze, Mr. Collins, except there are consequences. Choose the right path and you can become rich and powerful. Choose the wrong path and you'll wind up dead!"

He spewed the word "dead" like a threat, and then he stormed out of the apartment, making sure to slam the door. It was all Frank could do not to take one more shot.

The king of Gotham? Frank mused. *Man, this nutcase is even farther gone than I thought.* Yet as Frank showered, he couldn't shake the feeling that maybe he'd made a mistake—maybe he *should've* blown Cobblepot away when he'd had the chance. Guys like him had the potential of turning into lose threads someday, and that's why God created scissors, to cut loose threads.

Wow, something in Frank really *had* changed. He was starting to scare himself. What had happened to his conscience, his moral center? What frightened him most was that he didn't really give a damn.

TWENTY

Fresh clothes and a shower changed Frank's appearance, but he was still feeling the effects of last night's bender. He drank a lot of water, but it didn't help the nagging headache and nausea.

He got a call on his phone—Tommy Wayne again—and didn't pick up. He let the call go to his voicemail. When Tommy found out that Frank had stolen his painting and hightailed it to the tropics, he'd be shocked. It would be like a kick to the balls that he never saw coming, but Tommy was a big boy. He'd get over it.

During the drive out of town Frank had to piss like a racehorse, but didn't want to find a place to stop. So he peed into a large plastic soda bottle he kept in the car, just for such an emergency. In the old days, peeing in bottles was for long assignments like stakeouts, not twenty-minute drives. Yet more incentive for Frank to pack it in and sign out of Gotham, forever.

He knew a guy, Louie, who worked the desk at the Star Bright Motel. He didn't know if Louie would be working today, but when he entered the office sure enough the guy was there, on duty. Frank waited until he was finished checking in a couple. Cheaters for sure—they both had that giddy, kids-in-a-candy-store look, and then he gave Louie a big hug.

"Frank the man," Louie says. "What brings you to the Star Bright? Wait, you're not following that couple that was just here, are you?"

"No, but some other PI probably is," Frank said. "Actually, I'm here about somebody else. Guy who checked in today, named Duncan."

"Who?"

Uh-oh. Had Cobblepot sent him on a wild goose chase? *That friggin' bastard.* If he had, Frank was going to blow the little scumbag away.

"Duncan," Frank said. "At least I think—" He pulled out a fifty-dollar bill, the tail end of the emergency money he'd kept hidden at home. Louie looked at the computer monitor on his desk.

"Oh, wait, that guy. Yeah, he's here."

Frank gave Louie the fifty. It was just about the last money he had to his name, but it was okay—a lot more would be coming in soon.

"What room's he in?" Frank asked.

Louie pocketed the bill. "Two-oh-one."

"Thanks, buddy," Frank said. "How's your daughter doing by the way?"

"Getting married next month."

"Whoa, time flies," Frank said.

"You're tellin' me."

Frank left the office and headed outside. Mr. Duncan, aka Roberto Colon, was staying on the second floor. Frank went up the exterior stairwell, looking around casually to make sure there weren't any bystanders lurking about. This was just a precaution. The Star Bright was the type of motel that catered to cheaters and criminals, so when something suspicious went down, people tended to do the smart thing—look the other way and keep their mouths shut.

He spotted a guy getting into his car in the parking lot below. So when Frank got to the top of the landing he waited for the guy to drive away. Then, when the coast seemed clear, he took his gun out and approached Colon's room.

Someone was in the there. Although the curtains were pulled together, Frank could see a faint shadow moving inside.

So much for a polite entrance. He knew these rooms had windowed bathrooms and he didn't want to announce his visit, giving Colon a chance to get away. Also, he didn't know if just Colon was in there, or there were other people. Tommy had said there were three burglars, and there could be more.

The element of surprise was Frank's friend.

Staying low, he got into position. Then he reared back, led with his shoulder, and charged the door. He heard the lock give, ripping through the outer frame, and then the door swung open.

Colon—or the man Frank presumed was Colon—was lying in bed in just his boxers.

"What the f—" His hand shot toward the night table.

"Freeze or I'll shoot," Frank said.

Wisely the guy froze, his arm in the air. Keeping his gun aimed at Colon, Frank went over and grabbed the gun.

"Who the hell are you?" Colon said. "What do you want?"

"I think you know exactly what I want," Frank said. "Where's the Picasso?"

"Wait, what is this?" Colon said. "You didn't even show me a badge. Are you a cop? That's against the law, you know? I've got rights. You know, I can report you. They'll take your badge away."

"Shut up," Frank said. Then he heard movement, coming from the bathroom.

"Someone else here?" Frank asked.

"Lexi, run!" Colon shouted.

But at that moment the bathroom door opened and a young brunette in slinky lingerie came through. She looked familiar, though Frank wasn't sure why. He was more concerned with the gun she was aiming at him. She fired a shot at Frank. Frank fired back—hit her twice, both times in the head, and her body went down, falling back into the bathroom.

"*Nooo!*" Colon cried out.

"Shut up," Frank said.

"You didn't have to do that," Colon said.

"Would you have preferred it if I let her kill me?"

"Of course I would've, you sonuvabitch," Colon said.

"Who was she?" Frank asked.

Colon hesitated. "Friend of mine. What difference does it make to you?"

"Wait, I remember now," Frank said, letting his gun hand relax. "She's a pro. I've taken pics of her here before, screwing my clients' husbands."

"Who the hell *are* you?" Colon demanded. He reached toward the night table again. Frank fired, hitting him in the arm. Colon wailed in agony. "*Sonuvabitch!*"

"Shut your goddamn trap—or you want another?" Frank asked.

"You're crazy, man!"

"You're right," Frank said. "I am crazy. I snapped big time and, trust me, you don't want to push me too far. Where the hell is the painting?"

"Man, I have no idea what you're talking about? Painting? What painting?"

"The one you and your crew lifted from Wayne Manor."

"I have no idea what you're—"

Frank fired, hitting Colon in his other arm. He wailed again, and pressed back against the headboard. Blood was all over the bed sheets, spreading in a widening stain.

"Help!" Colon yelled. "Help me!"

"You're wasting your breath," Frank said. "In this joint, people run away from the word help. I got all the time in the world, but I'm warning you right now, if you scream again, the next bullet's going between your eyes. I'm asking you for the last time. Where's the painting?"

"You gotta tie tourniquets around my arms," he said. "I'm gonna bleed to death."

"Final chance," Frank said.

"Okay, okay," Colon said. "Belladonna has it."

"Who?" Frank asked.

"Belladonna, that's her name."

"What's her last name?"

"I don't know. She's an art dealer. I mean… I mean she sells stolen art."

"Where is she?"

"Please, I'm bleeding to d-death here, man. You gotta help me."

"If you want to live you better tell me quick."

"Duke Street, n-near the docks. It's a blue door. Gra-graffiti."

"That's where she lives, or where she works?"

"I don't know," Colon said. "Both maybe… Please, please help me. I'm begging you, man. *Please*." Colon was getting weaker, probably bleeding out. Even if Frank wanted to save him, he probably couldn't.

"Thanks, Roberto. You were a big help."

Frank shot him in the face.

The sudden silence was a relief. Frank had to kill him—he'd had no choice. A talker like him would've been a major loose thread. After he checked to make sure that Colon and the hooker were both officially finite—they were—he left the motel room.

He realized then that he hadn't asked Colon who

had hired him. But Frank didn't care if Hugo Strange was involved. Only Tommy Wayne cared about that, and Frank wasn't working for Wayne anymore.

He went into the motel office. Louie was still sitting at the desk.

"Thanks for all your help," Frank said.

"Anytime," Louie said.

Frank shot him in the face. Too bad, Louie was a good guy, and now he'd never get to go to his daughter's wedding. Well, whatever, there were worse tragedies, right?

Another loose thread snipped, Frank took the loose cash out of the cash box, put the key on the desk—wiped off his prints—and went back outside.

TWENTY-ONE

"How do we know he's in there?" Harvey asked Rick Powell, the GCPD Detective who'd been assigned the lead on the cop killer case.

"Anonymous tip," Powell said.

Harvey, Amanda, and about ten other GCPD detectives joined the stakeout outside an apartment building in the South Village. There were also dozens of officers on site, and a three-block radius had been cordoned off. Harvey had moved over to get the lowdown from Powell.

"This is a lot of resources to put into a glorified hunch," Harvey said. "The odds of an anonymous tip hitting are ten-to-one at best."

Powell was a stocky, arrogant cop who always thought he was the smartest guy in the room, just because he went to college while most other cops—like Harvey—rose up straight through the Academy. He gave Harvey a once-over.

"I know the difference between a hot tip and a cold

tip," he said with a little sneer, "and this one was the real deal."

"Yeah?" Harvey said. "And how do you know that?"

"Because I vetted it," Powell said. "The witness said the suspect told him he was going to kill a cop today. Other witnesses were at the scene and—"

"Sounds flimsy," Harvey said, not bothering to keep his voice down.

A few cops nearby were looking over, as it appeared as if Powell and Harvey were about to go at it.

"Yeah," Powell said. "Well, I don't give a crap if you think it's flimsy or not, since I'm the one calling the shots." His college-boy veneer was slipping. As far as Harvey was concerned, the only thing worse than having to play second fiddle, was having to play second fiddle to a jackass.

"Keep your voice down. You could be putting more cops in danger, for no good reason," Powell said. "Just get in position, Bullock, or else."

"Or else what? You'll make another jackass decision?"

Powell shoved Harvey, and barely budged him. Harvey shoved Rick back, nearly knocking him down. Of course, that was when Captain Essen came over.

"Bullock, that's enough," she said. "Over here."

Harvey had a flash of his grade school days, when he got called in to the principal's office just about every day—yeah, he and school didn't mix too well. Then he saw Powell smirk. He wanted to go after him again, beat him to a pulp, but he resisted.

"The guy's got a chip on his shoulder," Harvey said to Essen. "You know that."

"This isn't the time to act out on a personal grudge," Essen said. "There's a cop killer on the loose, and we've got to take him in."

"I have a better chance of hitting a straight triple in the first race today at Gotham Downs, than of the killer being in that building."

"That's yet to be determined," Essen said. "We received a promising tip, and the lead detective on this case determined it was worth following up." She glared at him, and added, "And I've had it with this pattern of insubordination. It's becoming chronic, and I'm giving you your last warning. Play with the team, Detective Bullock, or I'm gonna kick you off it."

"What's that supposed to mean?" Harvey said. "I've been on the force longer than you."

"Seniority only gets you so far," Essen said, "and you may have reached the finish line." With that she walked away to join Powell and the others. Harvey stood there and seethed, feeling humiliated, but he also knew there were some fights he couldn't win. This was one of them.

Amanda came over. "I can't leave you alone for five minutes without you finding trouble," she said, but she sounded concerned.

Then Powell signaled them all to get ready.

"Stand by." Then he added, "Suspect is moving, let's go."

"What do you want us to do, *boss*?" Harvey asked, oozing sarcasm.

"Cover the back," Powell said. He gestured, then he, Harvey, Amanda, and the other cops swarmed the building.

Powell and his partner went through the front, while Harvey and Amanda went around to the back. The GCPD had all of the possible exits—including windows and fire escapes—covered, and already had officers on the roof and the roofs of the adjacent buildings.

As soon as Harvey and Amanda entered the building, they heard a commotion in the front. They rushed over and saw Powell aiming a gun at a thin guy in jeans and a black leather jacket. The guy had thinning gray hair.

"I said put your hands on your head," he said to the guy.

"What's going on?" the guy said. "This is crazy. I-I didn't do anything."

"I need to see those hands," Powell said.

"Tell me what I did wrong," the guy said. "I have a right to know." He took a step toward Rick and reached into his jacket.

Oh, hell!

Harvey knew Powell was about to shoot.

"No!" he shouted, but it was too late. Powell fired three shots in quick succession. All the shots hit the guy in his chest, and he went down like a bowling pin. Amanda rushed over and squatted to examine him.

"He's gone," she said.

Then Harvey leaned over and checked the part of

the jacket he'd been reaching into before Rick shot him. He took out a pair of glasses and flung them onto the ground.

"Son of a *bitch*," Harvey said to Powell. "He was unarmed."

"So?" Powell said. "He was still the guy."

"We'll never know if he's the guy, now that he's dead," Harvey said.

"I better tell the others," Amanda said.

"Wait," Powell said. "Don't go anywhere."

Amanda stopped.

Powell took a spare gun out of his pocket, wiped it down, and then put it in the dead guy's hand.

"What the hell?" Harvey said. He wasn't beyond planting a gun to save his ass—he'd done the same thing before, and usually had a spare gun on him for just this purpose. But he only resorted to it when he knew, one hundred percent, that he was framing the right guy.

"Shut up," Powell said. Then he added, "Little finishing touch," and he took a book of matches out of his own pocket, putting it in a pocket of the dead guy's leather jacket.

Abruptly Captain Essen and a few other detectives entered. Telling Essen the truth, that Powell had planted evidence, wasn't even an option. There was an unwritten code in the GCPD to never point a finger at corruption, and Harvey never broke that code.

"We got him," Powell proclaimed.

"Great work, Detective." Essen was happy to get a

high-profile case off the books.

"I gotta get outta here," Harvey said to Amanda. Walking away, he added, "Can you believe that guy? Patting himself on the back after murdering somebody?"

"It's possible he was the killer," Amanda offered.

"Yeah, like it's possible I'll be the next pope," Harvey said.

"I think the odds are a bit better than that."

"Yeah," Harvey said. "Maybe a little."

"Well, if that's what you really think, you should tell the Captain," Amanda said.

"What'll that do except get me another beat-down?" Harvey said. "She's patting herself on the back, too—she did brilliant police work, she took a cop killer off the board. Bravo to the GCPD!

"The only way she'll ever even entertain the idea that they got the wrong guy is when the real cop killer strikes again," he spat, surprised at his own anger. "Even then she'll put a spin on it, say it was a copycat killer, there were two killers, just to keep internal affairs off her ass. Not that internal affairs would ever reprimand anything she does since they're basically a bunch of puppets over there."

"I don't get it," Amanda said. "If you genuinely believe we got the wrong guy, that the killer could strike again, you have to—"

"Keep my mouth shut," Harvey said. "There's only one word you need to know if you want to make it as a GCPD detective—silence. If you want to be a detective here, and have a career that lasts more than a couple of weeks, you have to understand that. We're in the business of closing cases, not solving them."

Captain Essen rushed up behind them.

"Detectives, wait." She caught up with them then added, "Just got a call in about the perp you were tracking, Roberto Colon."

"What about him?" Harvey asked.

"He was killed in a room at the Star Bright Motel this afternoon. There are two other casualties—a woman and the desk clerk."

"Wait, not Louie DePino," Harvey said.

Essen nodded.

"Goddamnit," Harvey said. "Jesus H, what the hell is going on in this town?"

"Friend of yours, I'm guessing," Amanda said.

"Old army buddy from the Great War," Harvey said. "Just got an invite to his daughter's wedding last week."

"I'm sorry for your loss," Essen said. She sounded like she meant it.

"So now that this case is solved, I guess we can go back to the Wayne robbery?" Harvey asked.

"Yes, you can," Essen said. "Do you have any idea who could've killed your friend and the others?"

Harvey looked at Amanda.

"Maybe the third guy in the crew," Amanda said. "The zombie."

Essen looked confused.

"She means the guy who was wearing the zombie

mask at the robbery," Harvey said.

"Well, then you have your new assignment," Essen said. "Go find that zombie."

It seemed like the rest of the GCPD, whoever hadn't been at the stakeout, was at the crime scene at the Star Bright Hotel. A triple homicide was a big deal, even by Gotham standards.

In the parking lot of the hotel, Harvey and Amanda approached a cop who had been one of the first responders.

"What do we got here?" Harvey asked, feeling déjà vu.

"The bodies—two in a room on the second floor, one the manager of the place."

"Who's the girl?" Harvey asked.

"Haven't ID'd her yet," the cop said. "Probably a hooker."

While Amanda went to talk to possible witnesses, Harvey went upstairs to check out the scene. Cops and medical examiners were working the scene, including that weird kid, Nygma.

"Hi, Detective Bullock," Ed said. "Exciting day today, no?"

Harvey glanced at the mess on the bed that used to be Roberto Colon.

"They let you out of the lab?" Harvey asked Nygma. "I didn't know you ever get to see the light of the day."

"Ha, ha," Nygma said, but he didn't really sound

pissed. "Actually, with the cop killer case, and it being a Sunday, we were short-handed, but I filled the void with my usual alacrity."

Harvey had no idea what the nut was talking about, and didn't really care.

"Where's the girl?" Harvey asked.

"Well, parts of her are in the bathroom," Nygma said, grinning.

What a freakazoid, Harvey thought.

Harvey approached where the woman's body was splayed, then stopped. Like Colon, she had been shot in the face. Although almost beyond recognition, Harvey still recognized her. He'd recognize that body anywhere.

"You gotta be kiddin' me," Harvey said.

"You know her?" Nygma asked. "Sorry, *knew* her?"

"Jeez Louise," Harvey said.

"Her name was Louise?"

"No, not Louise." She'd gone by the name Lexi Love, but Harvey had a feeling that probably wasn't her real name.

"She was a great love of yours," Nygma suggested.

"No," Harvey said, "she was not."

"Then lover with an 'r,'" Nygma said. "I'm a romantic myself. I pick up on these sorts of things."

Amanda entered and said, "Nobody's talking."

"At the Star Bright?" Harvey said. "What a surprise. Damn, we need to find the Picasso," he added. "The Picasso will lead us to the zombie."

Nygma had overheard this. "How exactly does a

Picasso lead to a zombie?" he asked.

"It's complicated," Harvey said.

"Oh," Nygma said, "I thought it was a riddle."

Harvey shook his head and rolled his eyes.

"We have to go to the hot art dealers in Gotham," Amanda said. "If the zombie has the painting, he's probably trying to sell it through a third party."

"Okay, so where do you want to start?" Harvey said. "Look in the Gotham phone book under 'H' for 'hot'?"

"May I hazard to make a suggestion?" Nygma asked. Harvey rolled his eyes again, then realized it was starting to hurt.

"I think you should focus on looking for fingerprints, or whatever you're doing here," Harvey said.

"I think you should talk to a woman named Belladonna."

"Maybe we can find somebody here willing to talk," Harvey said to Amanda.

"Wait," Amanda said. Then she said to Nygma, "Why her?"

"A case I worked on when I first joined the GCPD," Nygma said. "Several paintings were stolen from an auction house, and the criminals planned to fence them through Belladonna."

"I never heard of that case," Harvey said dismissively.

"It was Detective Powell's case," Nygma said. "A gang of criminals robbed a van transporting the paintings. If you haven't realized it yet, I'm gifted." He looked pleased with himself, like a child. "My mind is like a virtual encyclopedia."

"Oh yeah, okay, that case," Harvey said. "I remember it now, but I don't remember anything about Bella Whoever coming up."

"Belladonna," Nygma said. "And, well, that's because I've been doing a little investigating of my own. After you came inquiring about my dead friend, Byron Stone, I looked in Stone's arrest records. During his interrogation in the previous robbery, he mentioned that his fence would have been Belladonna. So while Belladonna wasn't actually a part of the case, in fact she was." Nygma grinned.

Amanda shot Harvey a look. "It's worth a shot."

He had to admit, it wasn't a bad lead.

"How are we supposed to find her?"

"You can start by going to her place of business. Eleven Duke Street."

"You're weird, Nygma," Harvey said. "But you can be helpful… sometimes."

"What does an ironic dying man say?" Nygma asked.

Harvey and Amanda had already left the room.

Nygma called after them, "Always happy to yelp!"

TWENTY-TWO

Frank liked this new dark side to himself. His whole career he'd been the good guy, and what had it gotten him? Not happiness, that was for damn sure—but now he was letting loose, breaking out of his shell, and it felt a lot like destiny. If he'd had any idea how great it would feel, he would've switched sides years ago.

Shooting the hooker had been like the gateway drug. He'd killed before—but always in the name of the law. Anybody could kill a bad guy, but killing an innocent person took *cojones*. And killing Colon? Even better, like moving up from pot to coke. The rush energized him, made him feel alive for maybe the first time ever.

People who hadn't killed in cold blood before couldn't identify—they had to experience it for themselves. But killing Louie, ah that was the clincher. Killing a stranger was one thing, but to a kill a friend, somebody who trusted you—that amped up this killing thing to a whole new level.

It was like moving up to crack, or angel dust.

During the ride to Belladonna's place, Frank kept replaying Louie's murder in his mind, recalling Louie's shock when he saw the gun, and that instant when everything he thought he knew and trusted about the world blew up in his face—literally! That look of total dismay and betrayal was a beautiful thing.

This whole killing thing could become addictive. It made Frank rethink his getaway plan, about retiring to the Mexican island. He'd got a taste of the thrill of murder, and it was hard to just walk away from it. He'd go into serious withdrawal.

Then he had a brilliant thought.

Why run away?

Quitting now would be like an athlete hanging it up after winning a gold medal. Yeah, it could be done, but why do it if he didn't have to? Frank had just got started—he had so much more to accomplish. He could stay in Gotham, get work as a hit man. It wouldn't be so hard to transition from detective work to killing. He'd have to solve mysteries, track people down, but when he found his targets, instead of bringing them to the cops, he'd knock them off. The day-to-day was the same—only the end result was different.

But would that be enough for him? Would it truly satisfy him? Maybe he was thinking too small. Instead of being a hit man, he could become a crime boss. Yeah, that was it. He could use the money from the Picasso to hire people to work under him, and create an entire crime empire. From his career in law enforcement he already knew the ins and outs of the Gotham underworld, so the transition would be easy.

Within a year—hell, maybe six months—he could take down Maroni and Falcone. That nut Oswald Cobblepot thought he was going to be the king of Gotham? Yeah, right. Frank Collins was going to be the next big name in crime.

"I want more!" he bellowed. "Give me more!"

When he got down to the docks, he drove around at maybe five miles an hour along Duke Street, looking for the building with the blue door—the one with graffiti on it.

He began to wonder if Colon had fed him a load of crap about Belladonna, the stolen art dealer. Frank had never heard of Belladonna before, and a criminal operating in Gotham, unbeknownst to Frank, was pretty unlikely to say the least. Under the circumstances, though, it also would have been unusual for Colon to come up with such a convincing lie. People with guns pointed at their heads tended to be at their most honest.

Then he spotted it—the blue door with graffiti on it, adjacent to a defunct fishery. Like all the buildings on this block, it looked as if it had been abandoned, or taken over by squatters, junkies, and street kids.

Pulling over, he parked the car and then walked briskly up to the door, filled with frenetic energy. He banged on the metal a few times with the side of his fist. No answer, nor any sign of life inside. He was wondering if Colon had steered him astray after all, when the door opened.

A woman stood there, about sixty, with dyed bright red hair, in a black velvet dress. Behind her it was dark—he couldn't see anything in the dimness.

"Sorry, we're closed."

She tried to shut the door, but Frank stuck his hand out to prevent her.

"Are you Belladonna by any chance?"

Suddenly she looked confused, maybe suspicious.

"Who sent you?" she asked.

"A friend said you might be able to help me out," Frank said.

"Are you a cop?" she asked.

Frank had gotten that question before. He had that "cop" look to him. Like he'd often told people, *"You can take the man out of the GCPD, but you can't take the GCPD out of the man."*

"No," he said. "I'm not."

He couldn't tell if she believed him.

"Well, I'm not open now, not officially," she replied, "but if a friend referred you, I don't want you to leave disappointed. If you'd like to do a reading, I can."

"A reading?" Frank was confused.

"A reading, your fortune," she answered, looking irritable all of a sudden. "I'm a fortune teller. That's why you're here, right?"

"Oh, a reading," Frank said. "Yeah, that's right. Have a little hearing loss, sorry—getting old sucks."

"It's fifty dollars for a half hour. Is that okay?"

"That's fine," Frank said. He would have agreed to any price, since he was planning to kill her anyway.

She looked him over again, sizing him up. If she was a fortune teller, she wasn't a good one, because she seemed to reach the wrong conclusion.

"Okay, come on in."

He had no idea what the deal was with this lady. Was she actually a fortune teller, and Colon had steered her wrong? Or was this whole fortune teller thing a front for her real gig as a crooked art dealer? He could have pulled his gun, tried to get her to talk, but he decided to hold off, and assess the situation first.

He stepped inside, and it took a minute for his eyes to adjust. Well, it sure as hell looked like a fortune teller's place—dim lighting, incense, a lot of red velvet. There seemed to be other rooms—she probably lived here, too. She led him to the area in the back where there were chairs.

"Sit, please," she said.

Frank sat on the plush chair. She sat across from him on a comfortable cane back chair with pillows.

For about a minute she sat in silence, with her eyes closed. Frank began to feel impatient, the frenetic energy making him antsy, and considered pulling his gun out, getting her to talk the old-fashioned way.

Then she opened her eyes.

"This has been a difficult period in your life. You've had to make difficult decisions. Money is very important to you."

Frank had never believed in psychics to begin with, but this seemed like a total load of crap. Difficult decisions? Money is important? There was nothing specific about it all—her comments could have applied to anybody who walked in the door. Did people really pay her to hear this crap? But he decided to play along, to see where it all was going.

Why the hell not? I can kill her anytime.

"Yes, it's all true," he said.

"Money has caused trouble for you in your life lately. Do you have debts?"

Frank thought about the bookies who wanted to kill him. But who didn't have debt? Everybody in Gotham owed something to somebody.

"Some," Frank said.

"You need to resolve this," Belladonna said. "It's causing stress for you. Also, you're deceiving someone, someone who has trust in you. This is causing you great anxiety."

Frank's thoughts went right to Tommy Wayne.

Okay, this was getting a little freaky.

"Who is it?" he said, deciding to test her.

"Someone you've known a long time. You're working on a project together. Are you a salesman?"

"No," Frank said.

"You're selling something for him, or selling yourself to him. I definitely see you selling, but you're not being straightforward with him. You're not giving him the best deal."

"What does this have to do with anything?"

"This man is in danger," she said, and her voice became agitated. "His wife is in danger, too. Do they have a child?"

Frank thought of Tommy's kid, Bruce.

"Yes," Frank said. The back of his neck started to itch.

"He's a strong boy. He's a fighter... but I see a lot of blood, destruction."

Okay, that was getting way off base again. Bruce Wayne? The kid was a pampered loser. What did he have to do with anything?

Finally, Frank had had enough.

"Do you see anything in my future about winding up rich," he asked, "and living on the proceeds of a stolen Picasso?" Abruptly he saw the fear in her eyes—the same fear he'd seen in the eyes of his other victims.

He took out his gun and aimed it at her face.

"Okay," he said, "where is it?"

"Where is what?" she asked.

"I'm warning you, I'm not in a game-playing mood," he said. "So there won't be any counting to ten, or second and third chances. Tell me where it is now, or I kill you and find it myself."

She stared at him, but not the way she had when he was reading his mind.

"It's worthless to you," she said. "Only I have the contacts needed to sell it." She sounded pretty sure of herself, too.

It was true, Frank had no idea how he'd sell a painting worth tens of millions of dollars, but he figured he'd worry about that later.

"I'm sorry," Frank said. "Well, not really."

"Wait!" she shouted, holding up one hand. Then she said, "Okay, I'll give you the painting."

"Where is it?" Frank asked.

"I'll show you." She stood, steady despite her age, gesturing for him to follow. He kept the gun aimed steadily at her, and followed her down a hallway into a dark room. Frank could barely see her, and didn't like this.

"Wait, hold on a minute," he said tersely. "Where are we going?"

"The painting's in here."

"Where's the light?"

A gun fired, then Frank felt the pain, ripping through his left shoulder. He fired back a few times. He didn't know if he hit her or not. Then she shot at him again, missing, and he saw her face in the flash.

His eyes were adjusting to the dim light, and he saw her ready to shoot at him again. He fired twice—both times hitting her in the center of the chest. When she hit the floor, he went over, wincing in pain. She was still squirming, making gurgling noises as she tried to speak. So he put one in her head, just to make sure she was a goner.

"Bet you didn't predict that," he said.

Looking around, he found a light switch and flicked it on. The pain in his shoulder was bad, but it was nothing compared to what she'd got. The bullet had grazed him, and there wasn't even much blood.

He seemed to be in a storage area—boxes of stuff against the walls. It was musty, and didn't seem like the place somebody would store anything valuable. He looked around anyway, and found a box of old books, then another one with dishes in it. It seemed like somebody had moved out of a house or an apartment and stored their stuff here.

He checked the other rooms. There was a kitchen, with dishes piled up on the sink, a bathroom, a living room with at least ten floor lamps, and random appliances in the corners—a toaster oven, a couple of microwaves, three blenders. Belladonna seemed more like a hoarder than an art dealer, and he had no idea where she'd kept the painting. He regretted that last shot, finishing her off with the bullet to the head. He should have tortured her a little, gotten her to talk.

Frank rechecked the rooms and found *nada*. Then, in the storage room, he moved the boxes around, to see if she'd hidden the painting there, but there was so much dust and cobwebs on the boxes, he quickly realized it was a dead end.

Then he had a thought and returned to the area where Belladonna had done the psychic reading.

Behind the chair where he'd been sitting there was a small alcove, hidden in the shadows. A ladder, like the kind on old bookcases, led to a loft-like area. Frank climbed up it and, sure enough, there was a painting in the corner, leaning up against the wall. Still in the frame, it had been covered with what looked like saran wrap, but didn't have any other protection. These guys were amateurs, not professional art thieves. That was for damn sure.

He moved it gingerly over next to the top of the ladder, wincing a little as his shoulder complained. As

Frank climbed down the ladder, reaching up to bring the painting with him, the excitement kicked in.

This was it. The beginning of the rest of his life. He had the painting—that had been the biggest obstacle. Now he just had to find a buyer, deposit the money in an offshore account, and he'd be able to get on with his life. What would it be like to have no worries?

Maybe he didn't want to be a hit man, or a mob boss. Why deal with all of the crap? During the day he'd just lie around in a hammock, with the waves crashing nearby, and he'd read books. He hadn't read a book in years, but he'd start. At night he'd drink and gamble and have sex with beautiful women. And that would be it.

No more pain in his life—just pleasure.

Then, when he reached the bottom of the ladder, he heard a noise. Footsteps. Somebody, or maybe more than one person, had entered the apartment.

Well, whatever. Frank had come this far, there was no way he would let anyone or anything prevent him from making his dream come true. He put down the Picasso and took out his gun. He stood with his back against the wall near the door, and waited.

The footsteps came closer... then the noise stopped.

"No... no..." It was a man's voice. By the sound of it, Frank figured the guy was probably in the storage room, and had discovered Belladonna's body.

Okay, enough of his crap, he thought.

He approached the room, gun aimed. Figured he'd blow this guy away, just like the others, then make some phone calls. He didn't know any art buyers, *per se*, but he had a lot of friends in low places, and it couldn't be that hard. Or maybe he could just head abroad, get the hell out of Dodge. Tommy Wayne had mentioned a big black market for art in Russia and North Africa.

Yeah, he'd start in Russia, get a quick deal, and then it would be hello happily ever after. But first things first—he had to get rid of this guy.

The storage room was dark again. Whoever had entered had turned off the light. As Frank's eyes adjusted, he still couldn't see much. Then, squinting, he saw a flash of what looked like polished metal, and then incredible pain hit.

He screamed maybe louder than he had since he was a baby. The pain emanated from his right shoulder, or where his right shoulder used to be. His entire right arm was gone, blood gushing like from a faucet. He crumpled to his knees—in shock, too, trying to figure out what had happened. Then the light flicked on and he saw the burly, bearded man towering over him, holding a meat cleaver.

Careless, he thought. *I got goddamned careless.*

"You killed my aunt, you son of a bitch," the man growled. "Who are you?" Frank tried to speak, but he was in so much agony he couldn't focus on his thoughts, or get his mouth to move the right way to produce words.

"Okay," the man said. "I see how it is."

He came down with the cleaver again and severed through Frank's left shoulder. More blood spattered and gushed. It seemed like the whole world had turned bright red.

"Who are you?"

Despite the pain and how dazed and weak he felt, he managed to gasp, "F-f-f-frank."

"Why are you here?"

Frank tried to answer, but couldn't. The man swung the cleaver again and off went Frank's left leg. Though the pain was excruciating, Frank didn't have the energy even to moan. He lay in a sticky puddle of red.

"Did somebody hire you?" the man asked.

Somehow Frank nodded.

"Who?"

Frank couldn't focus, then he saw the flash of the cleaver.

He was just a stump now, would be dead within seconds.

"Tell me who sent you here, and I'll let you live. Was it Thomas Wayne?"

If Frank had been thinking clearly, not in a delirious state, he would have realized that his reason to live had expired, and he had no reason to give the man any information.

But Frank nodded.

"I don't keep my promises," the man said.

Frank saw the cleaver coming down, right toward his neck.

The last images he had—the beach, a hammock, a drink with an umbrella in it.

The waves were crashing.

TWENTY-THREE

Harvey and Amanda arrived at Belladonna's and saw that the blue door, with graffiti all over it, was partway open.

"Looks like somebody might've beaten us to the punch," Harvey said.

With guns drawn, they entered the gloom, and instantly smelled something strange. They separated, checking out every part of the apartment or office or whatever the hell it was. Then Harvey entered a dark room and picked up on the stench of blood and feces. He took another step and *boom*—he slipped and fell right on his ass.

"What the hell?" he said, though it didn't take him long to figure out that he was in a puddle of blood. But whose? There didn't seem to be a body here, just a bunch of lumps of something, so how could there be so much blood?

Amanda rushed in. "Are you okay?"

"Yeah, fine." Harvey was embarrassed as hell,

trying not to show it. She fumbled around, then turned on the light. Suddenly Harvey was staring at a man's head, on its side in the puddle. He saw limbs, too, and the rest of his body.

Usually he had a thick skin when it came to gore, but everybody's got a limit. Harvey swung to one side and heaved. Then, again, and again. When it was finally over he tried to stand. After slipping and falling back down once or twice, he managed to get to his feet and back away from the mess.

"Are you sure you're okay?" Amanda asked. She didn't sound sarcastic. She sounded concerned.

"Yeah, fine," Harvey said. "Must have food poisoning. I knew something was wrong with that sausage I had for breakfast."

Okay, lame excuse, but he had to try to save face somehow. Looking around, he spotted a second body. An old broad with holes in her chest and a sizeable amount of her head blown away.

Amanda pulled out her cell phone and called in the homicide. Then, standing at the edge of the blood puddle, she craned over, looking at the decapitated head.

"Recognize him?" she asked.

Harvey didn't get how she was so unfazed about this. Maybe the most gruesome crime scene he had ever seen, and she was acting like it was another day at the office. Struggling not to throw up again, he took a closer look at the head.

Oh, crap. Then he said, "Can't be."

"Can't be who?" Amanda asked.

"Oh, man, it *is* him," Harvey said. "Frank Collins. A GCPD Detective back in the day. Worked as a PI for the past I don't know how many years."

"What would he have to do with a stolen painting?"

"No idea," he admitted. "I guess it's possible somebody hired him to look for it."

"Thomas Wayne?" Amanda asked.

"Possibly," Harvey said.

"And what about the other vic?" Amanda asked.

Harvey had been so distracted by the dismembered body, that he hadn't taken a good look at the body of the woman, lying further in the room. She was a mess, but at least she wasn't in six pieces.

"I don't get it," he said. "Why does the killer chop up one vic, but not the other?"

"Maybe he was angrier at one than he was at the other?" Amanda said.

"Or maybe there were two killers," Harvey said. "Or, I know—Frank killed the lady, I guess she must be Belladonna, and then another one killed Frank. Probably a guy, given the condition of the body."

Amanda shot him a look as if asking, *How can you be so sexist?* Harvey ignored it.

"But why would Frank kill her?" Amanda asked. "You said he was ex GCPD, became a PI. Why would he go around killing people?"

That had him stumped. Harvey didn't know Frank all that well—at the GCPD Frank had been ahead of Harvey's time, and they'd just crossed paths on a couple of cases after Frank became a PI. That Frank would murder somebody made no sense at all. He'd spent his life solving crimes, not committing them.

"Maybe the killer was trying to set Frank up," Harvey said.

"Why would the killer think that would work?"

"Most criminals are stupid," Harvey said.

"I think there are things going on here that we haven't figured out yet," Amanda said. "Like who was the guy in the zombie mask?"

"Well, it wasn't Frank Collins, I'll tell you that much," Harvey said.

"I don't think we can rule anything out."

"If you're saying you think Collins was part of the crew that robbed Wayne Manor, you're barking up the wrong tree," Harvey said. "Those guys were... are, whatever... career criminals. Two of them knew each other from Blackgate. Why would Frank toss away his whole career to work with a bunch of losers?"

"I agree, it doesn't make much sense," Amanda said, "but the facts remain—he came here for a reason, and now he's dead."

Harvey looked at Frank's eerie eyes again, and then he had to glance away again.

"Man," Harvey said, wincing. "I hate this feeling."

"If you need a mint I've got one in the car," Amanda said.

"Not *that* feeling," Harvey said. "The feeling that we're always two steps behind." Suddenly he saw a look on her face, as her eyes went wide. "What is it?"

"What weapon do you think the killer used?"

"Well, for the lady, my guess is a gun," he said. "For Frank, hmm, that's hard to say. If it was a knife, it was a sharp one."

"Remember how the walls in Thomas Wayne's study had been chopped up?"

"It was only a couple days ago," Harvey said sarcastically. "I've been known to black out, but my memory's not *that* bad." He saw where she was going.

"Thomas Wayne said the guy with the zombie mask had a meat cleaver," Amanda said.

"Good thinking," Harvey said. He looked again at the body parts. "So I guess we're looking for a zombie with a meat cleaver. Great. Just great."

"Basically, yeah," Amanda said.

Harvey looked at Frank's head, with the wide-open eyes that seemed to be staring right at him, and he couldn't hold back. He threw up again.

He went into the bathroom, washed up, and gargled. It helped… a little. Then he rejoined Amanda.

"Hey, about what just happened here—"

"I won't tell anyone, I promise."

He believed her.

"Thanks," Harvey said. He had to admit it—as a partner, she was starting to grow on him. She kicked ass, was tough as hell, and could keep secrets. That was a big trifecta.

There was noise at the front of the apartment, and the forensics crew arrived, along with a couple of uniforms. They did their thing, taking prints and collecting evidence from the scene. It became too crowded in the small space, and to Harvey's relief, he and Amanda retreated outside.

Later, they were back in the car, driving. The Gotham traffic was stop-and-go, with more stopping than going. There had to be an accident or something up ahead.

Harvey was absorbed in his thoughts, thinking about the friends and colleagues he'd lost over the years, and how it seemed like it was only a matter of time until his number came up.

"What's wrong?" Amanda asked.

"Huh?" Harvey asked. He'd heard her, but he was startled.

"You're not talking," Amanda said. "That means something's wrong."

"You're getting to know me too well," Harvey said.

"So what is it?" she asked. "You thinking about the zombie? What's going on?"

Harvey usually didn't like talking about his feelings. Whenever women asked him how he felt, he always clammed up, or changed the subject. He wasn't trying to be a jerk—if he knew how he felt he would've gladly told them—but most of the time he had no idea how he felt. That was how he got through life in Gotham and stayed sane. In Gotham, if you were aware of every feeling you had, felt the pain of every death, these were surefire ways to wind up in Arkham. In this town, denial was king.

"Guess I'm just thinking about things I shouldn't be thinking about," he said.

"What kind of things?" Amanda asked.

"You'd make a good shrink," Harvey said. The only worse thing than having to talk about your feelings was having to talk about your feelings to a shrink.

"That's what all my friends say."

"I don't know what surprises me more," Harvey said smirking, "that you have friends, or that you consider me a friend."

Amanda smiled.

"All right, if you really wanna know, I was thinking about that poor guy who got killed."

"Officer Warren?"

"No, but that sucked, too."

"Frank Collins?" Amanda asked.

"No," Harvey said, "Collins obviously somehow got too deep in his own dung, and paid the price for it. I mean the guy who worked at the motel, Louie DePino. He had a daughter—loved her, talked about her all the time. If a man gets killed, that stinks. If a man with a kid gets killed, that's tragedy."

"You ever think about having a kid yourself?" Amanda asked.

Back to acting like a shrink, but Harvey didn't mind.

"A kid deserves a better father than me," Harvey said.

"I think you're selling yourself short."

About ten seconds went by.

"How about you?" Harvey said. "I don't see you pumping out rug rats anytime soon."

"Why do you say that?"

"Well, you told me you don't have time for a relationship. If you don't have time to take care of a guy, how are you gonna take care of a kid?"

"Who said anything about a guy? I just need somebody with good genes to pass along."

"You mean like a test tube baby?" Harvey asked.

"No, but I'll get a sperm donor," she said. "A friend or someone to, you know, do the deed. Somebody who's strong, and sincere. That's a big thing for me—sincerity."

Harvey laughed. "So what're you gonna do? Hold interviews?"

"When I'm ready, I'll find the right guy." Amanda was serious, looking straight ahead, not at Harvey.

"Okay, so then what're you gonna do?" Harvey asked. "Quit the force?"

"I know how to walk and chew gum," Amanda said. "I'll take my maternity leave, then return to work. I see myself always being a cop. Actually, I want to be running the department someday."

"Great, then you'll be my boss."

"Unless you get there before me."

"Me? I have no interest in running anything," Harvey said. "I hate power."

"Have you told Lacey White that?"

"Nice one," Harvey said without smiling.

"I'm just busting your chops," Amanda said. "You don't like to be on the other end of a joke, do you?"

Harvey thought about it. "Does anybody?"

The cops must've cleared the accident up ahead and the traffic picked up.

A few minutes later Harvey got a call from headquarters. Forensics got a match on the print from the murder scene at Belladonna's place. The print belonged to a low level two-time loser thug named Nikos Petrakos.

"Looks like we found our zombie," Amanda said.

Putting on the siren, pumped for revenge, Harvey said, "Let's go nail this bastard."

TWENTY-FOUR

On Monday morning, Alfred dropped Bruce off at Anders Preparatory Academy for his first day back at school since the family trip to Switzerland.

"I'll be here to get you at three sharp," he told the boy, "and we'll go right to your tennis lesson."

"Right, how can I forget?" Bruce said. He wore his school uniform of dark pants, white shirt, tie, and jacket.

"Come on, tennis isn't so bad, mate. Maybe you'll be gracing the lawns at Wimbledon someday."

"I don't think tennis is my calling, Alfred."

"Okay, Wimbledon aside, everything doesn't have to be your calling. But, I reckon, there are things you can call your endeavors that may help you later in life. In tennis, for instance, you'll learn the importance of strategy, patience, planning, and you need to be quick on your feet."

But Bruce wasn't having any of it.

"I'd rather learn how to fight," he said, unwilling to give it up.

"Well, you have a great day, mate," Alfred said.

"You, too, Alfred." With that he headed along the pathway through the lush grounds, his book bag hanging over his shoulder. He passed fellow students—some from his classes, some from other grades. He acknowledged the kids he knew with a polite "hello" or a smile. In school he had many acquaintances whom he shared lunch with in the cafeteria, competed with during gym class, or worked with on science, math, and engineering projects, but he didn't have any close friendships.

It had always been that way for him—well, since kindergarten. He liked most kids, and most kids liked him, but when he wasn't in school, he preferred to spend most of his time alone, or with his parents and Alfred.

Some kids didn't like Bruce at all, and for no reason he could discern, they made nasty comments. Perhaps they resented him because he was the son of a famous billionaire, or they misunderstood his desire to spend time alone, and thought he was too uppity or aloof. He knew he wasn't imagining it, because he'd discovered some people talking about him behind his back.

He never quite knew what to do about it, however. When people were mean, he never felt upset or hurt. If anything, he felt sorry for them. He imagined that it must be an awful way to go through life, having to deal with so much anger.

There were two kids who seemed to have it in for Bruce—had since last year. Jake Wheeler and Andrew

Thompson. Jake was probably the most popular boy in the whole school. He was the star of the football, wrestling, and hockey teams, and had always exhibited the bravado that came with competition.

Andrew used to be a nice kid. In elementary school he and Bruce had played in the schoolyard together, and they always laughed and had a good time. Then, as Andrew got older and taller, all the girls thought he was good-looking and the popularity went straight to his head. He stopped hanging out with Bruce and his other friends, and became Jake's sidekick. Bruce didn't know what was going on with Andrew's life, but he figured that he had to feel pretty insecure in order to give up his entire identity to impress somebody else.

He approached the two of them, sitting on a wall, and Bruce saw Jake whisper something into Andrew's ear. Andrew looked at Bruce and smiled, but not in a friendly way. The smile reminded Bruce of the way that boy at the circus had smiled after bumping into his father. The smile reflected a hidden agenda. It seemed sinister.

Jake and Andrew got up and stood in front of Bruce, forcing him to stop walking.

"Hey, Bruce Wayne," Jake said harshly. "Where have *you* been?"

As always, Bruce didn't feel any fear or intimidation. He looked right into Jake's eyes.

"On a family vacation in Switzerland."

"A family vacation in the middle of the semester," Jake said. "Wow, I wish I was living your life. Well, not really, but…"

Jake laughed, and Andrew laughed with him, but it seemed to Bruce that Andrew didn't really want to laugh. He was just trying to get Jake's approval. It was rather pathetic.

"Seriously," Jake said. "I mean you get escorted to school every day by your butler, when all of the rest of us mere mortals have to take a school bus… So how do you get to take this time off school? Is it because your father pays them millions of dollars?"

"My father hasn't donated money to the school," Bruce said. "My family pays the tuition that everyone else pays."

"But you don't have to do the work that everyone else does," Jake persisted.

"I do the same work as everyone else," Bruce said. "When we're travelling, I'm home schooled."

"Ooh, home schooled in Switzerland," Jake said. "That sounds so fancy. So who home schools you? Does the richest kid in Gotham have a private tutor?"

"No, my mother tutors me," Bruce said.

"His mommy tutors him," Jake said mockingly to Andrew. "Does she still stick a pacifier in your mouth, and sing lullabies to you, too? Wait, maybe she still breast-feeds you. That would explain a lot."

Andrew laughed again. Could he really think Jake was funny?

"How is your mother anyway?" Jake asked Bruce. "Still hanging out at the hardware store?"

Bruce didn't respond.

"You know, the hardware store," Jake said. "I heard she charges a nickel a screw."

Jake and Andrew laughed, louder than before.

"I know what you're trying to do," Bruce said, remaining stone-faced, "and it won't work."

"Yeah?" Jake said. "I have to hear this. What am I *trying* to do?"

"You're trying to illicit a response from me," Bruce said. "You want me to say something like, 'Don't talk about my mother.' Or you'd probably prefer it if I just hit you, threw the first punch. Then we could get into it a fight and you wouldn't have to risk suspension. But the question you have to ask yourself is why you want to fight me?"

Bruce wondered if this was a mistake, challenging the kids, but couldn't stop himself.

"What do you get out of it? Does it make you feel more secure? Is that the real problem here, your insecurity? And not just you." He looked at Andrew. "In a way, you're worse than he is, because you don't think for yourself, you just go along with whatever Jake wants you to do. What a sad, powerless way to live your life. So no, I won't give you the satisfaction of responding to the insult about my mother, if that's what you're expecting. Now please, step aside. I need to get to my class on time."

Jake seemed a little confused, or maybe weakened, but then he sneered, trying to act like a tough guy again.

"What if we don't step aside?" he challenged.

"What're you gonna do about it, Billionaire's Son?"

Bruce didn't know *what* he'd do about it—that was the problem. Jake was a wrestler, was about six inches taller than him, and probably fifty pounds heavier. Most of his weight was muscle. Bruce would be lucky if he got a single punch in, and it probably wouldn't do much damage. Andrew wasn't quite as big as Jake, but still he was much bigger than Bruce. In a fight against both of them Bruce wouldn't stand a chance.

Then Mr. Sterling, the dean at the school, approached.

"What's going on here?"

Jake's expression changed—he seemed panicked.

"Oh, nothing, Mr. Sterling," Jake said. "We're just having a conversation, that's all. Right, Andrew?"

"Yeah," Andrew agreed. "Just a conversation."

"Such a follower," Bruce muttered, almost inaudibly.

"What did you say?" Mr. Sterling asked.

"Nothing," Bruce lied. "I didn't say anything."

Mr. Sterling looked back and forth—at the other kids, and at Bruce.

"Were they threatening you?" he asked Bruce.

Jake glared at Bruce as if to say, *"You better not squeal on us, or else."*

"No," Bruce said, maintaining eye contact with the other boy. "Not at all." He didn't stay silent out of fear—in fact, it was just the opposite. He wanted to show Jake and Andrew that they couldn't intimidate him, and if he needed to defend himself he could do it on his own, without a teacher's intervention.

"All right, let's get to class, boys," Mr. Sterling said. "First period's about to start."

Bruce had a feeling that he hadn't heard the last from Jake and Andrew—well, Jake in particular—but he didn't expect to have another confrontation so soon.

In English class the teacher, Mrs. Adams, had been impressed with Bruce's interpretation of Grendel in *Beowulf*. Bruce had entitled the paper, "Grendel and Our Endless Fascination With Monsters." After the class, he headed to the cafeteria for lunch. Alfred had prepared a roast beef sandwich with mustard and pickles, one of Bruce's favorites.

He was eating alone while double-checking the math homework that he would hand in next period, when he noticed Mr. Watson, the teacher in charge of supervising the cafeteria, talking on his cell phone.

"Okay, I'll be right there," he said into the phone, and then he left the cafeteria. As Mr. Watson exited, Jake and Andrew entered. Was this planned? Had Jake and Andrew prank-called some "emergency" for Mr. Watson to address, in order to get him out of the way? It sure seemed like it.

Jake looked around, then zeroed in on Bruce, eyeing him in a menacing way. He expected them to approach and challenge him to a fight, but instead they kept walking, stopping at the table where Dennis Riley was seated with some other kids.

Dennis was an easy target—a short, slender boy,

who looked much younger than fourteen. He could've passed for ten or eleven. He was also the smartest kid in the entire grade. Bruce had worked with him on a few projects, and they had always gotten along well.

From where Bruce was sitting, he couldn't make out what Jake was saying to Dennis, but from the larger boy's mannerisms he could tell that Jake was bullying him. Dennis seemed scared, and then Bruce could read his lips as he said, *"C'mon just leave me alone."*

But Jake didn't leave him alone—he kept challenging him, and then he spat on Dennis's sandwich and laughed. Of course Andrew laughed as well. So did several kids who had begun to gather round.

Jake was doing what bullies always did. They picked on the easiest target, so they could feel strong and powerful. But Bruce also knew this really had nothing to do with Dennis. Jack was putting on a show—for the kids in the cafeteria who were laughing and cheering him on, but mainly for Bruce. Jake knew that Bruce liked Dennis, and by picking on Dennis it would instigate some sort of response.

It worked.

Jake slapped Dennis's head, and Dennis screeched, "Owww!"

Bruce jumped up, rushed over, and with strength he didn't know he had he grabbed Jake by his muscular shoulder and pulled him away from his friend.

"Leave him alone," Bruce said.

While Jake's ulterior motive all along had been to lure Bruce into a fight, he still seemed surprised by the ease with which Bruce had separated him from his target. Instantly most of the kids in the cafeteria surrounded them. Some were shouting, egging Jake on.

"You gonna take that, Jake?" someone yelled.

Others began chanting, "Fight, fight, fight..."

"Look who it is," Jake said, "the billionaire's son."

"Why don't you just go away," Bruce said, "and stop acting like a jerk."

A bunch of kids said, "Oooooh."

"What if I don't want to walk away?" Jake said, trying to maintain his coolness and toughness. "What're you gonna do about it?"

"Then I'm going to fight you," Bruce said.

The oooohs got even louder, and some kids laughed.

Jake laughed, too. "I think that's the funniest thing I've heard all week," he said. "Billionaire boy Bruce Wayne says he's going to fight me."

"Ha," Andrew said. "Good luck with that."

"Why do you hang out with this jerk anyway?" Bruce said to Andrew. "You used to be a decent kid. We had a great time. Remember that sleepover at my house? We watched movies and told ghost stories and made popcorn. Went outside and watched the bats chasing insects. I'm sure you still have some goodness inside you. You don't need to spend your time following around an idiot like him."

At that Jake shoved Bruce, hard, causing him to stumble, almost knocking him down.

"Fight, fight, fight..."

"I think I've heard enough of you, Wayne," Jake said. "It's time for a beating."

Quickly Bruce raised his fists, like the boxers did, to try to protect his face, but Jake connected with a punch right below Bruce's right eye. It sounded like two rocks smashing together, and hurt like hell, but Bruce maintained his ground. He knew he didn't have the strength nor the ability to beat Jake in a fight, but he wasn't going to fall down.

A lot of the kids chanted and cheered, while others remained silent. No one turned away, however. Bruce didn't hope that Mr. Watson or another teacher came to break up the fight. He didn't want to be saved—he wanted to get out of this on his own.

"Is that the best you can do?" Bruce asked, tasting warm blood dripping over his lips. Again he raised his fists.

Jake gritted his teeth and unleashed another punch, this one more powerful than the last, hitting Bruce in the jaw. Once again, Bruce accepted the pain, but didn't give in to it. He felt dizzy, though, and while he didn't want to back down, he was afraid that if he took any more blows like that he would get knocked out.

All of the kids were shouting.

Jake had his fist cocked.

Then Bruce remembered Alfred telling him a story of when he was a teenager, growing up in London's East End. One night two guys had confronted him in an alleyway and attempted to mug him. Rather than fight both guys—which would have, as he had said "led to a surefire defeat"—instead he decided to focus on the weaker opponent.

"If you can't win the war, at least win the battle," Alfred had said. So, rather than focusing on how to absorb the next blow from Jake, Bruce turned his attention to Andrew, who was still standing alongside the bigger boy.

Yes, it was true that Andrew hadn't hit Bruce himself. However, he was complicit by supporting Jake while he was bullying Dennis. So without guilt Bruce charged at Andrew and tackled him like a football player, then began to pummel him in his face as hard as he could. He knew he was doing the right thing—giving Andrew some justice, some payback. Maybe in the future Andrew would make better decisions, better alliances for himself.

Suddenly everyone was cheering for Bruce.

"Hit him! Hit him!"

Bruce expected Jake to come to his friend's defense, but the big kid just stood to the side, watching, while Andrew screeched in pain. Maybe Jake had been caught off guard, and didn't know how to react, but Bruce suspected that it was Jake's true self coming out. Again Bruce heard Alfred's voice in his head.

"Bullies are often the biggest cowards."

Alfred hadn't, however, warned him about how much it would hurt his hands to punch somebody in the face. He'd never been in an actual fight before, but in movies, when people had fistfights in bars or wherever, they never seemed to hurt their hands.

Bruce figured he must be doing something wrong, or he needed gloves or some sort of protection, because with each crunching punch it felt like the bones in his hands were breaking.

"Okay, that's enough, *that's enough*."

Mr. Watson finally showed up to break up the fighting. He separated Bruce and Andrew. Bruce was happy and, yes, a little proud to see the blood gushing from Andrew's nose.

"Bruce started it," Jake said. "He just came out of nowhere and attacked Andrew."

Bruce didn't deny it, since this was technically true, nor did he try to place the blame on Jake. Mr. Watson would be well aware of Jake's prior bullying behavior, as he witnessed it frequently in the cafeteria. Then, when he consulted with Dean Sterling, they'd be able to connect the dots.

Meanwhile, Bruce was prepared to accept the consequences for his role in the conflict.

He, Andrew, and Jake were hustled off to the nurse's office. Jake was barely injured—just some scratches on his knuckles. Bruce's injuries required an ice pack, antibiotic ointment, and bandages. Andrew had gotten the worst of it—a possible broken nose, and both eyes were black and blue. Bruce hadn't realized he'd hit him so hard. He found it disquieting, but he still felt justified in what he'd done.

Dean Sterling called for each of the boys separately. When it was Bruce's turn, he entered the room and spoke before the dean could do so.

"I'm ready to accept whatever punishment you deem appropriate."

"Sit down, Mr. Wayne."

Bruce sat. "You don't have to call me Mr. Wayne. Bruce is fine."

"Why does it concern you?" Dean Sterling asked, sounding curious.

"Because I don't want any special treatment, just because I'm Thomas and Martha Wayne's son, and I was lucky enough to be born into fortunate circumstances."

Sterling maintained a serious glare.

"I assure you, you will *not* receive any preferential treatment from me, Mr... Bruce." He went on to explain that while he was very well aware who started the fight, and who has been causing trouble at Anders for a long time, that didn't abrogate the fact that Bruce had participated in the conflict.

"Fighting at Anders is prohibited under all circumstances," Sterling said, "and the punishment for a first offense is a one week suspension from school. Your family has already been notified, and your butler is on his way over here to pick you up."

"I understand," Bruce said. "If I were in your position, I'd do the same thing. I respect your decision, Dean Sterling."

"You don't seem very upset by any of this, Bruce, and I have to say, that's very concerning."

"I don't mean to concern you, sir."

Dean Sterling took a moment, then said, "I fear that,

if you were in the same situation again, you wouldn't do the right thing and notify me or a teacher that an altercation was taking place. I fear that you'd make the same decision you made today, and you'd get into a fight."

"Yes, I would choose to fight," Bruce admitted.

"Even though I just reminded you that fighting is against the rules of Anders Preparatory Academy?" Dean Sterling frowned.

"Those are Anders' rules," Bruce said, "not my rules."

"But as a student here, you must abide by the rules of the school."

"I'm afraid I can't promise that."

Sterling let out a deep breath. "And why can't you?"

"Because, while violence should always be a last resort, there are situations when violence is necessary, such as self-defense or to help someone in need. And if I find myself in one of those situations again, I'll make the same decision that I made today."

Sterling shook his head in frustration. "I'm extremely disappointed in you, Bruce," he said. "I hope you reconsider your attitude during your suspension. You're dismissed… Mr. Wayne."

Bruce was waiting with his backpack slung over one shoulder when Alfred pulled up in the Bentley. He got in the back seat and, without a word, they drove away. When they left the school grounds, Bruce saw Alfred's eyes looking up at him in the rear-view mirror.

"I don't think your mother will be pleased, Master Bruce."

Bruce had been expecting to receive his mother's wrath. Actually, he couldn't imagine anything that would upset her more than learning that he had been suspended for fighting at school.

"You're right, she won't be," Bruce acknowledged. "But I did what you told me to do."

"What was that, Master Bruce?"

"The story you once told me, about when you were a teenager in London. How when those two guys confronted you in the alley, you attacked the weaker one."

"I told you that?" Alfred sounded alarmed.

"Yes, you told me to win the battle, if you can't win the war."

"Ah, I think I remember telling you something about that now, didn't I? Guess I didn't expect you to take my words so literally, and apply them to a lunchroom brawl." Another pause, then Alfred said, "The boy you fought with. Is he in worse shape than you?"

"Yes," Bruce said. "I think I might've broken his nose." He didn't mention Jake.

Alfred didn't say anything for several moments, and Bruce thought a scolding might come.

But then he looked in the rear-view again and, maintaining the same deadpan expression, said, "Well done, mate. Well done."

TWENTY-FIVE

On Monday morning, Thomas tried several times but still couldn't reach Frank. Something was definitely off. It wasn't like him to just go off the grid like this—he was always punctual, almost obsessively so, with his updates. In more than twenty years of working together nothing like this had ever happened.

Was Frank okay? Had he been in an accident, or worse? Had he stumbled onto something, perhaps something involving Hugo Strange?

Wearing a well-tailored suit, Thomas came to the dining room where Martha was having her coffee, reading a novel—the same one she'd been reading lately, *Ethan Frome*.

"Good morning," he said, and he went over and kissed her.

"Oh, good morning," she said without looking up from the novel. "You came to bed late last night. You must be exhausted."

"Yes, I was working," Thomas said. "We have a

number of important meetings this week, as well as clients coming in from out of town." He looked around. "Is there more coffee?"

"Yes, I just made a fresh pot."

"Terrific." Thomas poured himself a cup.

"I woke up in the middle of the night, and saw you sleeping next to me," Martha said.

"Okay." Thomas didn't know where she was going with this.

"Your hair smelled of cigar smoke."

"Oh, right, I did smoke one while I was working last night."

"It's odd, though." Now Martha looked up from the book. "Sometimes *you* smell of cigars, but your office rarely does. It didn't this morning."

Instantly he was wary, but didn't want to show it.

"I open the windows when I smoke," he said. "For ventilation."

This made sense, didn't it?

"But cigar smoke is such a prominent odor," she persisted. "There was no hint of it in the room, and yet it was plain on you. Even with ventilation, there would be at least a faint odor in there."

"I, um, don't know what to say," he replied, and then he took a big gulp of coffee. "I should get to the office."

He retreated, but somehow knew he had lost that one.

* * *

Thomas drove to Wayne Tower, the Gotham home of Wayne Enterprises. He parked in his spot in the lot and then headed up the elevator to his offices on the fifty-eighth floor, the top floor of the building. Most people he passed said, "Good morning, Mr. Wayne," and he said "Good morning," back.

He used to love coming to work, especially on a Monday morning. It used to make him feel energized, hopeful, excited, but over the past few years—the past few months especially—the energy had changed. There was palpable tension and some employees, in particular certain board members, avoided him. This was due to the internal struggle over the direction of the company… and some felt it was time for Thomas to step down and hand over the reins.

After receiving an update from his assistant on various activities and negotiations, Thomas met with Lucius Fox, his most trusted employee—as well as one of his best friends. They began, as usual, with small talk, then the conversation turned serious.

"Did you have a chance to look into the security situation at Wayne Manor?" Thomas asked.

"I don't have a full report yet, but we're working on it," Lucius said. "At first glance, there doesn't seem to have been an external breach."

"'Seem' is a nebulous word," Thomas said. "Things aren't always as they seem."

"Well, let's just say that if indeed a breach took place, in all likelihood the source was internal—either at the house, or here at the offices," Lucius said.

Thomas shook his head in frustration.

"Any idea who?"

"The list would be too long to even speculate on," Lucius said. "It wouldn't have been easy to avoid detection, but any member of the board *could* have gotten into the system, if they had been hell bent on doing so."

Could Strange have somehow worked in collusion with a rogue board member?

"We have to make sure this never happens again," Thomas said. "It's more than my safety, or the security of my possessions. The safety of my wife and son is at stake."

"We have our top tech people working on the issue as we speak," Lucius said. "They're under orders to let me know as soon as they find something." He sounded certain, yet another thought occurred to Thomas.

"How do we know one of the tech people isn't corrupt?"

"We don't," Lucius admitted, "but what can we do, aside from requiring the entire company to submit to lie detector tests?"

"I hear you," Thomas said.

"We have to take this as a major wake-up call," Lucius said, his voice low. "We can't afford to be complacent any longer. Problems don't resolve on their own—they get resolved. This isn't just about a break-in at Wayne Manor. I'm concerned that persons within the company may be vying for power, and increasingly so—not just in Wayne, but within the political sphere. Gotham has become a dark place in which to live and work, socially and economically, and just because we're up here, above it all, doesn't mean we're immune to the repercussions."

Thomas frowned at his words, but didn't have a reply.

Later, when Lucius had left, Thomas tried Frank a couple more times, but still couldn't reach him. Frustrated by the lack of news, Thomas decided that the time for waiting was over.

He hadn't had any direct contact with Hugo Strange since a few weeks after Pinewood had been shut down. On occasion they found themselves at the same social functions, and Thomas scrupulously avoided talking to him. When that failed they had short, perfunctory conversations.

The last time had been at the Gotham Opera House, about three months earlier. Thomas had spotted him in the lobby before the performance, chatting with a woman whom Thomas knew was a major benefactor in the arts world. They made eye contact briefly, and then Thomas had asked Martha if she wanted to go to their seats.

Once there, Thomas glanced around but didn't see Strange seated anywhere. He didn't see him during intermission or after the show either.

He knew that Strange maintained medical offices downtown. He had returned to lecturing at Gotham

University, and practicing as a psychiatrist. From what Thomas had heard from various sources, he had a thriving career. How horrified would his patients be, though, if they knew the truth about their psychiatrist? It had been the source of endless torment for Thomas that he'd had to stay silent about Strange's psychopathy, and allow his colleagues and patients to be duped.

His mind made up, Thomas walked across town to Strange's office building, using the walk to organize what he was going to say, and rode the elevator to the twenty-seventh floor. When he arrived, he told a heavyset woman in a nurse's gown, sitting at the desk, that he needed to speak with Dr. Strange. Instead he was introduced to a heavyset middle-aged woman he didn't recognize.

"I'm Ethel Peabody, the doctor's… assistant," the woman said. "What can I do for you, Mr. Wayne?"

Although they had never met, or at least Thomas couldn't recall meeting her, he wasn't surprised that she recognized him. As a public figure in Gotham, even a local celebrity, he was known to many people he didn't himself recognize.

"You can't do anything for me, I'm afraid, Mrs. Peabody," Thomas said. "My business is with the doctor. Is he here?"

"Yes, but he's extremely busy right now."

"That's all right," Thomas said. "My schedule is flexible today, so I can wait."

"Perhaps you misunderstand." She sounded

irritated. "He won't have any time to speak with you today, but if you can tell me what this is in regard to—"

"I can't tell you anything," Thomas said firmly, "but I'll just sit here and wait for *Hugo* to become less busy. And if I can't speak to him today, I'll come back tomorrow and wait all day, and the day after tomorrow, as well."

Peabody stared at him for a long, silent moment.

"Wait a moment," she said. "I'll see what I can do." While Thomas sat in the waiting area, she went to the back of the office, then returned. A few minutes later, Hugo Strange entered.

Strange appeared much as he had in the Pinewood days. He'd always had an eccentric look—shaved head, a chinstrap beard, and he still wore round, tinted glasses, even when he was indoors. At the time Thomas had accepted it as the look of a quirky genius. With all that had occurred, however, it seemed—at least to Thomas—much more bizarre.

"Thomas Wayne," he said. "What a pleasant surprise."

He still had the same odd style of speaking, as well—talking in a low, almost monotone voice, and over-enunciating random words. He pronounced it "surpriiiiise." Also, there was a hint of ambiguity in his tone—not sarcasm, closer to passive-aggression. As always, it was hard to know what he was really thinking.

"We need to talk," Thomas said without pleasantries.

"I'm detecting a sense of urgency," Strange said. "Interesting. Please, follow me."

Thomas trailed Strange along a stale, fluorescent-lit corridor, and then they entered his office. It was well decorated, and had two exposures providing a spectacular view of Gotham, including the Wayne Tower off to the left. With his medical school diploma on the wall, and standard medical texts on the shelves, Strange's office looked like that of any other upscale psychiatrist. Thomas could understand why his patients trusted him.

Strange shut the door. Then he sat at his desk and motioned toward the guest's chair.

"It always brightens my day to see an old friend," Strange said. "Please, have a seat." But Thomas made no move to do so. Instead, he launched right into it, casting aside the speech he had planned on the way over.

"Were you behind the robbery at Wayne Manor the other night?" he asked.

"Excuse me?" Strange sounded baffled. "Wait, was there a robbery? At your home?"

"You heard me," Thomas said. "A Picasso was stolen Friday night. I think it was a cover."

"A cover?" Strange said. "A cover for what?" Thomas couldn't tell whether he was lying or not. Weren't all psychopaths natural liars? So he decided not to give ground.

"You know what I'm talking about," Thomas said. "You also sent a man to follow me on Saturday. Perhaps you have had people following me for some time."

"Following you? Why would I have someone following you?"

On the absurd chance that he might be speaking the truth, Thomas didn't want to give anything away about Karen Jennings, nor speak about Pinewood, or the experiments. For all he knew, their conversation was being recorded.

In fact, he was certain it was.

"Stop playing games, Strange."

"I'm detecting significant paranoia, and focused aggression," the bearded man replied. "Actually, I find the entire nature of this visit to be quite bizarre. I think it's quite rude, as well. I may have to ask you to leave, Thomas, if your behavior doesn't improve."

"I'm warning you," Thomas said, trying to sound as firm as he could. "I don't know what you're planning, but if you're planning what I *think* you're planning, it's a huge mistake." He paused to gather himself. "I have connections, I can use them if I want to. I'll make sure none of your plans come to fruition, and that you wind up where you belong—in prison."

"Interesting," Strange said. "So angry. And after such a long time. Quite anti-social. I can't think of any explanation for this other than you're having some sort of mental episode. I can't speculate myself on the cause of it, of course. That would be a severe conflict of interest, and quite unethical—you know how I am on ethics, Thomas.

"But if you'd like me to refer you to another psychiatrist, I can provide a name to your office… or your butler. There's an up-and-coming therapist named Leslie Thompkins who I hear is quite good at what she does. She sees private patients occasionally, and I believe she would take you on."

Struck by sudden doubt, Thomas wondered if it was possible that he had been wrong. Perhaps the break-in had nothing to do with Strange. Maybe Strange hadn't been searching for the documents on Pinewood. Maybe it had simply been a robbery by a gang of thieves.

I don't think so.

"I think you're lying," Thomas said. "It's not unexpected. For all I know you're recording this conversation, so why would you want to implicate yourself? There's no way you'd admit to having any connection to the robbery, or to having that man follow me on Saturday."

"Man?" Strange said. "What man?"

"You know who I'm talking about," Thomas shouted.

Then Strange stood. "You have overstayed your welcome, Thomas. You're clearly unstable, having some sort of an episode, and I suggest a full psychiatric screening. Miss Peabody will give you the contact information for Miss Thompkins on your way out. Please don't return again until you're healed."

"Stay away from me and my family, you son of a bitch," Thomas said. "And stay off my property."

He turned to go.

Then he heard Strange laughing.

Thomas wheeled around, livid, and asked, "What's so funny?"

"Humor," Strange said, "the most subjective

emotion. What makes one person laugh can make another cry. So, you're wondering, why did I choose to laugh? Perhaps there are two explanations. First, I remain baffled by your behavior. The bewilderment of others can, at times, be quite entertaining.

"Second, I find it amusing that you think you're in any position to put demands of any kind on me. Oh yes, I'm well aware of the power Wayne Enterprises wields in Gotham. I'm also well aware of my power over you, Thomas. Perhaps you're conveniently forgetting your involvement in the past—in *our* past. Without your financial investment, none of the unfortunate events would have taken place. In fact, an argument could be made that you're more culpable than I am."

"You son of a bitch," Thomas said.

"There, there, I think name calling is a non-productive way of expressing anger," Strange said. "You should work on that."

"I don't submit to blackmail," Thomas said.

"In that case," Strange said, "I'm warning *you*. If I do choose to pursue any creative, experimental medical endeavors in the future, that will be my own prerogative. And if you choose to try to stop me, you will suffer the consequences for your actions. But I don't have to tell you this—I think you're already aware of the dangerous line you're walking."

Staring at his reflection in Strange's tinted glasses—a face in each lens—Thomas wondered how he'd ever called this maniac a friend. Had something happened with Strange, from the first day they'd met till the time he conceived of Pinewood? Or had he always had a maniacal side that he'd kept hidden from Thomas?

"What are you thinking?" Strange asked.

"What happened to you?" Thomas asked. "How did you get this way?"

"Hmm, I wonder," the doctor said. "Are you asking me that question, or are you asking yourself that question? We have a psychological explanation for this phenomenon—it's called projection. I really think some intense psychoanalysis would do wonders for you."

"I think you're the one who's projecting, Hugo," Thomas said, and he left the office.

Several minutes later, walking along the busy street, Gothamites rushing past in both directions, Thomas decided it had been a mistake. He hadn't learned whether or not Strange was involved in the robbery and, worse, now the psychopath knew Thomas was on to him.

Strange was brilliant, crafty, and relentless. These attributes had once made him a great competitor as an athlete, but as a mad scientist he was alarmingly dangerous. One thing had become very clear, though—Strange wasn't going away on his own. If he was hell-bent on restarting a Pinewood-like program he would do it, and the only way Thomas could stop him was to go public. Strange assumed Thomas would never do it, as it could destroy his own reputation.

This is where Strange had gotten it wrong. If it meant saving lives and avoiding another Pinewood, Thomas was willing to do anything to stop him—even if meant turning himself in to the authorities and relinquishing control of Wayne Enterprises.

He tried Frank's cell, but the call went right to voicemail.

"For Christ's sake," Thomas said as he ended the call.

The streets were crowded. To avoid being recognized, he put on dark sunglasses. Still some passersby said, "Good morning, Mr. Wayne," and others acknowledged him with a smile and a nod of the head. He had gone a few blocks when his cell chimed. He checked his phone, hoping it was Frank with some goods, but the display told him otherwise.

Martha

He hit "accept."

"Hello," Thomas said, walking.

"You won't believe it." Martha sounded upset.

Thomas stopped. "What is it?" He wondered, *Has Strange contacted her? Has he threatened her in some way?*

"It's Bruce," Martha said.

No...

"Bruce?" Thomas's panic intensified.

"Yes, it's so awful," Martha said.

Had Strange sent someone to hurt Bruce? If so, Thomas planned to go back into that office building and kill him, strangle the son of a bitch with his bare hands.

"He was in a fight," Martha said.

"A fight? What kind of fight?"

"A fight in school. With two other boys."

Thank god. Just a harmless school fight. Thomas felt the tension lift.

"I knew that boxing would be a bad influence on him," Martha said, "and now look what happened. He gets into a fight, and gets suspended from school for an entire week. I mean, if he wasn't talking about boxing all weekend, reading about it in the papers, watching that fight on television, then he wouldn't have gone to school and gotten himself into trouble. It's awful, just awful."

Actually, it was the best news he'd heard all day, and he was eager to get more details about it from Bruce later on. In the past, Bruce had avoided fighting, often just running away from the bullies. But today, it sounded as if he'd taken a giant leap toward growing up, learning how to stand up for himself.

If Bruce was going to follow in Thomas's footsteps, and run Wayne Enterprises someday, he had to follow the example Thomas had tried to set for him. He had to be strong, resolute, a stoic.

"That's awful," Thomas said, going for an appropriately somber tone, mixed with disappointment. "I'll definitely have to have a talk with him about this when I get home."

"I hope you're serious," Martha said. "I'm just so

angry right now. Bruce is a smart boy, not some... some savage. This has been such an appalling day. I mean, given the news about that man Collins."

"What news?" Thomas said, startled by the sudden shift. "What about Frank?"

"Oh, I thought you saw it in the paper this morning, before you left. It was on the front page."

Thomas's gut tightened.

"What about Frank?" he asked.

"Oh no, you didn't know." She paused as if struggling for the right words, then went with, "He's dead, Thomas."

TWENTY-SIX

"It's troubling," Hugo Strange said. "Very, very troubling."

After Thomas left, Strange re-read the story in the *Gotham Herald* about the murders at the Star Bright Motel, and at the residence of the psychic known as Belladonna. Miss Peabody came into Strange's office and sat across from him.

"What did Mr. Wayne want?" Peabody asked.

Strange heard the question, yet he didn't feel compelled to answer it.

"It disturbs me when people don't follow orders," he said. "I wonder why that is." After a long pause, he added, "Perhaps it's because I'm such a perfectionist in my own life that I demand it in others. For example, my inherent sense of style. I would never let anyone else choose my wardrobe, or trim my beard, I must always do it myself.

"Perhaps it's because my father was such a bastard. I felt helpless as a child, watching him beat my poor mother on a nightly basis, so now I demand order and perfection in my life. I require control. When this doesn't happen it irritates me to no end."

"That's understandable," Miss Peabody said.

"Oh, but believe me," Strange said, "I thank my father for the man he made me today. He made me driven, I live to want to prove him wrong. He told me the night my mother killed him that I had been the biggest mistake of his life. He told me I would never accomplish anything, that I was destined for a life of failure. When I had to shut Pinewood down, his prediction seemed to come to fruition."

"So what are you planning to do about it?" Peabody asked. "Change your plans? Abandon them?"

"Oh, no, on the contrary, I intend to fast-track them." He grinned, and then said, "Ten years ago we were so close to a major breakthrough, to unlocking the greatest mysteries of genetic research. The secret to my success thus far is that I've never been a quitter. I always see things through to the bitter end. I knew that the time would come for me to resume my life's calling, and that time is now."

"But the robbery didn't work the way you wanted it to," Peabody said. "You didn't find Wayne's files, did you?"

"Oh, it's much worse than that," Strange said. "The thieves my contact hired stole a painting. If they had just found the files, Thomas wouldn't have even reported the robbery. What would he have said? That the files detailing his involvement in Pinewood had been stolen? But now Thomas wants his painting back, and the trail has led him to me. Can you imagine if the most important genetic research in the history of mankind was halted because some idiots stole a painting?"

"So what are you planning to do about it?" Miss Peabody asked again. He frowned at the repetition.

"Every doctor understands that you always need a plan B," Strange said. "My ultimate goal remains to take control of Arkham Asylum. I refuse to let anything stop me. Thomas Wayne wants to turn Arkham into a mental health facility, no doubt in another desperate attempt to redeem himself. He feels guilt for Pinewood, which seems to drive every decision of his life. He would make a fascinating case study in pathological guilt.

"I almost feel sorry for poor Thomas," he continued, "that he is bound by such useless emotion, and that he will never see his dream for Arkham come to fruition. The patients there will provide fertile ground for my future endeavors. But, I'm getting ahead of myself—right now there is some more housecleaning I need to do."

Strange went to the window, stared at gray, foggy Gotham. The whole city seemed to be smoldering.

"In this case, I actually need to let go of control," he said with his back to Miss Peabody. "My protection is in layers. The more layers, the less likely I'll get caught."

"Have you confirmed that Karen Jennings has been killed?" Miss Peabody asked.

"Negative," Strange said. "But if Karen is indeed

still alive, and I have my doubts, then she's living in seclusion, and thus is contained. I'm more concerned with other threats that are roaming around this city." Strange turned again toward Miss Peabody, and said, "Please make an appointment for me to see The Lady."

"Stop right here."

The driver double-parked in front of the luxury town house, and Strange exited. It was early evening, and the air was crisp. He went up the stoop, rang the bell exactly five times, and then the door opened. Alonso, the young butler Strange knew from his previous visits, stood there.

"Please, come in, Dr. Strange."

The place looked more like a bordello than the home of one of a discreet and expensive businesswoman. Exotic rugs, dim lighting, the scent of incense. Strange waited on one of the plush velvet couches, gradually getting annoyed. He enjoyed making people wait for him, but he didn't like waiting for others.

Finally, after an excruciating four minutes and twenty-three seconds—yes, he timed it—The Lady entered.

Strange didn't know her real name—and it was possible that no one did. She was a middle-aged woman, with elegance to her, although she was dressed the way her apartment was decorated. Gaudy, over-the-top. She wore a red dress, heels, and had on several gold necklaces.

"Dr. Strange, such a pleasure to see you," she said, coming over to him and kissing him European-style, on both cheeks.

"Thank you for having me," Strange said.

"Has Alonso offered you a drink yet?"

"No, he hasn't."

"He *hasn't*?" The Lady sounded appalled. Then she called out, "Alonso! Alonso!"

The butler dashed into the room. "Yes, my lady?"

"Why didn't you offer Dr. Strange a drink?"

"Oh." He sounded nervous, as if he feared consequences. "Well, because the previous times Dr. Strange visited here he didn't want anything to drink, so I assumed that this time—"

"Part of your job is to offer our guests drinks, Alonso."

"Y-yes, my lady," he said. "I-I won't make the same mistake twice." Then he said to Strange, "W-w-would you like a drink?"

"No, thank you," Strange said.

"You'll be punished for this, Alonso," The Lady said. "Now please leave us alone."

"Yes, my lady."

Alonso exited, still trembling. Strange had no idea what "punished" entailed, but the power dynamic fascinated him. He enjoyed observing Alonso's fear response. Fear was such an interesting phenomenon— so powerful.

"I'm so sorry about that," The Lady said to him. "It frustrates me to no end when one of my workers can't complete a simple task."

"I very much agree," Strange said. "Delegating always presents its challenges."

"Speaking of which," The Lady said, "I apologize for what happened with the man who followed Thomas Wayne last Saturday. The man I sent, Scotty Wallace, is one of my best, but I lost contact with him upstate. So I suppose he *was* one of my best."

"Was Thomas meeting with Karen Jennings, as I've suspected he has been?"

"I haven't been able to confirm that one way or another," The Lady conceded. "Since Wallace has disappeared, the only conclusion I can reach is either that he's incapacitated or dead, more likely the latter."

Strange considered this new information. "So the assassin disappeared while following Thomas Wayne. Is it possible that Wayne was responsible for his... disappearance?" Thomas Wayne was one of the last people whom Strange could imagine committing a murder. Then again, as Strange's experiments had proved, everyone has a monstrous side.

"Any explanation is possible," The Lady said. "It's also possible that Wallace killed Karen, and then wound up dead himself. Perhaps someone killed him or he was even in a car accident."

"A car accident would have been reported."

"Unless it occurred in a secluded area and hasn't been discovered yet," The Lady said. "Idle speculation is a waste of time. In any event, I feel as if I've failed you. I have a reputation to protect. I take pride in completing every job for which I'm contracted, and in having a nearly perfect close rate. I hope I have a chance to make it up to you, Dr. Strange."

"Oh, you most definitely will," Strange said. "In fact, I have another assignment for you. Except this person, I want him brought to me alive—and then killed in front of me."

"That's an unusual request," The Lady said, "and frankly quite risky."

"I understand that," Strange said, "which is why I'm prepared to pay double my usual fee."

"I see." The Lady took a beat, then said, "And who is this person whom you want brought to you?"

"Nikos Petrakos," Strange said. "He's a known criminal in Gotham. You shouldn't have too much trouble tracking him down." He knew she wouldn't ask questions about Petrakos. She was only interested in one thing—money.

"I have the perfect man for the job," The Lady said, "but because of the risks I'm going to be forced to charge four times your usual fee."

"Given that you didn't complete the last assignment, I think four times is excessive," Strange said, "don't you?"

"Four times, and that's my final offer," The Lady said.

Strange didn't have leverage. He needed her now, would need her again, and she knew it.

"In that case it's a deal," Strange said.

* * *

Strange returned to his office to see a couple of patients. He was getting ready to leave for the evening when Miss Peabody buzzed him.

"There's a man on the phone for you," she said. "He said you're expecting his call."

"Put him through," Strange said. The call connected. "Yes?"

"I got him," the man said.

"Fantastic," Strange said. "Where can we meet?" The man suggested meeting outside an old shoe factory in North Gotham.

"I'll be there," Strange said.

Strange brought Miss Peabody along to the meeting. When they arrived at the factory, they didn't see anyone there. The area around the complex of buildings was barren, seemingly deserted. Several lights from atop the main building illuminated the area.

"Are you sure this is the place?" Miss Peabody asked, sitting next to him in the car.

"Positive," Strange said. He parked up closer to the front of the factory when a car approached behind him, and pulled up perhaps twenty feet behind.

"Wait here," Strange said to Miss Peabody. He unfastened his seat belt, opened the door, and got out.

Heading toward the other car, he stopped in between the two vehicles. The driver, presumably The

Lady's man, was a balding, overweight person in his fifties with a bushy mustache. He got out of the car, and there was no one else in evidence.

"Hugo?" the man said.

"Yes."

"He's in the trunk."

Strange followed the hit man to the back of the car. He lifted the lid to the trunk, revealing the bound and gagged, surly, dark-haired guy. Nikos Petrakos was trying to scream, but could only make muffled noises. He had multiple bruises and cuts on his face, some of them still oozing blood.

"Ah, fantastic," Strange said.

"Wasn't easy," the hit man said. "Lotta heat out there. The cops are looking for this guy, too."

"Can you remove the gag, please?" Strange asked.

The man said to the guy in the trunk, "You better not scream, or else." Then he removed it.

"Can you give us some privacy, please?" Strange asked. The hit man walked away. Then Strange said, "Greetings, Mr. Petrakos."

"Who… who are you?" Petrakos asked. His voice was hoarse, probably from choking on his own blood.

"I'm the man who hired you to break into Wayne Manor," Strange said.

"But-but a guy named Geno hired us."

"Yes, but I hired Geno," Strange said. "I know, it's very unusual, you were never supposed to find out who you were working for. But now that two of your partners are dead, that's irrelevant, isn't it?"

"So… so what do you want with me?"

"You made a big mistake stealing the painting. That wasn't part of the mission statement."

"The painting wasn't my idea, I swear."

"Yet you used your aunt as the fence."

Strange saw the fear in Petrakos's dark eyes.

"Yes, I did my research," Strange said. "I always do."

"That… that was a coincidence," Petrakos said.

"I'm a psychiatrist," Strange said. "I've observed abnormal behavior my entire adult life. I know when someone is lying to me, so don't even attempt to do it. It will save us both valuable time."

Strange was a master of manipulating people, a skill he took great pride in, and he had Petrakos under his control.

"Okay, yeah, I suggested taking it to my aunt," Petrakos said. "But I swear the whole stealing the painting idea was Roberto's idea."

"You're telling the truth," Strange said, "but the fact remains, you went along with it, so you're as guilty as the others. Much more importantly, you've also put my plans in jeopardy."

"I'm sorry," Petrakos said. "Really I am."

"Now you're lying again," Strange said. "I can't blame you. Any man bound in a trunk with a hit man standing just a few feet away will say anything he can to save his life."

"Please," Petrakos said. "I didn't meant to hurt you, or anyone. I was just trying to make a few bucks, get a better life. I'll do whatever you want. If you want the painting, you can have it. I'll tell you where it is."

"I don't care about the painting, I care about discretion. Your accomplices are dead, your aunt is dead. Does anybody else know about any of this?"

"Why should I tell you?" Petrakos sneered. "You're just going to kill me anyway."

"I'm a psychiatrist, not a murderer," Strange said. "I have no interest in killing you. After we finish this conversation, I will simply hypnotize you into forgetting everything you know about me, and erase this entire unfortunate incident. You'll wake up on the side of the road, and you'll be able to resume your life."

"Are you serious?" Petrakos said. "You'll really let me go?"

"I'm a man of God, and you have my word."

"But how do I know you're not lying? That you're not just saying this stuff so I'll tell you what you want to know?"

"Your concern is entirely valid," Strange admitted, "but I'm afraid, given your circumstances, you have no leverage in this situation."

"What does that mean?"

"It means you have no choice," Strange said. "You have to trust me."

"All right," Petrakos said. "All right, nobody else knows. The painting is in my apartment. I was gonna take it away to sell it, when this guy beat me up and threw me in the car." He nodded toward the hit man, and winced in pain at the motion.

"You're not lying," Strange said. "Where's your apartment?"

"It's actually my friend's apartment, but he's away, went down south to visit family."

"What's the address?"

"Four-seventeen Holland Street."

"Thank you," Strange said, "you've been very helpful." Then he said to the hit man, "Kill him."

"What?" Petrakos said. "*Wait*. What's going on? I thought you were a man of God."

"I lied," Strange said.

"No," Petrakos said. "Please, don't. Plea—"

The hit man fired into the trunk three times. Then there was sudden silence.

"Thank you," Strange said. "Job well done. Please make sure the body is never found."

"I will," the hit man said.

"And I may have another job for you soon," Strange added, "Be prepared." Turning and walking across the gravel ground, he returned to the car where Ms. Peabody was waiting, and they drove away.

"Only one person left to eliminate now, and the slate will be clean," Strange said.

"Are you sure you want to do that?" Miss Peabody asked.

"Are you questioning my judgment?"

"No, of course not, doctor."

He had Miss Peabody well trained, under his control. He smiled.

"I didn't think so."

TWENTY-SEVEN

Alfred normally didn't make it a habit to eavesdrop on conversations, though in some cases, when the conversations escalated into outright arguments, such occurrences were unavoidable.

The conversation this afternoon hadn't reached argument level yet, though unfortunately it seemed to be headed in that direction.

Alfred had been in his bedroom, writing a letter to an old mate, when he heard Thomas's heavy, distinctive footsteps on the stairwell, and then he heard him enter his bedroom. The conversation started up right away, and while Alfred couldn't make out much of anything they were saying, Martha sounded upset, so it must have been about Bruce's fight and suspension from school.

Martha had already shouted at Bruce about it— Alfred had never seen her angrier, in fact. Perhaps Thomas was defending Bruce, though Alfred had had enough experience with women to know that when one gets angry, the best strategy is to retreat into silence.

The worst thing to do is take an opposing position, which seemed to be the path Thomas had followed.

Alfred opened the door to his room, with the intention of going downstairs, when he found Bruce with an ear to his parents' door. His eyes went wide at being caught, though wisely he kept quiet.

"Let's go, Master Bruce," Alfred whispered. "Give your parents some privacy, all right?"

"But they're arguing about me," Bruce protested, also whispering.

"All the more reason you should leave them alone, mate. It'll only get worse if they find out you're listening in. Your father will defend you, and then your mother will get even angrier at him for taking your side and not respecting her authority. It's a vicious cycle, you see?"

Bruce considered this.

"You're right, Alfred."

The two of them went downstairs, then outside, walking along the grounds of Wayne Manor.

"I hate when my parents argue," Bruce said. "Especially when I know it's my fault."

"You don't have to take responsibility for everything."

"My mother says I should feel bad for what I did," Bruce said. "I believe she's talking about guilt, and yet I don't feel any guilt for the boy I beat up. Does that mean something's wrong with me?"

"No, it just means you've got the killer instinct."

"You really think?'

"Yes," Alfred said, "and you should be bloody

proud of it. Killer instinct can't be taught. In that respect, it's like having perfect pitch or a knack for languages. You either have it or you don't, and you, Master Bruce, have it."

"How about you, Alfred? Do you have it?"

"I usually prefer to be a bit more modest about myself, but yes, I reckon I do have it."

"I don't think I have it," Bruce said. "I never want to kill anyone."

"I didn't say I want to kill," Alfred said. "That's not necessary to have the instinct, though there are certain circumstances where killing is necessary."

"In boxing the goal isn't to kill," Bruce suggested. "The goal is to win. Maybe it should be called winner's instinct. I think the ability to fight and not kill is what separates us from animals."

"That might be true for boxing," Alfred said, "but you'd reconsider your position if you were ever in a war. Believe me, when you're on a battlefield and see a mate, even a loved one murdered in front of you, it changes something in you."

"It's horrible that you went through that," Bruce said, "but if I was in a war, it wouldn't change anything in me. I still wouldn't want to kill anyone."

Alfred stopped walking, so Bruce did as well. They had made it about halfway up the long drive.

"Okay, let's say, God forbid, someone caused harm to a loved one," Alfred said. "Let's say one of your parents, for instance, was murdered. That won't happen, of course, but if it did, and you passed the killer on the street, what would you do?"

"I can't even imagine that," Bruce said. "I love my parents so much. But if I saw the killer, I wouldn't kill him. I might beat him up if I knew how to fight, or make sure that he goes to jail so he couldn't hurt anyone else. But what would killing him do except put him out of his misery? And isn't misery worse than death? I'd definitely let him live."

"Well then, it sounds like you're a better man than me, mate." Alfred put an arm around Bruce's shoulders as they headed back toward the house.

TWENTY-EIGHT

Tracking down Nikos Petrakos turned out to be much more difficult than Harvey and Amanda had anticipated. In between his stints at Blackgate, he had had six known residences. They checked out each one of them, but came up empty each time. Harvey threw Fish Mooney a call, but even she had no idea where Nikos had shacked up.

By Monday evening it was looking bleak. It had been more than twenty-four hours since the killing spree at Belladonna's and the Star Bright Motel, which translated into plenty of time for Petrakos to slip out of Gotham, and maybe the country. The only positive was that the APB had come up empty, too, so hopefully that meant the guy was still in town.

Adding another wrinkle to the case, according to ballistics, the gun used in the Star Bright Motel was the same gun found on Frank Collins's body. Also, on Collins's cell there were missed calls from Thomas Wayne. So Collins must have been working for him, or had been trying to track down the Picasso for himself.

Word on the street was that Collins had a big-time gambling problem. Harvey had made an appointment to talk to Wayne first thing in the morning, where he hoped to get some answers. For the moment, however, he was spending his Tuesday night home in bed, sleeping, when he got a call.

From headquarters.

"Just got a tip on the Picasso," the duty officer said.

Still half-asleep, Harvey had been in the middle of a weird dream where he was wearing a wedding dress, being chased across a field by a bunch of football players, screaming in a language that sounded like Chinese.

He shook his head to chase away the images.

"A tip," he said. "From who?"

"The caller didn't say, but he sounded legit. The address is four-seventeen Holland."

"Wait," Harvey said, waking up some more. "Did you say a tip on the Picasso or Petrakos?"

"Picasso," the cop said.

As skeptical as he was about tips, this one seemed intriguing. After all, the APB had been for a missing person, not a missing painting, so maybe somebody knew something. Harvey got dressed as fast as he could, thankful that the dream had almost fully faded from his memory, and headed to the address.

He called Amanda, and she was on her way as well. Then he called for backup, including a team from the GCPD bomb squad, just in case the tip was some kind of set-up. It was past two a.m. when he arrived at the modest two-family house in a middle-class area of Gotham. A couple of lights were on downstairs.

"This better be worth it," Amanda said. "I'm exhausted."

"*You're* exhausted?" Harvey said. "I feel like I've been running on fumes for the past thirty-five years." The bomb-sniffing dogs didn't raise a ruckus, but they found some fresh blood on the walkway leading to the front door. Harvey didn't know what this meant— maybe it didn't mean anything.

With him leading the way, they busted in.

"GCPD!" Harvey announced, with his gun drawn.

The room was empty, but the TV was on—a middle-of-the night infomercial. They checked the rest of the apartment, but the place was definitely empty. Relieved that they hadn't been set up, they searched for the Picasso.

Harvey was searching the closet near the front door when Amanda called out.

"Harvey, come here." He went to the bedroom, where she was holding up the painting of a guy in yellow on a horse. He stared at it for a few seconds.

"*That's* worth a gazillion dollars?"

Early the next morning, after a few hours of shuteye, Harvey and Amanda rang the doorbell at Wayne Manor. Harvey was holding the painting. The butler Pennyworth answered and greeted them.

"Detectives." Then he glanced at the painting and added, "You've brought an old friend, I see. Well done."

"Is Thomas Wayne here?" Harvey asked.

"He is indeed," Pennyworth said. "This way, please." He led them into Thomas Wayne's study, where Harvey glanced around and gave a low whistle.

"Whoa, nifty repair job."

The butler left, so he and Amanda sat on the couch, waiting. Pennyworth returned with Wayne, who was dressed in jeans and a navy polo shirt.

"I can hardly believe it," Wayne said. "In all honesty, I never thought I'd see it again." He examined it closely, especially the signature. "It's the original," he announced. He looked at Harvey and said, "I'm impressed. I have to admit, I didn't think you'd find it."

"Never underestimate the GCPD," Harvey said.

"Actually, we got a tip about it," Amanda admitted.

Harvey shot her a look that said, *Thanks a lot*.

"A tip?" Wayne seemed intrigued. "A tip from who?"

"We don't know," Amanda said.

"It was anonymous," Harvey said. "We were hoping you might know who could've contacted us? Do you have any guesses?"

"No," Wayne said. "I have no idea."

"Are you sure?" Harvey pressed. "I mean, think about it, because honestly there've been a lot of holes in this case that are, well, hard to explain."

"I wish I could help you, but I have much less information than you do," Wayne said.

"What about the alarm system?" Harvey asked.

"You have any new theories about how it might've been disabled?"

"As far as we can tell, someone must have hacked into the system somehow," Wayne replied. "I've had discussions with my engineers, and the software people at Wayne Enterprises, and if there was a breach, it won't happen again."

"Of course, that's what you thought before it happened the first time," Harvey said. "The thing is, these guys were low level thugs. I'd be surprised if they knew how to turn on a computer, much less how to hack into one."

"Well, you're the detective," Wayne said, sounding a little irritated. "I guess you'll have to figure that part out, won't you?"

Harvey sort of smiled, trying to play off the jab Wayne had just landed.

"Do you know a PI named Frank Collins?"

Wayne hesitated, then said, "Why do you ask that?" Harvey couldn't tell if the hesitation confirmed that Wayne knew Collins, and was trying to figure out what to say, or if he was just confused. He glanced at Pennyworth, but the butler was hard to read, as well.

Then Harvey said, "Just trying to figure out what he was doing down at this Belladonna's place, and why he got killed. He must have been investigating the robbery, and when we checked his phone, we saw some missed calls you made to him."

"I was hoping to keep this confidential," Wayne said, "but yes, I did hire Frank Collins to help find the

Picasso." Harvey noticed that Pennyworth seemed surprised by this.

"I was shocked when I heard what happened to him," Wayne continued. "It's awful—a tragedy. I'm completely baffled how it could have happened. I know that sounds trite—whenever someone does something horrible, out of the blue, friends and family always say there were no signs, that they never saw it coming. But in this case it's true."

"Why didn't you tell us he was working for you?" Harvey asked.

"Private investigators are called private for a reason," Thomas said. "Martha and I wanted that painting back—it has great sentimental value. I was devastated when I heard that Collins was killed, of course. He was a good man."

"For a good man, it's possible that Frank Collins killed three people at that motel," Harvey revealed, "including a guy at the desk who was a good friend of mine."

Wayne seemed stunned by the revelation, and for a long moment he didn't say anything.

"I'm sorry for your loss." He sounded sincere, but somehow Harvey didn't buy it. Why should he be?

"Did Frank give any indication that he might snap?" Amanda asked.

"No," Wayne said. "Absolutely not. Never. I would never, ever, have hired him if I thought he might become unhinged in any way. He's always been entirely professional, a stand-up kind of person. But

I don't have to tell you two that. He was a GCPD detective, for God's sake. Obviously he didn't seem unhinged when he worked for you."

This was true, Harvey realized.

"Well, this just keeps getting stranger by the day," he said. "Two of the guys who broke in here the other night are dead, and the other one is missing, which already is pretty freakin' weird. The fact that the PI was killed with a meat cleaver seems to connect his murder back to the robbery, given the way they left the walls. But to be perfectly honest, I'm not sure where any of this gets us." He looked at Wayne and Pennyworth, then at Amanda, then back at Wayne.

"Did Collins tell you *anything* about what he may have discovered?" Amanda asked.

"No," Wayne said. "He didn't tell me anything, I had very limited contact with him after I hired him to help find the painting, which was quite frustrating, in fact. I spoke with him briefly on Sunday morning, and he said he was making progress on the case, and would update me soon.

"I hadn't had any contact with him since that call," he continued, "and I have no idea how he or the others wound up dead. That said, if there's any way I can possibly assist in the investigation, I'd be happy to. But if you don't have any more questions right now, I have a lot of work to do this morning."

"I understand." Harvey stood. "We'll be in touch."

Pennyworth led them back to the front door and wished them a great day. They walked back toward their car.

"So? What do you think?" Amanda asked.

"He's hiding something," Harvey said.

"I got that, too," she said. "But what?"

"Who the hell cares?"

Harvey's gut told him that Wayne was holding back, but nobody was squeaky clean in Gotham, not even Thomas Wayne. Everybody had secrets, and it wasn't his job to uncover all of them.

"He got his pretty picture back, and everyone who got killed was a lowlife—even the damned PI," he growled. "Let's go get some breakfast."

TWENTY-NINE

That evening, Thomas hung the Picasso in its old spot on the wall of his study.

"A little to the left," Bruce said.

Thomas shifted it ever so slightly.

"Bit to the right," Alfred said.

Thomas adjusted it again.

"More to the left," Bruce said, "just a fraction of an inch."

Thomas did it.

"Bit more to the right now," Alfred said.

"All right, that's enough," Thomas announced, and he got down from the ladder.

"It still looks crooked," Bruce said.

"Well, I think we're going to have to leave it that way, and learn to live with it," Thomas said.

"I don't know." Bruce stared at the painting. "I think it will always bother me."

"Well, I think it's past your bedtime now, isn't it?" Thomas replied.

"But it's only nine o'clock," Bruce protested.

"You're being punished remember?"

"Oh, right," Bruce said. "I forgot."

"Forgot?" Alfred responded. "Or chose not to remember?"

"It's not like there's a difference," Bruce said. "Goodnight, Dad. Goodnight, Alfred." He gave his father a hug, and left the study.

"What would you say to a glass of Scotch?" Thomas asked Alfred.

"I'd say hello."

Thomas poured the drinks and put on some music—Chopin's Nocturne in B Major. Alfred had already sat on the couch and Thomas sat across from him in a leather armchair.

"It must be nice to have the painting back," Alfred said.

"Yes, it is," Thomas said, "but I have to say, it's shocking about Frank. I considered him a good friend, and it's awful when a friend betrays you that way. Have you ever been betrayed?"

"I've lived a long life," Alfred replied. "I reckon I've experienced just about everything."

"Well, it's not the first time it's happened to me," Thomas said, thinking about Hugo Strange. "Maybe I'm too trusting, or I don't pick up on the signs well enough. Going forward, I'll need to keep my ears and eyes open a little bit wider."

There was a lull in the conversation as they sipped the Scotch, listening to the Nocturne.

"You know I usually don't discuss personal matters with you," Alfred said, "as I prefer to respect your space in such matters. And if I overstep my boundaries, I'll blame it on the Scotch, so I have my built in excuse. But I don't want to look back at this time with the regret of knowing I could've said something, but I didn't."

"What're you getting at?" Thomas asked. He tensed, wondering what was coming. Alfred shook his glass, the ice clinking against the side.

"You know, Martha has felt in the dark lately," he said. "You're aware of that, aren't you?"

"Yes, I'm aware of that," Thomas said, vaguely relieved.

"Just saying," Alfred said, "if you ever need a mate to chat about anything with, I'm always here."

Thomas took a moment, perhaps studying Alfred's sincere expression.

"Did she tell you anything specific?"

"You know I don't like to get in the middle of these sorts of things, so it's probably better you ask her that. But I know she's sort of, well, curious about your trips to the country."

"Oh, that," Thomas said. "I've assured her there's nothing... er... romantic going on. You can be sure of it, as well."

"I have no doubt about that, sir," Alfred said.

"I just like to get away, to get fresh air now and then," Thomas said. "I hike, I sit by a lake and stare at the water. It helps to reenergize me. Everybody needs to get out of Gotham once in a while to gain some perspective on things, and I'm no exception." He kept his tone as casual as he could manage, and thought he was pulling it off.

"I understand, sir," Alfred said. "I'm just trying to alert you to an expanding rift that may be occurring in your marriage, so you can give the matter the proper attention it deserves. Do a bit of mending, I suppose."

"Then there's you and Martha," Thomas said.

"What about me and Martha, sir?"

"You've been spending a lot of time together lately. I saw you talking the other day."

"What day was that, sir?"

Thomas couldn't remember. "It doesn't matter."

"What are you saying, Mr. Wayne?" Alfred seemed offended. "I hope you're not implying that you think your wife and I—"

"No, of course not," Thomas said quickly. "I know that's ridiculous." In reality, however, the thought *had* occurred to Thomas—more than once. He wasn't a fool, after all. He knew he'd been aloof, evasive, not giving Martha the attention she deserved.

He'd been neglecting his marriage as well, not working hard enough on getting things back on track. Meanwhile, Alfred was a strong, handsome, well-travelled, sophisticated man. While he didn't think either of them would ever cross the line, Thomas couldn't deny the possibility. Every day, husbands and wives deceived one another.

And friends betrayed friends.

"Well, you can rest assured," Alfred said. "I'm not

an idiot, you know."

"But…" Thomas paused. "I have to admit, I have been a bit jealous."

"Jealous?" Alfred seemed shocked. "By God, of what?"

"Okay, jealous is too strong a word," Thomas said. "But when I see you and Martha talking sometimes, you seem like good friends."

"I reckon that's because we are good friends."

"Right, and that's what's been missing with us lately," Thomas said. "I've been so wrapped up in Wayne Industries, and trying to deal with…" He almost blurted out Hugo Strange's name, but caught himself in time. "…other outside forces in this city that, admittedly, it's had an effect on my marriage. We're not as close as we once were."

"Then perhaps it's a good time to take a holiday."

"But we were just away in Switzerland."

"That was with Bruce and me, as well," Alfred said. "I'm suggesting that you go alone, just the two of you."

"This is a tenuous time at work," Thomas said. "There are so many things demanding my attention. I can't just take off for Europe."

"How about a beach holiday then?" Alfred said. "A long weekend. Getting away for a few days would do you some good, and give things in Gotham a chance to cool off."

"What needs to cool off?" Thomas asked noncommittally.

"I'm not referring to anything specific, sir," Alfred

said. "It's just an overall sense I have. From my days on the battlefield, I've gotten quite adept at detecting when trouble is looming. Anyway, I think jetting off to an island for a romantic weekend could be a good idea for you and the missus. Getting away from these forces you mentioned, it might be a good thing."

"Running from problems never solves them."

"I'm not suggesting that you run away," Alfred said. "I'm suggesting taking a break, that's all. A bit of perspective never hurt anyone. You yourself said you go to the country for perspective, so all I'm suggesting is that you get the perspective as a couple, for a change. I'm suggesting this as a man who has loved and lost, so I'm aware of the importance of doing things together, rather than individually.

"And, without overstepping my boundaries here, while it feels as if things in Gotham haven't yet come to a boil, they're headed in that direction," he added. "It may be good to let things simmer for a bit."

"Thank you," Thomas said. "I'll think it over, though I still don't think leaving is the answer. It's good to know that you're looking out for me and my family, and watching my pot to make sure it doesn't boil over."

"I guess we've officially beaten that metaphor to death now, haven't we?" Alfred said.

Thomas smiled.

"Well, I should retire myself." Alfred finished the rest of his drink in a swallow. "In all seriousness, sir, I do think you should consider it. It would do you and the missus a world of good."

"In all seriousness, Alfred, I will." But, the truth was, Thomas had already made up his mind.

When Alfred left the study, Thomas poured himself another glass of scotch. Sipping it, he stared at *Le Picador* on the wall, as Chopin played on.

He wasn't going anywhere.

THIRTY

Harvey took a sip of lukewarm coffee, reading the report on the Picasso robbery. Captain Essen had just signed off on it.

On the surface it seemed like a cut-and-dried case. A few ex-cons got together to rob Wayne Manor, and the bad guys wound up dead. Things happened like that all the time—dumb criminals fighting with each other, fighting over money, or to prove who had the biggest cojones. In this case, there were a bunch of unanswered questions.

How had they gotten codes to the alarm? That was the big one. Did they hack into Wayne's system? If so, how? And what did Frank Collins want out of all of this? Why did Collins go psycho, and shoot people up at a motel? Why did he snap?

Where was Nikos Petrakos?

Who made the anonymous tip?

And why?

"You know how to read?"

Harvey looked up, saw Amanda standing there, smirking. Was he imagining it, or was she getting prettier? When they had started working together, he'd barely noticed her, looks-wise, because he'd been so worked up about the idea of having a female partner.

Now that he'd seen her in action, and saw how good she was at her job, she'd become a lot hotter. Or that's how it seemed, anyway. Where were those hips last week? And how about those lips? How come he hadn't noticed that sexy pout?

"I'm just full of surprises," Harvey said.

"Everything in order?" Amanda asked.

"Seems to be," Harvey said.

"You sound skeptical."

"I'm *always* skeptical," Harvey said. "Somehow a case doesn't feel wrapped up when there are more questions than answers."

"We can still try to figure out what went down at that hotel."

"No, that's not likely to go anywhere," he replied. "Waste of time." Abruptly he shifted his eyes downward. Yeah, okay, he was looking at her chest. So what, he couldn't help it. Why did it bother him all of a sudden?

"What're you doing?" Amanda asked.

"What do you mean?" he said. "I'm closing the books on the Wayne robbery."

"No, I mean, you've been looking at me differently all day."

Damn. Harvey thought he'd been more subtle than

that. Then again, he shouldn't have been surprised, since the words "subtle" and "Bullock" didn't exactly go together.

"I was just noticing that shirt," Harvey said. "It's a nice color."

Amanda put her chin to her neck and checked herself out.

"White's a nice color?"

Crap. Why hadn't he come up with a better line?

Well, too late now, had to go with it.

"Yeah, I love white," he said. "White is pure, innocent, vaginal." He heard it as soon as he said it. "I mean virginal—virginal." Like that made it any better.

Thankfully the Captain came over at that moment.

"Shooting at a DJ's Drugstore on Davidson."

"We're on it," Harvey said, grabbing his coat and fedora.

The drugstore wasn't far—Harvey and Amanda got there in less than five minutes by car. Compared to their recent cases, this one was like a walk in the park. Some young thug had attempted to rob the store, and the owner blew him away with a sawed-off shotgun. Harvey and Amanda talked to the owner, looked at the body, then it was taken away in a bag.

Boom, just like that, case closed.

Heading back to their car, Harvey said, "Wouldn't it be nice if every case was this open and shut?"

"How about a drink?" Amanda asked.

"My favorite question," Harvey said. They went to Harvey's favorite watering hole—Old City, downtown. Before they knew it, they were through the second round.

It was the first time they'd gone out drinking together, and Harvey was impressed by how Amanda was throwing back the Guinnesses—two pints so far, halfway into number three. It was nice to not talk to her about police work for a change, too. They had some good small talk going—Harvey told her funny stories about his old man and his brother, and she told him about growing up all over the country because her father had been in the military.

"I was wrong about you, Bullock," she said abruptly.

"Yeah?" Harvey said. "How's that?"

"Well, to be honest, when I first got the assignment to work with you, I wasn't thrilled about it. For one, your reputation preceded you."

"Hey," Harvey said, "I've worked long and hard to build up a lousy reputation. It's a work of art, like a Picasso."

"I'm getting to a compliment, bear with me," Amanda said. "I thought you were lazy actually."

"That's a compliment?"

"Thought," Amanda said. "Past tense."

"Ah, gotcha," Harvey said. "That's a little bit better, I guess."

They smirked, teasing each other.

"What I mean," Amanda said, "is the *way* you went about police work—roughing people up, paying bribes, cutting corners. But now I see you're just a product of your environment, and a good product at that. I'm learning from you every day, and I can't wait to see what the future brings."

"Man," Harvey said, "if I wasn't such a hardened Irishman I'd be tearing up right about now."

"Tears aren't allowed in Ireland?" Amanda said.

"We've been through so much misery, nobody has any tears left," Harvey said. "That's why we drink— we're all trying to rehydrate."

"Now I get it," Amanda said. "I don't know how I've made it through my life without discovering the origins of the drunken Irishman. That clears up so much of the mystery, I'm not sure there's anything else for me to learn."

Harvey smiled.

"Seriously though," he said, "I was wrong about you, too. Want to know the truth? I thought you were weak."

"Weak?" Amanda pretended to be offended. "Weak how?"

"Look at you," Harvey said. "I could bench press you without breaking a sweat."

"Bet you think you could beat me in an arm wrestle, too."

"Let's not get crazy," Harvey said. "You know some karate, but that's a skill. But arm wrestling? We're talking about brute strength."

"So you think you can beat me then?"

"No, actually, I *know* I can."

"Let's do it, then." Amanda put her elbow on the bar.

Smitty, the bartender, looked over. So did a few other regulars.

"I don't want to be embarrass you," Harvey said, "but if you insist."

He elbowed up.

"Need a judge?" Smitty asked.

"Sure," Amanda said.

Now a little crowd—maybe ten people—formed around them. Harvey and Amanda clutched hands. Jesus, his hand was like twice the size of hers.

"I feel like I should give you a head start," Harvey said.

Amanda looked focused, like she was in some kind of Zen state. He figured he'd take it easy on her—keep it a tie for like ten seconds before taking her down.

"On three," Smitty said. "One, two…

Three!"

The back of Harvey's hand hit the bar—it was over.

In shock, he had no idea how she'd done that. He'd *tried* to hold her, but he never had a chance. The guys in the bar were laughing, making wisecracks.

"Maybe he *let* her win," one guy suggested.

Another guy yelled out, "Rematch!"

"What do you say?" Smitty said to Harvey. "Want to go again?"

Harvey knew he'd get destroyed in a rematch, so he made it into a joke.

"No, I concede, I concede." He held up his hands,

palms out. "What can I say? She beat me fair and square. Guess it just wasn't my day."

"Yeah, well I think he let me win," Amanda said to everyone.

Harvey looked at her. She had a serious expression, but he could see the smile in her eyes.

As the crowd dispersed, he said, "Why'd you lie like that?"

"I wanted to beat you," she said. "I didn't want to humiliate you."

"But how'd you do that anyway?" Harvey said. "Some kind of magic trick?"

"No, it's just a matter of focus," she said. "The mind is the strongest muscle."

He thought about that for a long moment. She waited, probably figuring he was searching for a good wisecrack.

"I'm gonna do something now that I don't do very often," Harvey said.

"Pick up the check?"

"More surprising than that," he said. "I'm going to apologize to you. I know I was a little, well, resistant to working with a woman, but I was wrong. You're like a secret weapon nobody sees coming. Any cop would be lucky to have you as a partner."

"Aww, thank you, Harv, that's such a sweet thing to say." She hugged him. "You almost made me tear up, and that's saying a lot."

"And," he added, "you're the first woman I've hugged in ages who I didn't want to take to bed."

Crap, Harvey thought, *Come on, filter, where are you for Chrissakes?*

Amanda pulled back, looking surprised, but not upset.

"Hey, that was the Guinness talking, not me."

"So you didn't mean that?" she asked.

"No," he said.

"So you *do* want to take me to bed?" She looked offended.

Suddenly Harry was confused.

"Okay, you really want me to be honest?" he asked.

"Yes, go ahead," she said, "I want to hear it."

Harvey gulped down the rest of the pint. "Okay, yeah, I think you're sexy as hell, especially when you're beating the crap out of people, but that doesn't mean I want to take you out. I'm dumb, yeah, but I'm not stupid enough to mix business and pleasure."

"I guess there's a compliment in there somewhere," Amanda said.

"See, this is why I don't like to be honest with women," Harvey said. "Whenever a woman asks me to be honest I wind up getting into trouble."

"I'll be honest with you about something," she said. "I'm starving and I'm in the mood for a big, juicy steak. How about you?"

Harvey smiled, wondering how she had gone from total pain in the ass to his total fantasy woman.

"Let's do it," he said.

They paid the tab, and then went across the street to a steakhouse. There they devoured a couple of

T-Bones, and each had a couple more beers.

"How're you matching me pint for pint?" Harvey asked. "You got a wooden leg or something, or you just focusing your energy?"

"Why am I matching you?" she said. "Maybe *you're* matching *me*?"

Good point.

"Touché."

Later, they left the steak house and wobbled back to the car. Laughing, they had their arms around each other's waists. Harvey didn't even know how his had gotten there.

That was how he knew he was having a good time. When they got in the car, she looked good and he felt good.

What the hell? he thought, and suddenly they were kissing. Holy crap, it felt good, it felt *right*. How had this incredible woman been right under his nose all this time and he hadn't noticed?

Then the logical side of his brain kicked in.

"Wait, this is a bad idea."

"Why?" She didn't want to stop.

"Because the GCPD's like a fish bowl, and rumors spread like viruses. Hell, people are probably already talking about us."

"I'm good at keeping secrets," Amanda said.

That was all Harvey needed to hear.

They started going at it again—kissing, grasping at

each other. If she had some domme in her, he mused, this would be pretty much perfect.

Then something weird happened.

They were suddenly wet, and Harvey's eyes stung.

"What the hell?" Harvey said.

The car stunk of gasoline. Was there some kind of leak?

Oh, shit.

On the passenger side, beyond Amanda, he saw the hand reaching into the car with a lit match. Amanda saw it, too. Harvey grabbed her, opened the door on his side, and they rolled out on to the street.

But she was burning like a log. Her clothes and hair were on fire. Although he knew the fire could spread to him, too, he didn't care. He put his coat over her, trying to smother the flames, and then he grabbed her again and rolled with her, back and forth, along the street. The flames subsided, but it was too late—Amanda's wide-open eyes were staring at nothing.

"No!" Harvey screamed, so loud his ears hurt!

Then he glanced toward the burning car, realizing the danger, but he didn't have time to react. The explosion propelled him backward, maybe ten feet, and landing hurt his back like a son of a bitch. He struggled to get up, making it to his knees, then he looked over and saw the feet and legs of someone, standing about ten feet away. He shifted his gaze higher.

It was Ryan Maxwell, the guy he'd met in front of the liquor store the other day, the guy who had *begged* to get sent back to Arkham.

"You?" Harvey gritted. His brain was overloaded with a lot of ideas, all at once, but one thought dominated. *I could've prevented all of this.* If he'd just taken Maxwell in on some trumped up charge, three cops—including Amanda—would still be alive.

"I told you I was gonna get back to Arkham, one way or another," Ryan said.

"That's why you killed three cops?" Harvey finally managed to stand up. "Are you freakin' insane?"

"Yes I am, actually," Maxwell said, "but I already told you that. You can't really blame me for this one, though. If you morons at the GCPD hadn't killed the wrong man, an innocent man mind you, then this murder could've been prevented."

Harvey pulled his gun, and aimed it at Maxwell.

"You killed a great lady," Harvey said, "and you're gonna pay for it."

Maxwell didn't seem concerned. "You can't shoot me," he said.

"Yeah," Harvey said. "And why can't I?"

"Because there are witnesses." Maxwell gestured with his jaw to his right. Harvey looked over and saw several people there, watching.

"I'm unarmed," Maxwell said. "If you shoot me, you'll lose your job, or you might even go to jail. You know what happens to cops at Blackgate? You'll have a real ball in there, hanging out with the guys you sent to prison."

Harvey knew he was right about losing his job,

especially because a couple of guys in Internal Affairs already had hard-ons for him.

"See," Maxwell said. "You have to arrest me. It's a win-win situation for both of us. You'll get the credit for solving the cop killer case, and maybe it'll even get you a promotion or a raise. Meanwhile, I'll be found insane, and hopefully get to stay in Arkham for the rest of my life. Oh, Arkham, how I have missed thee so."

Maxwell was right about that, too. He was obviously loony tunes, so any judge would commit him. Then Harvey had an idea.

He flashed his badge at the observers. "GCPD," he bellowed. "Get the hell outta here, right now! This guy's a maniac."

Everybody scattered.

Maxwell knew he was screwed.

"I'm a mentally ill man," he said. "Anybody who'd kill innocent cops has to be c-crazy, right? I'm a danger to myself and to others, I need r-rehabilitation. You, as a moral man, have to understand that."

"If you think I have morals, you really are crazy."

He blew Ryan away.

Just to make sure, he went over to the body, and pumped a couple more into him.

"Son of a bitch," he said, and he spat on the creep's stupid, dead face.

Then he went over to Amanda, and stared, numb. Another partner had bitten the dust—wasn't the first, and wouldn't be the last. He was glad he hadn't fallen in love with her, that he'd dodged that bullet. This was why he didn't share his feelings, why he didn't like to even *feel* his feelings.

This was why he didn't get close to anyone.

The pain wasn't worth the gain.

THIRTY-ONE

"How about we go to the shooting range today?"

A week had gone by since the Picasso had been recovered, and things seemed to be returning to normal. Thomas had gotten back into a routine at work, Bruce had finished serving his suspension from school, and he and Martha had been getting along well.

Thomas had checked in with Karen Jennings by phone, and there hadn't been any fallout from the killing of Scotty Wallace. He was convinced this meant that Strange hadn't discovered the location of the cabin, nor had anyone else.

Perhaps his visit had yielded its desired effect, and Strange had reconsidered any plans he'd had about restarting genetic testing. If that was the case, the status quo of the past ten years between had been restored.

"I'd fancy that quite a bit," Alfred replied. So at around noon, on a bright sunny day, they headed out in the Bentley—Alfred driving. They passed the gate, where Nigel had returned to duty. With his face covered in bandages, he still managed a smile.

"Have a wonderful day, Mr. Wayne."

"Thank you, Nigel," Thomas said. Then he said to Alfred, "You were right about him. He's a dedicated, trustworthy employee. We need men like him in Gotham."

The shooting range they frequented was about an hour's drive south of Gotham. They merged into traffic on the highway, and Alfred glanced repeatedly in the rear-view mirror. His brow wrinkled.

"I think we're being followed, sir." He had a matter-of-fact voice, with no fear or real concern in evidence.

"Really?" Thomas replied, adopting the same tone. "Perhaps I have a stalker now. I guess I should feel special."

"I'm afraid I'm quite serious, sir."

Thomas looked over his shoulder at the red van directly behind them. The driver was a young brunette.

"The van?" he asked.

"No, the black car travelling behind the van," Alfred said.

Thomas couldn't see it.

"Are you sure?" Thomas asked.

"Afraid I'm almost positive," Alfred said. "I noticed the car when we were a few blocks away from the manor. I didn't want to alarm you initially, but I have been looking out for it ever since. After he followed us for the first two turns, I was willing to strike it up to coincidence. But when he followed us on to the highway, as well, I'm afraid the odds of a coincidence diminished significantly."

"Well, there's only way to find out for sure," Thomas said. "Try to lose him."

"As you wish, sir," Alfred said. He accelerated and cut over to the left lane. After passing around a dozen or so cars, he veered back into the center lane and slowed. Looking back, Thomas couldn't see the black car.

"Looks like he may not have been following us after all," Thomas said.

"I wouldn't be so sure."

Sure enough, the black car cut over from the left lane, as well, securing a position behind the Bentley, but with a couple of cars in between. Thomas still hadn't been able to catch a glimpse of whoever was in the front seat.

"Did you see the driver before?"

"Dark hair, sunglasses, mustache, mid-thirties perhaps," Alfred said. "Do you have any idea why someone could be following you?"

Thomas flashed back to the shooting of Scotty Wallace—in particular, the blood spattered wall.

"No, none at all," Thomas said.

"I see," Alfred said.

"Do you think you can lose him?" Thomas asked.

"We'll find out," Alfred said.

When an opening was available, Alfred cut over to the left lane again and accelerated, faster than the previous time. Guiding the Bentley like a race-car driver, he weaved through traffic, hardly varying his speed. The black car, however, followed every move.

The Bentley was in the left lane, the black car trailing, as they approached the next exit.

"Let's try something, shall we?" Alfred said. At the last possible moment, without reducing his speed at all, he cut in front of a car in the center lane, and another car in the right lane, and made it onto the exit ramp. It didn't seem as if the black car could mimic the maneuver in time, yet, the driver somehow managed to brake a bit, shift over to the right, and then began to spin out. The car actually turned 360 degrees, then wound up on the exit lane, as well.

"Bloody hell," Alfred said. "This bloke either knows how to drive, or he's the luckiest man alive."

"What now?" Thomas asked.

"I have some other tricks up my sleeve." They were along a two-lane road in a hilly, suburban community, with the black car about fifty yards behind. Then Thomas looked again and saw that the black car was only twenty-five or so yards behind.

"He's gaining on us," Thomas said.

"Is he now?" Alfred said.

The car ahead of theirs was obeying the speed limit. Although the lines were double yellow, and they were approaching a bend, Alfred slipped into the oncoming lane and passed the car.

Around the bend came a speeding van.

Thomas, thinking this was the end, cried out, but Alfred managed to avoid a collision with perhaps less than a foot to spare, and got back into the correct lane.

"If you do that again, I think I might have a heart attack," Thomas said.

"Well, in that case I suggest you brace yourself."

Thomas glanced to his left and saw the black car, pulling alongside. The driver was middle-aged, a little older than Alfred had guessed, and had a bushy mustache.

"Jesus," Thomas said.

"Not a bad name to summon up under the circumstances," Alfred said.

The black car sideswiped theirs. Alfred lost control for a moment as the Bentley swerved toward the narrow shoulder, but then he regained control. The black car was still alongside, and now the passenger-side window had been opened. The man was aiming a gun at Alfred and Thomas.

"Duck!" Alfred shouted.

Thomas bent his head toward his lap as far as it would go as a bullet pinged off of part of the car, maybe the roof.

"Bastard," Alfred said.

Out of the corner of his eye, Thomas saw that Alfred had his gun out now. He fired at the man several times, and the man fired back. Then Thomas heard honking.

"Bloody hell," Alfred said. "Hold on."

Thomas took a peek and saw that a school bus was speeding toward the black car, and a head-on collision was imminent. Then Alfred fired, hitting the man in the head, and the black car spun out of control, down an embankment, as the school bus sped past.

Alfred pulled over.

"Are you all right, man?" he asked Thomas.

"Fine," Thomas said.

Alfred was about to get out of the car when Thomas grabbed him.

"What are you doing, sir?" Alfred asked.

"Let's just go?" Thomas said. "Forget about this."

"Are you mad?" Alfred said. "We have to find out who it is, and call for medical help."

"He's probably dead," Thomas said.

"We don't know that for sure," Alfred said.

Without loosening his grip, Thomas said, "I don't want my name in the papers, Alfred? Do you understand? It's not good for Wayne Industries, especially on the heels of all the other drama of late."

"Somebody tried to kill you, sir," Alfred persisted.

"He could've been trying to kill *you*," Thomas replied.

"Me?" Alfred said. "Why on earth—?"

"You shot somebody the other night," Thomas said. "A friend could be out for revenge."

"I reckon that's a possibility," Alfred admitted, "but it's more likely that it's related to whatever you've been up to—"

"Drive away," Thomas said. "That's an order."

A grimace crossed his features for a moment, but Alfred maintained his professionalism.

"As you wish, sir."

* * *

After driving about a mile, they passed a couple of speeding patrol cars headed in the opposite direction.

"Perhaps you should reconsider going on holiday," Alfred said.

"If I go, I'll still have to come back, and then what?" Thomas said. "Yes, I have enemies—you can't be the richest man in Gotham without accumulating enemies along the way. The corruption in this town runs so deep, you have no idea, Alfred. But I'm doing work now—good work to make Gotham a better place for everybody. I firmly believe I can make that happen, as long as I stay the course."

"I understand, sir," Alfred said. Even if Alfred didn't understand Thomas's position, he at least had to understand that this wasn't an argument he could win.

"Well, it's a good day for shooting anyway," Alfred said. "Since we've already had a warm-up, we might as well carry on."

At the shooting range, Thomas couldn't focus. Usually he was a great shot, but today he could barely hit the target. Alfred saw he was struggling.

"Would you like to take a break, sir?" he asked. Thomas, aiming his gun, didn't answer. He imagined that his target was Hugo Strange—with a demented, maniacal grin and those odd tinted glasses.

He fired five shots.

All were bulls-eyes.

THIRTY-TWO

As he hung up the phone, Thomas considered killing Strange for real. Not by himself—hiring someone, a professional. He recalled how Frank had floated the idea as a possible solution to the overriding problem. Pinewood, and all of its horrible consequences, had been weighing on Thomas for years.

What a relief it would be to simply give someone a wad of cash—problem solved. He wouldn't have to live his life in fear, which would help to make him a better husband and father. He could drive up to the cottage in the country and give Karen Jennings the great news—that the man who had created Pinewood Farms was dead.

"You're free to leave here now, and do whatever you want with your life," he would say.

While the fantasy had its appeal, in the end it was only that—a fantasy. Thomas understood how people reached the level where murder seemed like an acceptable option, but even so the idea went against everything for which he stood. He didn't condone murder under any circumstances.

If Strange were arrested and sentenced to death, that would be one thing, but Thomas wasn't a vigilante. He wouldn't stoop to his enemy's level.

However, Thomas didn't want to make himself a sitting duck, either. So he had called Strange—from a phone booth so the call couldn't be traced—and made his position clear. In a firm, concise message, he instructed him to back down, or the police would be called.

It had come to this. Risking his company, his reputation.

But by God, his family would be safe.

Risky as it had been, his call may have had the desired effect.

It had been weeks, and Strange had slipped back into relative obscurity. Perhaps the loss of two assassins had been enough. Mad as he was, maybe Strange had realized that if he kept making failed attempts, he would eventually get caught. Perhaps he had decided that he had too much to lose, and not enough to gain.

Thomas knew this was wishful thinking.

Strange wouldn't just walk away from what he considered his life's work. At the same time, however, Thomas refused to live his life in constant fear. He didn't want his family to live in constant fear, either.

Alfred provided some protection, but they couldn't take Alfred everywhere.

At one point, after the incident on the highway, he had considered hiring twenty-four-seven bodyguards for each member of the family, and placing full-time armed security around Wayne Manor. Then paranoia had kicked in, and he decided there was no one he could trust—not fully. As his experiences with Frank Collins had taught him, anyone could cross over to the dark side, when offered the right price.

That, too, had passed, and a welcome sense of normalcy returned. Bruce was doing well in school, making some new friends, and Martha threw herself into social issues, diverting her fire toward positive pursuits and away from Thomas.

He, in turn, focused on his work at Wayne Enterprises. The company was doing well, though with expected and unexpected ups and downs. One Friday afternoon the stock dropped, losing nearly twenty percent of its value. This was particularly unusual because it came on a day when the Exchange as a whole was soaring. As a major blue-chip company, Wayne rarely bucked the trends.

An emergency board meeting was called, and the records were examined with a fine-tooth comb, but no one could suggest any reason for the drop. The balance sheets had never looked better, and none of their subsidiaries seemed to be dragging them down. So while Thomas was concerned, he wasn't seriously concerned.

This, too, would pass.

***

Two months had gone by since the Picasso had been recovered, and Thomas and Martha decided they needed a break.

Both had been working nonstop for days on end, so after a complex checking and re-checking of their calendars, a date night was settled upon—one which would take them to the theater.

Both had been laboring hard, as well, to repair the damage to their relationship, and it seemed to be working. While Alfred didn't get the "beach holiday" he'd proposed, he was clear in his approval of their new lifestyle.

Thus, a play was chosen—one which they both would enjoy. At least Thomas *hoped* he would enjoy it. At least it was Martha's cup of tea. They were dressed and ready to go when Bruce came out of his room.

"Can I come with you?"

Thomas and his wife were holding hands.

"I thought you wanted to stay home and watch television with Alfred?" Martha said.

"But I haven't been out all day," Bruce said. He gave her his most appealing look. "Please." It struck Thomas that she never stood a chance, and he would end up outnumbered.

Martha looked at him.

"Okay," he said, "but I have an idea. How about we go to a movie instead? I'm sure we could get an extra ticket for the Brecht, but honestly, I'm already bored just thinking about it." To his surprise, Martha let out a deep breath.

"I'm so glad to hear you say that, sweetheart," she confessed. "I feel the same way, but thought for sure you were eager to see it."

"Then a movie it is," Thomas announced. "There's a new musical comedy that's gotten some excellent reviews. It looks like great fun."

"I'll be happy to see anything," Bruce said.

"Sounds like we have a plan," Martha added.

Alfred offered to drive them, but Thomas insisted on giving him a night off. It was foggy, drizzly evening, the roads slick.

They parked in a private lot Thomas had used, several blocks from the theater. As they were leaving the lot, joining the passersby on the crowded sidewalk, Thomas saw a tall, middle-aged balding fellow watching them. At Thomas's gaze the man seemed uncomfortable, and walked away in the opposite direction. Thomas was relieved, as he didn't want to subject his family to the paparazzi, or some opportunist trying to profit from his fame.

The movie turned out to be kind of pedestrian, but at least Martha seemed to like it—laughing out loud at some of the jokes—and so did Bruce. Thomas wished they had gone to the Brecht, instead, and he even nodded off a couple of times. When the movie ended, it was like the completion of a two-hour prison sentence.

As they left the theater, the air was heavy and damp. It had been raining and it looked as if it could start again. Nevertheless, their spirits were high, and the other bystanders seemed to share in their pleasure.

An older couple approached, and recognized them.

"Look, the Waynes," the man said, keeping his voice low.

"Where?" the woman asked, glancing around.

"Right there," the man hissed, nodding.

Another fellow passed, accompanied by his son.

"Hello, Mr. Wayne."

Thomas nodded in acknowledgment. Normally he didn't mind being recognized, but for some reason the attention tonight made him uncomfortable. They continued along the busy street, then approached an alley. It was a shortcut to the parking lot, and was generally very busy.

"Let's go this way," he suggested.

Martha seemed hesitant.

"It's shorter," Thomas insisted. "The car will be right at the other end of the alley, and it's about to rain again." Sure enough, the first drops were beginning to fall.

Bruce and Thomas both looked at Martha. She nodded, and they turned down the alley. As they did Thomas thought he saw a dark shape flit past overhead. He thought it might be a person on the fire escape, but decided it likely had just been a cat.

There were fewer people in the alley than he'd expected.

"So what did you think?" Martha asked her husband. "Did you enjoy the movie?"

"I thought it was okay," Bruce offered.

"I couldn't wait for it to end," Thomas said.

"Oh come on, Tom, it wasn't that bad," Martha protested.

"Childish drivel," Thomas said. "Movies these days, I don't know."

"Well, I thought the acting was fine, and the music was lovely. Didn't you think so, Bruce?"

"Sorry, Mom, I have to agree with Dad," the boy replied. "It was kinda lame." Thomas reached over and ruffled his son's hair.

"There's no such word as 'kinda,'" Thomas said.

"You two, so judgmental," Martha said. "Just once I'd like—"

She stopped abruptly, and Thomas saw why. A tall man was approaching, wearing a ski mask. He carried a gun.

Uh-Oh. Thomas's fight-or-flight instinct kicked in, and he realized it had been a huge mistake to take the alley rather than the street.

"What's up, folks," the guy said. Then, before they could respond, he added, "Gimme your money."

The tone was friendly, but the attitude was menacing. The guy stopped walking, blocking the Waynes' way, so they had to stop, as well. Thomas recalled the man he'd seen earlier, lurking near the parking lot. Could this be the same person?

This didn't feel random.

Just like the break-in hadn't felt random.

"No problem," Thomas said, pulling out his wallet and handing it over.

Even so, he prepared himself. If taking a bullet was to be his punishment, he was ready to accept his fate. Thomas's own life was secondary, so long as no harm came to Martha and Bruce.

"The necklace," the man said.

"Oh," Martha said, "but—"

"Give it to him, Martha," Thomas said.

He hoped that maintaining a calm demeanor would help them avoid violence, but his gut told him otherwise. This wasn't just a mugging. He recalled the drop in the stock—had Hugo somehow engineered it? He should have hired someone to kill Strange, weeks ago, when he'd had the chance. Would this be the consequence of remaining a moral person?

For trying to do the right thing?

The man ripped the necklace off of Martha's neck, and the pearls clinked onto the cobblestones. Thomas stared at the man's evil eyes, searching for hope that wasn't there. This man was a stone cold killer, who had crossed the line of morality so many times there was no way back for him.

Thomas wanted to buy time, but he knew he was out of it. Alfred wasn't here to save him today, nor could anyone else.

He had deluded himself into believing there were solutions to Gotham's problems. He may have been the most powerful man in the city, but he had no power now. He had lost control of the situation, the same way he'd lost control of his company. What he wanted to happen didn't happen anymore. He had no free will.

Perhaps he'd never had any.

As the man's trigger finger twitched, one thought became clear, like an absolute truth:

No one is safe in Gotham.

ACKNOWLEDGMENTS

Special thanks to Steve Saffel, Gabrielle Heller, and the entire *Gotham* team at Warner Bros. and Fox.

ABOUT THE AUTHOR

JASON STARR is the international bestselling author of many crime novels, thrillers, and comics. His novels include *Cold Caller*, *Twisted City*, *Lights Out*, *The Follower*, *Panic Attack*, and *The Pack*. His work in comics for Marvel and DC has featured Wolverine, The Punisher, Sand, The Avenger, Doc Savage, and Batman. In addition, for Marvel he authored the original prose novel, *Ant-Man: Natural Enemy*. He has won the Anthony Award for mystery fiction twice, as well as the Barry Award. His latest crime thriller, available in the U.S. and U.K., is *Savage Lane*. He lives in New York City.